Vampire Academy
THE ULTIMATE GUIDE

Vampire Academy
THE ULTIMATE GUIDE

MICHELLE ROWEN

with

RICHELLE MEAD

razOr
bill

An Imprint of Penguin Group (USA) Inc.

Vampire Academy: The Ultimate Guide

RAZORBILL

Published by the Penguin Group
Penguin Young Readers Group
345 Hudson Street, New York, New York 10014, U.S.A.
Penguin Group (USA) Inc., 375 Hudson Street, New York, New York 10014, U.S.A.
Penguin Group (Canada), 90 Eglinton Avenue East, Suite 700, Toronto, Ontario, Canada M4P 2Y3
(a division of Pearson Penguin Canada Inc.)
Penguin Books Ltd, 80 Strand, London WC2R 0RL, England
Penguin Ireland, 25 St Stephen's Green, Dublin 2, Ireland (a division of Penguin Books Ltd)
Penguin Group (Australia), 250 Camberwell Road, Camberwell, Victoria 3124, Australia
(a division of Pearson Australia Group Pty Ltd)
Penguin Books India Pvt Ltd, 11 Community Centre, Panchsheel Park, New Delhi – 110 017, India
Penguin Group (NZ), 67 Apollo Drive, Mairangi Bay, Auckland 1311, New Zealand
(a division of Pearson New Zealand Ltd)
Penguin Books (South Africa) (Pty) Ltd, 24 Sturdee Avenue, Rosebank,
Johannesburg 2196, South Africa

Penguin Books Ltd, Registered Offices: 80 Strand, London WC2R 0RL, England

10 9 8 7 6 5 4 3 2 1

ISBN 978-1-59514-451-5

Library of Congress Cataloging-in-Publication Data is available

Printed in the United States of America

Vampire Academy
THE ULTIMATE GUIDE

Index

PART ONE:
BOOK RECAPS

CHAPTER 1: *Vampire Academy*   2

CHAPTER 2: *Frostbite*   35

CHAPTER 3: *Shadow Kiss*   74

CHAPTER 4: *Blood Promise*   110

CHAPTER 5: *Spirit Bound*   145

CHAPTER 6: *Last Sacrifice*   178

PART TWO:
THE WORLD OF VAMPIRE ACADEMY

CHAPTER 7: *Characters*   225

• MAIN CHARACTERS:

ROSEMARIE "ROSE" HATHAWAY

VASILISA "LISSA" SABINA RHEA DRAGOMIR

DIMITRI BELIKOV

CHRISTIAN OZERA

ADRIAN IVASHKOV

MASON ASHFORD

EDISON "EDDIE" CASTILE

JANINE HATHAWAY

IBRAHIM "ABE" MAZUR

JILLIAN "JILL" MASTRANO DRAGOMIR

SYDNEY SAGE

NATASHA "TASHA" OZERA

VICTOR DASHKOV

• OTHER CHARACTERS

CHAPTER 8: *Love and Friendship*   253

• ROSE & DIMITRI:

PRIVATE LESSONS   ADDICTED TO LOVE   FINDING BEAUTY

• ROSE & ADRIAN: THE WARRIOR & THE BAD BOY

• ROSE & LISSA: BEST FRIENDS FOREVER

• LISSA & CHRISTIAN: THE PRINCESS & THE OUTCAST

CHAPTER 9: *Allies and Monsters*   272

MOROI
- ELEMENTAL MAGIC

  EARTH   AIR   WATER   FIRE   SPIRIT

- ST. VLADIMIR'S ACADEMY

  MOROI CLASSES   DHAMPIR CLASSES   SHARED CLASSES

- MOROI ROYAL COURT

  MOROI ROYAL COUNCIL   THE 12 MOROI ROYAL FAMILIES

DHAMPIRS
- GUARDIANS
- MARKS & TATTOOS

  PROMISE MARK   MOLNIJA MARK   ZVEZDA MARK

ALCHEMISTS

STRIGOI
- HOW STRIGOI ARE CREATED
- HOW STRIGOI CAN BE KILLED

CHAPTER 10: *The Quiz*   288

CHAPTER 11: *Glossary*   300

PART ONE:
BOOK RECAPS

CHAPTER 1

Vampire Academy

RICHELLE ON *VAMPIRE ACADEMY*

The idea for *Vampire Academy* was first conceived back in 2006. I was already working on two adult series and really wanted to do something for young adults. Since my first two series dealt with demons and fairies respectively, I thought I'd give vampires a try in order to be different—little knowing what a phenomenon they'd become in the next year! I knew from some college courses that a lot of the best vampire mythology could be found in Eastern Europe, so I went digging around the stories from that region and eventually discovered Moroi, Strigoi, and dhampirs. Really, all I had to work with was a snippet from that myth, but I was able to build an entire culture and history for my books surrounding those three races and their interactions with each other.

The idea of a young woman in love with her instructor was a story I'd wanted to do for some time. Rose's character and personality were, in some ways, inspired by one of my adult characters: Eugenie from the Dark Swan series. Eugenie's another action heroine who's not afraid to get in a fight, but she's a twenty-something woman who has already come to terms with who she is and who she wants to be. I began to wonder what it'd be like to write about a younger character, one who was kickass and not afraid to stand up for her beliefs but who was still growing, finding her identity, and also learning what it means to control her fighter impulses. I was fascinated by the idea of that journey. Rose and her fierce devotion to her friends were the results of my experiment, and she soon developed into the vivid and unique character we love today.

First line: I felt her fear before I heard her screams.

LOST AND FOUND

In the middle of the night, two years after running away from their boarding school, Rose Hathaway and Lissa Dragomir have been found . . . and there's no escaping *this* time.

Where are they going? Back to St. Vladimir's Academy, the last place they want to return to. They'd run away to escape a looming threat that had put their lives at risk, and returning could mean they'll have to face those dangers head-on.

The majority of the students at St. Vlad's are Moroi—peaceful, living vampires who follow a nocturnal schedule. Even though sunlight doesn't kill them, they're still stronger at night. All Moroi have abilities in elemental magic—earth, fire, air, or water—but in their teens, they will begin to specialize in one of the four. Also enrolled at the school are dhampirs—those who are half Moroi and half human. Dhampirs train to become the bodyguards of the Moroi after graduation, guarding them against the evil, undead Strigoi. Rose is a dhampir who's been unofficially protecting her best friend, Lissa, a Moroi, while they've been out on their own. Keeping Lissa safe is Rose's number-one goal. That they've been found means Rose has failed—and she's damn mad about that.

Rose might be tough, but she stands no chance against the ten guardians the school has sent to find them, especially the one who seems to be in charge: Dimitri Belikov. The attractive guardian stops her easily. Rose is ready to fight hard to protect Lissa but lacks the skill to go head-to-head with someone as strong and experienced as Dimitri. Rose quickly learns that Dimitri's nobody to mess with—the proof is marked right on his skin.

> *He leaned forward to pick up something, revealing six tiny symbols tattooed on the back of his neck:* molnija *marks. They looked like two streaks of jagged lightning crossing in an* X *symbol. One for each Strigoi he'd killed. Above them was a twisting line, sort of like a snake, that marked him as a guardian. The promise mark.* —*page 13*

Total badass. Too bad he's the one dragging them back to St. Vlad's. Anyone else, Rose might be able to handle.

Through their psychic bond, Rose senses Lissa's terror about going back to the school. The bond was created after the car accident that killed Lissa's parents and brother Andre when the girls were fifteen. It only works one way, though. Rose can sense Lissa's thoughts and feelings, but Lissa can't do the same.

The car accident left Lissa as the only remaining member of the Dragomir family, and therefore her continuing survival is vital to her race. The Dragomirs are one of the twelve royal Moroi families—important and influential families that rule the rest of the Moroi and from which the Moroi king or queen is chosen.

Rose wishes she could help ease the fear her best friend feels about being discovered and captured, but there's nothing she can do. They're headed back to St. Vlad's whether they like it or not.

At the school, Headmistress Kirova calls an uncomfortable meeting to decide the girls' fates. Unsurprisingly, the rebellious and outspoken Rose is blamed for convincing Lissa to run away from the safety of the Academy and putting her life in danger all this time, but that's not the truth. Rose took Lissa away in order *to* protect her, but she can't tell anyone that. Trust is not something Rose hands out easily.

Joining them in the meeting is Victor Dashkov, gravely ill with Sandovsky's syndrome, a terminal illness that afflicts Moroi. He is also from one of the royal Moroi families and had promised Lissa's father that he'd watch out for her. He's like an uncle to Lissa. When Dimitri reveals to those present at this meeting that the girls share a rare psychic bond—which he noticed during their capture—it's a secret that Rose doesn't want anyone else to know about.

Victor shows great interest in what a bond like this could mean.

> *"That is a gift," murmured Victor from his corner. "A rare and wonderful thing."*
>
> *"The best guardians always had that bond," added Dimitri. "In the stories."*
>
> *Kirova's outrage returned. "Stories that are centuries old," she exclaimed. "Surely you aren't suggesting we let her stay at the Academy after everything she's done?"*
>
> *He shrugged. "She might be wild and disrespectful, but if she has potential—"*
>
> *"Wild and disrespectful?" I interrupted. "Who the hell are you anyway? Outsourced help?"* —*pages 21–22*

Actually, some might just say the Russian's a good judge of character. But other than that, he's also Lissa's sanctioned guardian now and, as such, he is invested in the Dragomir princess's safety.

As a novice guardian herself, Rose is way behind in her classes, which puts her at a major disadvantage compared to other students in her senior class. A bit reluctantly, Dimitri agrees to tutor Rose before and after regular classes to help her catch up. Rose doesn't exactly like this guy—well, not *yet*, anyway—but she needs to stay in school in order to keep Lissa safe. And this? Well, this might be the only way she can do that. However, if she steps out of line just *once*, she's out of there—and for the immediate future she's basically on house arrest, grounded from doing anything fun or social except going to class and training with Dimitri. Looks like she's going to have to rein in those "wild and disrespectful" ways if she wants to stay out of trouble.

Sure. That could happen.

BACK TO SCHOOL

Since there's no rest for the wicked, Rose and Lissa are sent to their separate classes immediately. Classmates seem shocked to see the beautiful but rebellious Rose Hathaway back at St. Vlad's. Rose gets a chance to reconnect with some of them, including Mason Ashford, a fellow novice guardian, who was a good friend of Rose's before she and Lissa ran away.

"Hey Mason, wipe the drool off your face. If you're going to think about me naked, do it on your own time."

A few snorts and snickers broke the awed silence, and Mason Ashford snapped out of his haze, giving me a lopsided smile. With red hair that stuck up everywhere and a smattering of freckles, he was nice-looking, though not exactly hot. He was also one of the funniest guys I knew. We'd been good friends back in the day.

"This is my time, Hathaway. I'm leading today's session."

"Oh yeah?" I retorted. "Huh. Well, I guess this is a good time to think about me naked then."

"It's always a good time to think about you naked," added someone nearby, breaking the tension further. Eddie Castile. Another friend of mine.   —page 28

Mason gives her some info about the enigmatic Dimitri Belikov. Among the students, the Russian's considered a god around school when it comes to fighting. She's going to learn a lot from him—but it's really going to hurt.

Terrific. But if it gets her what she wants, then it's totally worth it. She's determined to be Lissa's guardian after graduation, but first she's going to have to prove herself to everyone . . . and not everyone is happy she's back. An instructor named Stan Alto gives Rose an extra-hard time in class, reminding her harshly that she has a lot to catch up on and there are many people to whom she must prove herself. To protect Lissa, she needs to stay in school, and to stay in school she's going to have to work damn hard.

Later, Victor Dashkov finds Rose to tell her that he's on her side. To him, it's obvious that Rose kept Lissa safe all this time because she's skilled and dedicated. He seems to know a lot about the psychic bond the girls share because he's studied up on the subject, but he's eager to know more. Rose feels bad for the sick man—at this point she believes he only wants the best for Lissa's future.

But that isn't what *everyone* wants. A bitchy rival named Mia Rinaldi makes her presence known. She's taken over Lissa's spot with the popular "royals" at St. Vlad's, and Lissa and Rose seem to be no longer welcome in those circles—not if Mia has anything to say about it. Mia's even currently dating Lissa's ex-boyfriend, Aaron, and hates both Lissa and Rose on sight. Later, they'll learn that this hatred stems from Mia's hurt feelings at being used and discarded by Lissa's brother, Andre. Mia, despite having non-royal bloodlines, is determined to be a part of the popular crowd and sees Lissa as a threat.

Great. Yet another person Rose needs to protect her friend from.

It's not just bitchy blond enemies who are a problem now that the girls have returned to St. Vlad's. They're the main focus of student gossip and rumors today. One topic everyone wants to know the answer to: What did Lissa do for blood while they were away? As a vampire, she has to drink blood regularly to survive.

The truth is that she fed from Rose, but a dhampir giving her blood to a Moroi, even a friend in need, is viewed as big-time wrong—and dirty. There's a nasty term for a dhampir who gives up both her neck and her body for the addictive bite of a Moroi guy—a *blood whore*. While what she and Lissa did isn't nearly that bad, it's best to keep this secret to themselves.

Luckily, the girls are not only greeted at school by gossip, conflict, and potential enemies. They also have a few allies who are very happy they're back, like Victor's daughter, Natalie Dashkov, who's been assigned as Lissa's new roommate. She's super boring and unpopular, which pleases Rose since it'll help keep Lissa out of danger. Ever since the car accident, Lissa's been very fragile—being back at school with backstabbing, fake friends—aka the popular crowd she used to socialize with—might prove too much for her. At the first sign of trouble, a worried Rose plans to get Lissa out of the school if that's what it takes to protect her.

CHRISTIAN AND THE ATTIC

But Rose can't be with Lissa *all* the time—at least not physically. However, sometimes she can be pulled into Lissa's head through their psychic connection and see and hear the world through Lissa's eyes. That's what happens when Lissa wanders into the school chapel's attic in a search for solitude.

Instead of solitude, Lissa finds Christian Ozera. Christian's parents chose to become Strigoi—the evil, immortal enemy of Moroi. Even though he's from a royal bloodline, this stigma has branded Christian a social outcast—not to mention a jerk—and Lissa isn't too thrilled to be around him.

However . . . there's something about him that's *kind* of intriguing. The taunting, snarky Christian seems very insightful, especially when he easily guesses that Lissa fed from Rose while they were away. She's afraid he's going to tell, to use it against her, but he's not that kind of guy. He promises not to say a word and then magically warms the air when Lissa seems chilled—Christian's elemental magic specialty is fire.

Other than her secret ability to heal—which isn't really tied to any of the four elements—Lissa hasn't specialized in any one element yet.

Hmmm. Lissa decides that maybe Christian's not so bad after all, especially when he volunteers to share this secret hiding place with her whenever she wants to use it. And, you know, his ice-blue eyes are rather striking…

When Rose snaps out of the bond, Dimitri's in front of her and seems worried about what's happening. His concern takes her by surprise, and she explains that it's just the bond between her and Lissa at work. Suddenly he isn't the hardass guy she originally met. Maybe there's more to Dimitri than meets the eye—not that what meets the eye is bad at all. Her twenty-four-year-old instructor's tall, dark, Russian, and…*super hot.*

Feeling his eyes on me like that made something flutter inside of me—which was stupid, of course. I had no reason to get all goofy, just because the man was too good-looking for his own good. After all, he was an antisocial god, according to Mason. One who was supposedly going to leave me in all sorts of pain.

—*page 64*

Yes, pain for Rose is yet to come with Dimitri. Physical . . . and otherwise.

Right now? Just the physical kind.

Later, Rose makes a point to lecture Lissa about staying away from creepy Christian. If she's interested in dating, Rose thinks she should direct her attention back to her ex, Aaron, who would be a much safer choice of potential boyfriends—plus, stealing him away from the annoying Mia would be a total bonus.

Rose gets permission to go to church, even though she's not exactly what you'd call religious. She just wants to do something social—being grounded sucks. There she learns in the sermon about St. Vladimir, the patron saint of the school, someone who was "filled with spirit," which allowed him to heal the sick.

Healing . . . just like Lissa can do.

The priest mentions his "shadow-kissed" guardian Anna, and this also gets Rose's attention since Ms. Karp, a former teacher, had once called Rose the same thing in reference to her connection to Lissa. She wants to know more about St. Vlad, and the priest suggests she look up the subject of Moroi saints in the library.

Great, extra homework.

When Mia continues to be a pest by insulting Rose's fashion sense—which, admittedly, has slipped a bit in the past two years—Rose vents to Mason in the library about the girl who's quickly turning into her nemesis. Mason has inside info on Mia—her parents are basically servants, working for Moroi royalty. Huh. So even though Mia acts like a princess, she sure isn't one in real life. Putting her Mia issues aside, for the time being anyway, Rose and Mason research Moroi saints, as the priest suggested, and Rose learns that Anna and St. Vlad had a bond that allowed her to see into his heart and mind. It's intriguing information, but over the next weeks, while training with Dimitri regularly and attending all her classes, she forgets all about it.

A DEADLY WARNING

When a fox with a slit throat is discovered in Lissa's dorm room, Rose sees this as a serious and disturbing red flag. Lissa, who has a deep love for animals, immediately reaches for the poor thing to try to help it. But Rose restrains her. It reminds her too much of a dead raven Lissa also wanted to save once . . .

She turned to me, eyes almost wild. "Rose . . . do you remember . . . that one time . . ."

"Stop it," I said. "Forget about it. This isn't the same thing."

"What if someone saw? What if someone knows? . . ."

I tightened my grip on her arm, digging my nails in to get her attention. She flinched. "No. It's not the same. It has nothing to do with that. Do you hear me?" I could feel both Natalie's and Dimitri's eyes on us. "It's going to be okay. Everything's going to be okay."

—page 99

They have no idea who'd leave such a gruesome gift. Is this somebody's idea of a stupid joke? Or is it a threat? And from whom? Mia? Or could it be someone with even darker intentions?

In class, a Moroi jerk named Ralf taunts Lissa about the fox. Other students know Rose and Lissa were brought back against their will to the school, so a new rumor is circulating that Lissa killed the fox so she'd be considered crazy enough to get expelled. Rose warns Ralf off, but he doesn't take the hint . . .

At least not until he bursts into flames courtesy of Christian's fire magic. Looks like Christian is getting a bit protective of Lissa. And he knows the stakes, too. Using magic in class is forbidden, and he gets kicked out for defending Lissa. But rather than impress Rose, all it does is convince her that Christian's a serious danger to her friend. However, Rose worries it's possible Lissa doesn't feel the same way and that she might be starting to like the outcast. Later, Rose slips into her friend's head—this is the first time she's been able to do this with conscious effort—to see if her suspicions are correct. Yup. Lissa's in the attic again with the fire starter himself.

To most Moroi, like Lissa, their elemental magic is peaceful, *not* something to be used as a weapon. Obviously, Christian feels differently. Moroi used to fight with their magic, to defend themselves against Strigoi rather than depend entirely on guardians. Some have forgotten, but others haven't. This will soon become a very hot topic—no fire-magic pun intended—in the Moroi world.

Christian knows Lissa uses compulsion on others—and he's right. Compulsion is the ability all Moroi have to mentally influence someone else—only some Moroi, like Lissa, are much stronger in it than others. It's how the girls got by in the human world for so long. Same thing as lighting someone on fire, really. Both are forbidden abilities.

> *"What are you going to do then?" she asked. "You going to turn me in?"*
>
> *He shook his head and smiled. "No. I think it's hot."*

—page 114

Despite herself, Lissa can't help but be attracted to Christian. And it's not just that. When she's with him, she feels . . . at peace. Like she can be herself without trying to hide what she really is.

It's always been Rose and Lissa against the world, but now it looks as if her best friend has found someone else. Rose can't help but feel jealous about this.

The best way to deal with feeling cast aside? Hook up with a hot guy. Sounds like a plan. The hot guy in question is Jesse Zeklos, a Moroi who's always found Rose gorgeous and with whom she's fooled around a bit in the past. And right now, she definitely needs a bit of an ego boost.

That night, they find a private place to make out. When Jesse's sharp fangs brush against Rose's skin, it reminds her of what it feels like to be bit—really, *really* good. The endorphins in a Moroi's bite make the act totally addictive. However, the last thing she needs is for everyone to start thinking she's a blood whore—she hasn't even gone all the way with anyone yet. Moroi guys love hooking up with dhampir girls, but it almost never leads to anything serious like marriage since Moroi like to keep their bloodlines going with other pure Moroi. And yet . . . she's not totally pulling Jesse away and he's starting to get encouraged.

But then the door bursts open. It's Dimitri. Uh-oh.

> *"Mr. Zeklos, do you have permission to be in this part of the dorm?"*
>
> *"No, sir."*
>
> *"Do you know the rules about male and female interactions around here?"*
>
> *"Yes, sir."*
>
> *"Then I suggest you get out of here as fast as you can before I turn you over to someone who will punish you accordingly. If I ever see you like this again"—Dimitri pointed to where I cowered, half-dressed, on the couch—"I will be the one to punish you. And it will hurt. A lot. Do you understand?"* —*page 120*

Dimitri successfully chases Jesse away and then turns his dangerous gaze on Rose. But then, as he studies her body, currently clad only in jeans and a bra, his gaze shifts to something more like ... *desire.* Suddenly the thought of Dimitri touching her is all Rose can think about. Which, of course, she realizes is *way* wrong. He's seven years older than she is. *And* her instructor. And ... there are *a lot* of other reasons she shouldn't be thinking of him this way—or vice versa.

> *What was I thinking? Was I out of my mind? Embarrassed,*
> *I covered my feelings with attitude.*
> *"You see something you like?" I asked.*
> *"Get dressed."*   —*page 121*

The heated moment passes and Dimitri's all business again, chastising Rose for not taking her reinstatement at the school seriously. If she really wants to protect Lissa, she needs to focus. And she will. She wants Dimitri to teach her to *really* fight. So far all she's had are remedial lessons with him as he's attempted to catch her up on everything she's missed out on in the last two years.

She wants to really learn how to fight?

Fine. They'll start tomorrow.

MS. KARP AND THE RAVEN

Her many issues and interactions with Dimitri are very distracting, but Rose's first priority is her best friend's safety now that they're back at the school. What happened with the dead fox in Lissa's room weighs heavily on Rose's mind. It's much too similar to what happened two years ago just before they ran away.

Back then, Ms. Karp, a young, pretty teacher at the school who always acted a bit loony, caught Rose and Lissa in the woods with booze in hand. Busted. The three of them then found a dead raven on the ground and Lissa, seemingly transfixed, reached for it . . . and brought it back to life with her touch!

Another time, Ms. Karp had healed one of Rose's injuries. Was the ability to heal the raven—and Lissa's need to do the same with the fox—the same kind of thing? It's the first sign that there are some strange similarities between Ms. Karp and Lissa. Just like Lissa, Ms. Karp never specialized in a specific element with her magic like all other Moroi do.

Their teacher was disturbed by the incident with the raven and made them promise not to say anything about it. She warned Rose never to let Lissa attempt to bring something back to life again. Ms. Karp's paranoia worked, instilling Rose with a fear of anyone finding out about Lissa's ability to heal—to the point of bringing animals back to life. It would put her friend in jeopardy.

With the dead fox, it was clear to Rose that Lissa wanted to resurrect the dead fox too—but that would risk others finding out about Lissa's strange and secret ability.

But does someone already know what it is?

FALLING FOR DIMITRI

Rose tries to focus on her next session with Dimitri, the first where they're going to work on taking her training to the next level. She's supposed to hit him, but he easily knocks her to the ground, which is frustrating. When he turns his back, Rose tries to attack, but he's able to grab her and pin her to the ground.

It's full body contact with the gorgeous Russian.

All of a sudden, it occurred to me that he was still holding me down. The skin on his fingers was warm as he clutched my wrists. His face hovered inches from my own, and his legs and torso were actually pressing against mine. Some of his long brown hair hung around his face, and he appeared to be noticing me too, almost like he had that night in the lounge. And oh God, did he smell good. ——*page 141*

It's a very sexy moment, and Rose realizes she's seriously crushing on her gorgeous, older mentor. Bad idea! It's absolutely the *last* thing she needs right now with the rest of the problems she's dealing with!

Thankfully, there's something else for Rose to focus on. Queen Tatiana, the leader of the Moroi world, is coming to the school on an official visit in celebration of All Saints' Day, and the school is buzzing in anticipation and excitement of this. Rose isn't too impressed, though. Visits from the queen and her royal party are fairly common, but after being given permission to attend the event, it does give her the chance to socialize with others at the royal banquet.

This doesn't go so well—not for Lissa, anyway. During the welcoming assembly, the queen pauses to speak with the last remaining Dragomir—but their conversation quickly takes a nosedive when the queen intimates, in front of everyone, that Lissa shamed her family name by running away. Lissa is mortified.

Mia, of course, makes a point to mock Lissa for this public embarrassment. Rose jumps to Lissa's defense as always and, in a heated moment, disses Mia's family for being "servants." Dimitri breaks up the verbal sparring, sending Mia on her way, and he begins to escort Rose back to her dorm to avoid any further trouble. As they leave, Rose notices Christian making a beeline for her distraught friend, but she stops him before Lissa sees him. Rose thinks Christian's a bad influence and decides to lie to him, to tell him Lissa doesn't like him and thinks he's a freak. The lie works perfectly, and a hurt Christian steers clear of Lissa that night.

Later, Rose is awakened by Lissa's emotions flowing through their bond—she's incredibly upset. When Rose makes it to her friend's dorm room, she sees that someone has left another horrific gift for Lissa—a dead rabbit. This time there's a note attached warning Lissa that the sender knows what she is and that she won't survive if she stays at the Academy. The grave message is enough to put her over the edge, and she resorts to her old method of dealing with stress. Cutting herself helps refocus her pain. This is a very bad sign for Rose, since this isn't the first time Lissa's done this. It happened before they ran away from the school, and it means Lissa's becoming more mentally fragile by the day. Rose is very worried about her friend.

As desperate as Rose is to help Lissa, the next day she has other major problems she can't ignore. There's now a devastating rumor going around that Rose had sex with both Jesse and his friend Ralf...*and* she let them drink her blood. Everyone's saying that Rose Hathaway is a blood whore. Rose is willing to bet the mastermind behind this little catastrophe is Mia—Jesse and Ralf are just her meathead tools.

But this realization doesn't help matters. The damage is done.

A sickening feeling settled in my stomach. I thought about the friends and respect I'd managed to eke out, despite our low profile. That would be gone. You couldn't come back from something like this. Not among the Moroi. Once a blood whore, always a blood whore. What made it worse was that some dark, secret part of me did like being bitten. —*page 173*

Sickened by the rumors, Lissa resolves to protect Rose from now on, just as Rose has always protected her. She begins to use her compulsion to get everyone to shun Mia and accept Rose again.

And it actually starts to work. Before long, the rumors about Rose begin to fade—and not only that, Lissa's accepted back into the popular crowd and has successfully stolen Aaron away from the vengeful Mia. While she's not in love with her ex, it's a way to snub Mia and hang out with the royal students again now that she isn't trying to keep a low profile around school anymore—which hasn't really gained them anything. Besides, dating-wise, it's not like Christian is even acknowledging her existence anymore, so what difference does it make if she dates Aaron? Lissa, of course, doesn't realize that Christian is only distancing himself from Lissa because of what Rose told him.

But the more Lissa uses compulsion to fix things, the darker her moods become. Rose finds herself worrying more and more about Lissa's ever-diminishing emotional stability, and this sends her straight back to researching the story of St. Vladimir. The similarities to Lissa and Ms. Karp are striking—like them, he was able to heal. But his talents didn't end there. He could also bring *people* back from the dead. Rose needs to know more, but information on the saint is extremely hard to find.

Fortunately, there's a box of St. Vlad's writings in the chapel's attic—Rose remembers Christian pointing out a box to Lissa that he said was "full of the writings of the blessed and crazy St. Vladimir." Rose sends Mason, who's been helping her research St. Vlad at the library, with a message to Christian to bring them to her. He does, which is a bit of a surprise given their unfriendly relationship, especially in regard to Lissa.

Rose reads St. Vlad's diary and is intrigued when he mentions his gratitude toward his "shadow-kissed" guardian, Anna, and his ability to heal. It scares Rose to read that the more he used his powers, the crazier and more depressed he became, leading to an attempted suicide. It's more proof that there are similarities between St. Vlad, Lissa, and Ms. Karp, especially in light of Lissa's increasingly darker moods . . . Rose's concern for Lissa is turning to real worry.

It only gets worse when Lissa has a big party in her room. She gets drunk, and her emotions begin to run rampant. It reminds Rose of another party two years ago when Lissa had gone over the edge—and nearly used her compulsion to force a jerk of a guy to bludgeon himself to death with a baseball bat after he'd abused a helpless human feeder.

Luckily, Rose managed to stop her then, but the darkness and anger coming from Lissa scared her deeply. Before they left the school last time, Ms. Karp had eventually gone completely insane from the darkness that ruled *her* mind. Rose didn't want the same to happen to her best friend.

This is why Rose had insisted they run away two years ago. With everything happening—the dead animals, the warnings, the overuse of compulsion—are they headed down that road again?

Rose does more research on St. Vladimir and is struck by one phrase in particular: St. Vlad was said to be "full of spirit." Just like

Ms. Karp and Lissa, he never specialized in an element whereas all other Moroi will specialize in fire, air, earth, or water magic.

When Rose tells Lissa what she's learned, Lissa is edgy, defensive, and quick to argue. However, she finally agrees to stop compelling people and using her healing ability to see if it makes a difference in her moods.

Even though Lissa has been dating the popular, good-looking Aaron in order to regain her status in the school's royal social stratosphere, get revenge on Mia, and work her influence on everyone to clear Rose's reputation, Rose isn't so sure anymore that he's the best choice of boyfriends. He's boring. *Christian*, however, isn't boring and might actually be good for her friend.

> *He was creepy and dark and liked to set people on fire, true. On the other hand, he was smart and funny—in a twisted way—and somehow had a calming effect on Lissa.* —page 222

Damn. Rose had messed it all up. She now knows she made a big mistake about lying to Christian about Lissa's real feelings, letting anger and jealousy get the best of her. Lissa was better when she was friends with him, and she seems worse off without him in her life.

Rose apologizes to Christian for lying, but even if he believes her, he's not sure he wants to be friends with Lissa anymore. After all, she's been acting very *royal* by hanging out with her old, snobby friends and seemingly embracing her old elitist "Princess Lissa" ways. That's definitely not the outcast Christian's scene, even if there are reasons behind Lissa's actions other than a grasp at her previous popularity. Rose then relates her worries about Lissa and how she won't listen to Rose's advice, but she might listen to Christian. Finally, reluctantly, he agrees to talk to her and try to help her, even though he thinks that any big problems—like Lissa's secret cutting—should be discussed with Kirova or Dimitri.

> *"Lissa wouldn't like that." I considered. "Neither would I."*
>
> *"Yeah, well, we all have to do things we don't like. That's life."*
>
> *My snarky switch flipped on. "What are you, an after-school special?"*
>
> *A ghostly smile flickered across his lips. "If you weren't so psychotic, you'd be fun to hang around."*
>
> *"Funny, I feel the same way about you."* —*page 227*

But before Rose has time to hope things might get better, the girls receive another threat in the form of a dead dove. They still have no idea who it's from or what they want other than trying to scare the girls away from the school.

FIELD TRIP

Despite their mounting problems, a few days later the girls are invited on a shopping trip with Natalie and her ailing father, Victor. Since Rose is still basically "grounded" as punishment for running away, Dimitri suggests they justify the trip away from the school by treating it as a training exercise—Rose's first official day in the real world as Lissa's unofficial guardian. In the future, she's reminded by another guardian along for the day, both she and the gorgeous Dimitri will be required to guard Lissa together—so they better start practicing.

"Yup. You're going to be Dimitri's partner."

A moment of funny silence fell, probably not noticeable to anyone except Dimitri and me. Our eyes met.

"Guarding partner," Dimitri clarified unnecessarily, like maybe he too had been thinking about other kinds of partners.

page 233

On the trip, Rose complains that she doesn't get to carry a weapon like the other guardians do. Dimitri isn't so sure she's ready to kill a Strigoi yet. It's not an easy thing to do, especially because a Strigoi might be someone she knows from the past—killed, and then brought back to life as a member of the evil undead. Despite how difficult it might be, they both strongly agree that if either of them were turned Strigoi—monsters who have lost all morals and who kill innocent people—they'd want someone to kill them.

Conversation on the ride turns to others who've had to face the same horrible task—hunting someone they once loved—and one example hits very close to home. Until now, Rose has kept a secret from Lissa. The princess is shocked to hear that Ms. Karp—the teacher who seemed to have so much in common with Lissa—ultimately chose to become Strigoi. Rose learned this the night she decided they had to run away to help keep Lissa safe from her abilities, since the more she used them, the worse they'd get. After turning Strigoi, Ms. Karp was then hunted by her former guardian lover, Mikhail Tanner.

It's a sobering conversation, and Rose suddenly isn't sure if she'd be able to do the same—to hunt down and kill someone she loves. Little does she know that it's something she'll have to face head-on in her not-too-distant future.

Trying to focus on more pleasant pursuits, the group gets to shopping, which is difficult with Rose acting as Lissa's guardian. It's tricky trying on cool clothes when you're trying to guard your best friend from potential threats. In fact, it's impossible. Lissa takes the initiative and buys Rose a sexy black dress to wear to the upcoming school dance. Lissa also spots a beautiful gold and diamond necklace with a pendant the shape of a rose that she thinks would be perfect for Rose's outfit—she always loves to buy Rose "rose" stuff—but it's sadly far outside of even the Dragomir princess's price range.

Rose is in a good mood when they return to the school. She hops from bench to bench on the way back to their dorms—but suddenly, the wood gives way and she feels searing pain as her ankle snaps. After blacking out, she wakes in the clinic with a concerned Dimitri nearby who is relieved she's okay. Strangely, her ankle isn't broken like she thought it was.

By her side in the clinic, Dimitri has a couple of gifts for Rose. The first is a small box and a note from Victor congratulating her on a successful first day as Lissa's guardian. She opens the box and peers inside, surprised to see gold and diamonds glinting out at her. It's the expensive rose necklace she and Lissa had seen at the mall. Wow . . . talk about generous!

Also generous is Dimitri's gift—although it didn't cost nearly as much. It's Rose's favorite lip gloss. She can't believe he noticed. She's touched by the thoughtful gift and, without really thinking about it first, Rose gives him a hug . . . and things heat up quickly.

At the first touch of his skin on mine, I shivered. He wound
a lock of my hair around one finger, just as he had in the gym.

Swallowing, I dragged my eyes up from his lips. I'd been contemplating what it'd be like to kiss him. The thought both excited and scared me, which was stupid. I'd kissed a lot of guys and never thought much about it. No reason another one— even an older one—should be that big of a deal. Yet the thought of him closing the distance and bringing his lips to mine made the world start spinning. —page 251

Unfortunately, any kissing potential is interrupted by the doctor coming to check on Rose, who appears to be fine. Dimitri wonders out loud if perhaps Rose simply has excellent healing abilities— he's heard of how she emerged unscathed from the car accident with Lissa's family.

In that moment, Rose comes to a shocking realization. Lissa can heal animals—she's seen it herself. She must have healed Rose's broken ankle today, going against the promise she'd made not to use her abilities again. Then something even bigger occurs to her. Lissa must have also healed Rose's injuries after the car accident. That's why they both walked away unharmed.

Through their bond, Rose mentally finds an upset Lissa in the attic with Christian. Lissa's surprised to see him in their hiding spot, especially when he's clearly been trying very hard to ignore her.

A snarky Christian tells Lissa that lately she's been acting a lot like her brother, Andre, who was a royal jerk. *He's* the real reason Mia has had it out for Lissa all this time. According to Christian, Andre used Mia and threw her away. Lissa refuses to believe it and thinks Christian must be lying about her beloved brother just to upset her. She bets Christian's just upset that Lissa would date someone like Aaron, who she doesn't really like, rather than him.

> *"I like him."*
>
> *"Like or* like*?"*
>
> *"Oh, there's a difference?"*
>
> *"Yes. Like is when you date a big, blond moron and laugh at his stupid jokes."*
>
> *Then out of nowhere, he leaned forward and kissed her. It was hot and fast and furious, an outpouring of the rage and passion and longing that Christian always kept locked inside of him. Lissa had never been kissed like that, and I felt her respond to it, respond to him—how he made her feel so much more alive than Aaron or anyone else could.*
>
> *Christian pulled back from the kiss but still kept his face next to hers.*
>
> *"That's what you do with someone you like."* —*page 259*

Lissa feels the desire between them, but her dark emotions are raging out of control from using her healing ability on Rose's ankle earlier. She yells for Christian to get out and, even though they'd both agreed to share the attic, he begrudgingly does as she wishes. Her mood continues to plummet and she ends up cutting herself again. This time, she slices deeper than ever before. And Rose, through her bond, senses it's too far.

Rose rushes to tell Dimitri what she's seen—he's known about their bond since day one, but not many other people do. She's not risking this secret right now as much as she's betraying Lissa's confidence, but her friend is hurt and needs help before she loses too much blood. It's Rose's attempt, yet again, to protect her friend.

However, when Lissa is brought to the clinic for treatment, she's furious that Rose told on her. To Lissa, it feels as if the only person in the world she trusted has betrayed her—even though Rose only did so to save her life.

With all the drama, Rose almost forgets about the school dance. Having her best friend hate her guts doesn't make the thought of being social very appealing, but Rose lets Mason convince her to go anyway. He's been a loyal and supportive friend all along, and he never believed in the "blood whore" rumors for a moment. As much as she'd rather stay home, she reluctantly puts on her new, sexy dress and the rose necklace from Victor. And she has to admit—she looks pretty damn good. It's a sentiment that Dimitri seems to share; when they cross paths on her way to the dance, he can't seem to take his eyes off her.

Mason has a surprise for Rose at the dance that he's personally arranged. He gets Jesse and Ralf to admit—once and for all—that they were lying about Rose being a blood whore. Well, *duh*. Rose already knew that, but at least now everyone else will too. But that's not all! How did Mia get the boys to lie about what happened? She slept with them—*both* of them.

Jesse . . . *and* Ralf? Um, *eww*!

The secret is out and Mia is mad as hell. She's ready to blame everyone for her mistakes and share her pain—which all stemmed from her treatment at the hands of Lissa's brother. Mia confronts Lissa and tells her point-blank that her craziness is going to get her locked up. Rose, automatically defending her best friend even when they're not speaking, responds by punching Mia in the face and breaking her nose.

Rose has never been all that great at impulse control.

Devastated by Mia's taunts and that everyone heard them, Lissa flees the dance, and Rose yells for Christian to go after her. She'd do it herself, but she's being escorted by guardians back to her dorm room so she doesn't get in any more trouble.

Once in her room, a worried Rose reaches out to Lissa through their bond. In the chapel attic, Christian is soothing Lissa and her mood is improving . . . but suddenly guardians bust in. They knock Christian out and kidnap Lissa!

THE NECKLACE

Rose knows she needs to find help immediately, but her thoughts suddenly become fuzzy. Something tells her to go to Dimitri, so she heads to his room. It's very hard for her to focus, especially when he answers his door bare-chested and fresh from the shower.

Rose's desire for Dimitri skyrockets and she can't seem to control it. Dimitri grabs her wrists to stop her from crossing a line between them, but the second his hands land on her skin, he's also seized by whatever force is affecting Rose. Now he wants her too. Badly.

> *"Do you think I'm pretty?"*
>
> *He regarded me with utter seriousness, like he always did. "I think you're beautiful."*
>
> *"Beautiful?"*
>
> *"You are so beautiful, it hurts me sometimes."* —page 283

Things get hot and heavy between them—fast! Before too long,
Rose is naked and Dimitri isn't far from it. She's overwhelmed with
desire for him and thinks she'll lose her virginity to him—which
is totally okay with her. But when Dimitri removes her necklace,
the voice urging her to be with him is gone. The attraction is still
there—no doubt about it—but the need is less intense. They realize the necklace is charmed with a compulsion spell—in this case,
lust. When Dimitri throws it out the window, clarity returns, and
with it, Rose remembers that Lissa is in terrible danger!

They race to tell Kirova what Rose saw through the bond, but
the headmistress doesn't believe her. At least, not until an injured
Christian staggers in.

The group moves immediately into action to rescue Lissa. Dimitri insists Rose come along because through the bond, Rose can
tell the direction that Lissa and her captors are headed.

She's able to see who took her best friend—it's Victor Dashkov!
Kind and helpful, practically a member of Lissa's family, Victor
Dashkov!

He's the one who gave Rose the charmed necklace—he was trying to stop her from intervening in this kidnapping. Through the
bond, Rose sees and hears what a shocked and frightened Lissa is
now experiencing—that Victor knows about Lissa's ability to heal
and wants her to do the same with his disease.

Victor has suspected this for a while—ever since the car accident that killed her parents. Rose watches on and is as stunned as
Lissa is when he reveals something the girls weren't fully aware of
until this very moment. In the accident that killed Lissa's parents
and brother . . . Rose also died. But there was a difference—Lissa
brought Rose back to life with "spirit." It's what forged the psychic

bond between them. Because of this, Rose is "shadow-kissed."

Just like Anna—St. Vladimir's guardian, Rose realizes. St. Vlad also used spirit to bring Anna back from the dead.

It turns out that Victor and his daughter, Natalie, have been leaving the dead animals for Lissa in an attempt to test her abilities in spirit, which is the fifth magical element Moroi can specialize in. Since it's so rare, it's been forgotten over the centuries by nearly everyone in Moroi and dhampir society.

It was important for Victor to prove that Lissa was, in fact, a spirit user because only a Moroi who possessed spirit could keep his disease at bay. Victor is determined to receive regular healings, regardless of the cost to Lissa's mental and physical health.

But it's all for the greater good. Or so he claims. Victor was next in line to the throne, and he thinks he can regain his status once he's healthy again. He has big plans for the future of the Moroi race.

When Lissa refuses to help, Rose watches with horror through the bond as Victor has her friend tortured by one of his air-user henchmen who magically suffocates Lissa until she finally agrees to do as he wishes.

Lissa uses her healing ability to heal Victor, and he becomes stronger and stronger. Meanwhile, Lissa only gets weaker from using so much spirit magic.

RESCUING LISSA

Rose is sickened by what is happening to her best friend and feels helpless that she's unable to protect her from the pain. She directs the guardians to the cabin where Lissa is being kept. Before they storm in, Dimitri tells a furious and frustrated Rose to stay behind in the SUV. But alone in the car, Rose realizes they won't find Lissa—the bond shows her that Lissa has escaped the house and is now on her own in the wilderness.

She needs to find her friend . . . and fast. When Rose finds her, Lissa is backed up against a tree by a pack of Victor's psi hounds, psychically connected wolf-like beasts. They turn on Rose when they realize she's there. In the nick of time, Christian—who stowed away for the trip in an attempt to save the girl he's fallen for—arrives to help fend them off, but he's violently attacked.

Alberta, the head of the school's guardians, swoops in and shoots the dangerous animals. Christian is badly hurt . . . and dying. Lissa wants desperately to heal him, but she's too weak from healing Victor.

Before, Rose might have hesitated to let her friend feed from her in public, risking being labeled again as a blood whore, but there's no question what she needs to do to help Lissa to save Christian. Her friend needs blood to regain her energy and her magic; Rose offers her neck to the cause, and it's enough to give Lissa the energy to save Christian.

The other guardians capture Victor and hold him prisoner under full-time guard at school. They realize Natalie is also to blame. Not only did she help plant the dead animals, but, as an earth-magic user, just like her father, she was the one responsible for rotting the wood that broke Rose's ankle. It was another attempt to get Lissa to use her healing ability, proving once and for all that she is a spirit user.

In the wake of her kidnapping, Lissa realizes what she really wants. For starters, she wants *Christian*—the boy who has stood by her side, in the attic and out, the one who stowed away in the back of a van in order to help rescue her. She breaks up with Aaron and officially starts dating the social outcast, not caring what damage this relationship might do to her royal reputation.

Not everyone's romantic life is quite as happy. Dimitri makes sure Rose is aware that what happened because of the lust charm was wrong and stupid.

> *"Even if you choose not to tell, you need to understand that* it was a mistake. *And it isn't ever going to happen again," he added.*
>
> *"Because you're too old for me? Because it isn't responsible?"*
>
> *His face was perfectly blank. "No. Because I'm just not interested in you in that way."* —*page 314*

Ouch. Rose is heartbroken to know that Dimitri doesn't return her feelings for him. In the end, what she feels is just a stupid schoolgirl crush, but it's one she can't seem to shake no matter how hard she tries.

And she tries very hard. She even goes to visit Victor in his cell to ask him to break the lust compulsion that makes her still want to be with Dimitri. But instead, Victor tells her startling news: the spell only works on feelings already present—feelings *both* of them would have had to share. Before Rose can figure out what this means, she hears a commotion down the hall. Natalie has arrived to help her father escape and there's something very different—and very *scary*—about her.

She's been turned into a Strigoi. And now she's more than strong enough to throw Rose against the wall when she attempts to get in her way. But luckily, before Natalie can finish her off . . . Dimitri arrives.

32

He manages to stake Natalie, saving Rose. While other guardians race to recapture Victor, Dimitri takes an injured Rose to the clinic. On the way, she wants to know if what she's learned about the lust charm is true. Does Dimitri really feel something for her? Yes, it's true. He *does* want Rose . . . but they can't be together.

"[Y]ou and I will both be Lissa's guardians someday. I need

to protect her at all costs. If a pack of Strigoi come, I need to

throw my body between them and her."

"I know that. Of course that's what you have to do." The black

sparkles were dancing in front of my eyes again. I was fading out.

"No. If I let myself love you, I won't throw myself in front of

her. I'll throw myself in front of you." —page 324

He's right. Even though Rose still desperately wants Dimitri, she knows she must protect her best friend over anything else. It's her job.

But Rose can't be resentful because Lissa is there to help her heal the injuries she sustained from fighting Natalie. Still, Lissa's dark moods are a serious problem. She agrees to go on depression medication to help. One downside of this is that she'll be blocked from using spirit magic, but it's worth it to regain her shaky sanity.

Being on meds is one way to lose touch from the magic. But there's another—Natalie had said during her short confrontation with Rose that becoming Strigoi was worth giving up the magic of being Moroi.

This makes something click into place for Rose.

Ms. Karp's spirit magic is what had driven her insane. She didn't become Strigoi because she was mad—she did it to *escape* from

33

the madness. It's a chilling realization for Rose, especially since Ms. Karp and Lissa seem similar to her in so many ways. Is Lissa inevitably headed down the same dangerous path? Would Lissa ever make the same tragic decision as their teacher did to escape the side effects of having such a powerful ability?

But St. Vladimir didn't turn Strigoi. After going to the chapel and asking the priest some questions, Rose learns that St. Vlad lived for a very long time. After all, St. Vladimir was lucky enough to have Anna as his "shadow-kissed" guardian to help him stay strong and never give in to his madness . . .

And Lissa has Rose.

* For quiz answers, see p.298.

CHAPTER 2

Frostbite

RICHELLE ON *FROSTBITE*

Starting *Frostbite* was a little rough. I knew what the running plotlines were going to be, but establishing them was tricky. The writing of this book was also taking place in a tumultuous time in my own life, which made it even more difficult to just really focus and get out the words I wanted. I think I rewrote the beginning of *Frostbite* about three times! What's surprising to a lot of people is that, despite the beginning difficulties, the book's ending was pretty much set in stone. I wrote it in one energetic burst, and it was good to go. I'd known from the day I started writing the first VA book what the path of the series would be, and this ending—as harsh as it was—was essential both for the story and Rose's growth. Terrible, traumatic endings would eventually become a normal thing for me in all of my series, but this was the very first one I ever wrote. Again, knowing it was needed for the series, I didn't feel a lot of guilt over what happened, but I was a little amazed in looking back at it that I had actually created something so heart-wrenching.

First line: I didn't think my day could get any worse until my best friend told me she might be going crazy. Again.

SCENE OF THE CRIME

Rose definitely has her hands full at the moment.

First, Lissa confides in Rose that her darkness is returning, despite the depression meds she's on that cut her off from using spirit, including her ability to heal others.

Second, Rose is off to take her Qualifier, which is an important interview to determine her commitment to being a guardian. It's nerve-racking, but there's one very bright side about the test . . . and that's who's going with her.

> *Dimitri stood there, looking as gorgeous as ever. The massive, brick building cast long shadows over us, looming like some great beast in the dusky predawn light. Around us, snow was just beginning to fall. I watched the light, crystalline flakes drift gently down. Several landed and promptly melted in his dark hair.*
>
> *"Who else is going?" I asked.*
>
> *He shrugged. "Just you and me."*
>
> *My mood promptly shot up past "cheerful" and went straight to "ecstatic." Me and Dimitri. Alone. In a car. This might very well be worth a surprise test.* —*page 11*

However, when they arrive at the test location, something is horribly wrong. A royal Moroi family, the Badicas—and their dhampir guardians—have been slaughtered by Strigoi.

Dimitri tells Rose to wait in the car while he goes inside to investigate. Never one to follow orders, Rose finds a silver stake buried in the ground and heads into the house to see the victims for herself, horrified by the bloody massacre. When she finds Dimitri, he's angry she didn't stay safely outside, but he questions her about where she found the stake. Strigoi can't touch the charmed silver—but its magic would be enough to breach the protective wards around the house that are placed there to keep Strigoi out. Dimitri surmises that humans could have helped the Strigoi by planting the stake and allowing Strigoi access to commit the murders. Rose can't believe a human would help a Strigoi to do something this horrible . . . would they?

After Dimitri calls in a group of guardians to investigate the murder scene, Rose catches a glimpse of something horribly disturbing as they continue to survey the house. The Strigoi have left a warning on a mirror—

And it's written in blood.

It's a message that Moroi royal families are targets and the Badica family is only the first. Rose is enraged. And now, she's even more afraid for Lissa—the last of the Dragomir line. Not only will Lissa have to deal with her inner darkness and worry for her sanity, but now she must also fear for her life.

News of the tragedy reaches the Academy quicker than Rose and Dimitri can return. When she gets back, Mason tells her that plans are already underway for a school trip to a huge ski lodge that will include both students and their parents. The school rapidly organized this in order to gather Moroi somewhere safe while the Strigoi responsible for the Badica massacre are hunted down. While the idea of a getaway sounds fantastic to Rose, it's sobering to know that the only reason the trip was planned is because people were murdered.

Rose now knows Lissa's in direct mortal danger from these dangerous Strigoi, so she wants to step up her training with Dimitri and learn how to use a silver stake. But when Rose has trouble figuring out exactly where the heart is—kind of important when you're required to put a stake through one—Dimitri tells her to study up if she really wants to get to the next level. Sometimes Dimitri can be devastatingly sexy, and sometimes, like now, he's just really annoying.

Just because they have a deeper connection—not that they can act on it—doesn't mean he's going to go easy on her.

MOMMY DEAREST

Family members start to arrive for the big ski trip, along with their guardians. To Rose's deep dismay, among them is her estranged mother, Janine Hathaway.

The novices are excited to hear Janine, a famous guardian with a high Strigoi kill count, speak to Rose's class about her legendary field experience. Well, all the novices *except* for Rose. Janine left her in the Academy's care when Rose was just a kid and never looked back—choosing to pursue her career as a guardian rather than be a devoted mother. And Rose's father? Other than him being Turkish, Rose has never met him and knows absolutely nothing about him at all.

Rose and Janine haven't spoken in more than two years, and Rose can't get past her animosity toward the woman she feels abandoned her—one who didn't even bother to give her the heads-up that she was on campus.

Janine tells the class an epic tale about a kidnapping that occurred at a royal Moroi ball. Two Moroi were abducted, and guardians tracked them to a hideout where Janine performed a hat trick—staking, decapitating, and burning her Strigoi foes.

Everyone is in awe of this incredible guardian. Rose, however, rudely questions the decisions her mother made, making it seem like Janine was out more for glory than for the safety of the Moroi victims.

> *The tightness in her lips increased, and her voice grew frosty.*
> *"We did the best we could with an unusual situation. I can see*
> *how someone at your level might not be able to grasp the intri-*
> *cacies of what I'm describing, but once you've actually learned*
> *enough to go beyond theory, you'll see how different it is when*
> *you're actually out there and lives are in your hands."*
>
> *"No doubt," I agreed. "Who am I to question your methods? I*
> *mean, whatever gets you the* molnija *marks, right?"* —page 56

That's enough snark to get Rose booted from the class for having a bad attitude. All too soon, though, she'll realize just how
right her mother is . . .

For now, she's just pissed off and ready to hit something. Hard. In
her after-school session with Dimitri, she proves she now knows
exactly where the heart is—she studied up, like he asked her to.

Later in their practice, he surprises her:

> *When he suddenly extended his hand and offered the stake to*
> *me, I didn't understand at first. "You're giving it to me?"*
> *His eyes sparkled. "I can't believe you're holding back. I figured*
> *you'd have taken it and run by now."*
> *"Aren't you always teaching me to hold back?" I asked.*
> *"Not on everything."*
> *"But on some things."* —page 60

He's made it very clear that too much stands between them right now—the age difference and the fact that protecting Lissa takes top priority over any potential romance. Still, she finds herself wishing things could be different. Just because Rose knows it's true doesn't make it any easier to be near him.

Especially when he notes how similar Rose and her mother are. It's the *last* thing she wants to hear because, hello? *So* not true. She still feels like Janine's story earlier was all about bragging about her fierce reputation and her impressive number of *molnija* marks.

Dimitri wants to show Rose something that might change her mind—not all marks are badges of honor.

He takes her to a small, run-down cabin in the woods that surround the school. It's an abandoned watch post for school guardians. Lissa and Christian are skating on a nearby frozen pond, and they're with another woman who seems to know Dimitri. She even calls him by a nickname: Dimka.

This is Rose's first introduction to Tasha Ozera, Christian's aunt, a woman whose beautiful face is marred by a large scar she got protecting Christian from his Strigoi parents.

She's way different than other Moroi, who shy away from physical conflict. Tasha teaches martial arts classes. And even though she's a royal, she has no guardian. When she mentions she's going shopping later, Dimitri offers to go with her for extra protection.

Before they leave, Rose lets Dimitri know that she *gets* it. Tasha's shown her that when it comes to fighting Strigoi, the marks don't matter—*molnija* or scars. What matters is doing the right thing to save others.

Dimitri didn't say anything, but he gave me a sidelong glance.

I returned it, and as our eyes met, I saw the briefest glimpse of the old attraction. It was fleeting and gone too soon, but I'd seen it. Pride and approval replaced it, and they were almost as good.

When he spoke, it was to echo his earlier thoughts. "You're a fast learner, Roza."
—page 76

When Rose goes to her before-school practice the next day, she's greeted by her mother. Apparently, Dimitri only just returned from taking Tasha shopping and is still sleeping. Instead of canceling the session, Janine's offered to take over today. She wants to see what her daughter can do.

Oh, it's so *on*.

It's the chance Rose has been waiting for, to take some of her frustrations out on the woman herself. As they spar, Rose doesn't hold back on how she feels.

"Did you go all Darwin and select the guy most likely to pass on warrior genes to your offspring? I mean, I know you only had me because it was your duty, *so I suppose you had to make sure you could give the guardians the best specimen you could."*

"Rosemarie," she warned through gritted teeth, "for once in your life, shut up."

"Why? Am I tarnishing your precious reputation? It's just like you told me: you aren't any different from any other dhampir either. You just screwed him and—"
—page 82

41

—and she gets a fist to the face, which sure feels more personal than part of any training session.

Rose heads directly to the Academy's med clinic to get checked out. She's okay—apart from a big black eye. Great. Just in time for the ski trip, too.

Lissa isn't entirely sympathetic to Rose's plight when she learns that Rose provoked the punch—although it still doesn't excuse what Janine did. If it weren't for her anti-depression meds, Lissa could use spirit to heal Rose. Lissa wishes she could use her magic in a controlled way that doesn't destroy her mentally and physically. Bitterness over this comes through the bond, which quickly intensifies to something darker and uglier. Uh-oh. Are the meds really starting to weaken?

Lissa's mood brightens during their talk when they switch to a different topic. Namely, Rose's potential romantic future . . . with *Mason*. After all, the guy's crazy about her.

Lissa has no idea yet that Rose is really interested in Dimitri. Rose wants to tell her the truth about her crush on her older mentor and how her feelings were very nearly returned in full. She and Lissa have always told each other everything. Why should this be any different?

Rose is about to spill all her secrets about Dimitri and her hesitation to date other guys like Mason when Lissa interrupts her to go meet her boyfriend, Christian, for their date. Later, a burst of emotion shoots through the bond and—*bam!*—Rose is in Lissa's head experiencing her world firsthand. And Lissa and Christian's date is getting hot and heavy.

The two are taking their relationship to the next level. Since Rose *really* doesn't want to virtually lose her virginity to Christian while being stuck in Lissa's head, she manages to get out of Lissa's head and escape the romantic encounter just in time.

That Lissa and Christian are taking their relationship to the next level leaves Rose with an ache in her heart. Christian's officially replaced her as the most important person in her best friend's life . . . and this makes her feel very alone.

A KISS FROM A ROSE

Rose wears her hair down for her next session with Dimitri to make her bruise less visible. When it gets in the way, Dimitri almost brushes it away from her face—he has an ongoing love of her beautiful hair—but he stops himself.

Rose can see he wants to touch her. He *is* still attracted to her, despite being on his best and most professional behavior lately.

With concern, he asks if her bruise hurts—and her attention momentarily shifts from her sexy instructor back to her annoying mother, darkening Rose's mood. Dimitri suggests she make peace with Janine and control her hatred. This *isn't* what Rose wants to hear. She challenges his Zen-like behavior. Despite his protests, she knows Dimitri doesn't always want to stay in control . . . *especially* when he's around her.

And you know what? Rose is ready to prove this once and for all.

Before he realized what was happening, I kissed him. Our lips met, and when I felt him kiss me back, I knew I was right. He pressed himself closer, trapping me between him and the wall. He kept holding my hand, but his other one snaked behind my head, sliding into my hair. The kiss was filled with so much intensity; it held anger, passion, release . . .

> *He was the one who broke it. He jerked away from me and*
> *took several steps back, looking shaken.*
>
> *"Do* not *do that again," he said stiffly.*
>
> *"Don't kiss me back then," I retorted.* —*page 112*

Rose has definitely succeeded in shaking Dimitri's composure. And, just like that, their session is *over*. He cancels the next two sessions too, and, despite his other excuses, Rose is sure it's because of their very dangerous kiss.

On Christmas morning, with the upcoming ski trip on everyone's mind, Rose goes to an on-campus brunch hosted by Tasha. Who should be there but Dimitri? She hasn't seen him since their kiss. Rose realizes she should have expected him—he's Tasha's friend after all. He seems to make a point to steer away from Rose, keeping his attention totally on Christian's aunt.

Lissa gives Rose a present of a *chotki*, which is like a rosary, only bracelet-sized. It's a Dragomir family heirloom that belonged to her great-grandmother's guardian, so it's only appropriate that Lissa pass it on to her own (soon-to-be) guardian and best friend Rose.

Tasha also invited Janine to the brunch—which Rose is less than thrilled about and only makes her more agitated. Rose hasn't seen her mother since she punched her in the face two days ago. And since that time, there have been no visits, no apologies. *No big surprise.* Now, with her mother in attendance, talk turns to such festive topics as how to decapitate a Strigoi and—as always—everyone except Rose seems fascinated by Janine's tales of being a guardian.

After the party, Rose is on her way back to her dorm when Janine catches up to her. She has a Christmas present for her daughter. It's a piece of jewelry too: in this case a strange glass pendant that looks like an eye—which she'll later find out is called a *nazar*, given to Janine by Rose's real father. It's a generous and heartfelt gift, but Rose doesn't know or appreciate that yet.

And that's when Janine drops a bombshell on Rose's lap in casual conversation: Tasha has requested Dimitri as an official guardian. And she has her eye on something more . . . Apparently, Christian's aunt is *romantically* interested in Dimitri and willing to have dhampir children with him—something very few Moroi women would be willing to do. Hooking up with a Moroi woman is the only way Dimitri can have kids since dhampirs can't procreate with each other.

This news hits Rose like another punch to the face, stunning and sickening her. The thought that Dimitri could be leaving the Academy, leaving *her*, to be with Tasha instead is too much for her to bear. It's one thing to accept that *she* can't have him, but imagining him with someone else?

It's the worst Christmas *ever*.

RESORT LIFE

If the news about Dimitri has done one thing, it's made Rose look at Mason with a bit more interest. After all, if Dimitri can move on with Tasha, then she should be able to do the same, right?

They reach the gorgeous resort, all decked out—including human feeders—for a large group of holidaying vampires. Wards are set, guardians are in place, and the ski slopes are on a nocturnal schedule. Even though the reason they're there is because of the Badica massacre, it's kind of hard *not* to have fun.

Rose and Mason challenge each other on the slopes in dangerous feats of bravery. Rose sees firsthand that Mason's a major risk taker and he loves to face danger head-on. That risky behavior will soon lead to very bad things for him. Today, however, it's just a sprained ankle.

After Rose helps the injured Mason back to the lodge, she meets someone who will soon become one of the most important people in her life....

Adrian Ivashkov is a very good-looking but arrogant, cigarette-smoking Moroi royal who seems intrigued by the pretty girl he immediately nicknames "little dhampir."

Rose's first impression of Adrian? He's a jerk. And the Ivashkovs' arrogant family reputation certainly doesn't help change Rose's opinion of him. And yet—she's not scurrying away. Adrian's also charming and handsome and has an air of danger to him that she's drawn to.

Rose's nemesis Mia Rinaldi picks that moment to stroll by, sneering about Rose being with yet another guy. She even tries to give the handsome Ivashkov a bit of advice when it comes to the dhampir:

"Rose only hangs out with guys and psychopaths," said Mia. Her voice carried the usual scorn she harbored for me, but there was a look on her face that showed Adrian had clearly caught her interest.

"Well," he said cheerfully, "since I'm both a psychopath and a guy, that would explain why we're such good friends."

"You and I aren't friends either," I told him.

He laughed. "Always playing hard to get, huh?"

"She's not that hard to get," said Mia, clearly upset that Adrian

was paying more attention to me. "Just ask half the guys at our
school." —pages 139—140

When Rose not-so-gently reminds Mia that *she's* the one known for sleeping with guys so they'll do favors for her, an embarrassed Mia quickly skulks away. Rose is left alone with Adrian, who seems genuinely interested in her.

He's not only interested in *Rose*, though. He's also curious to know more about Lissa and how she's doing after being kidnapped by Victor Dashkov. This makes Rose end the conversation immediately. It doesn't matter how charming Adrian is; Rose doesn't like discussing Lissa's fragile mental health with *anyone*.

But abruptly shutting down the conversation isn't nearly enough to stop Adrian in his tracks. Even though Rose makes a swift beeline for the lodge, her brash attitude and good looks have definitely captured the young Lord Ivashkov's interest.

"Rose Hathaway, I can't wait to see you again. If you're this charming while tired and annoyed and this gorgeous while bruised and in ski clothes, you must be devastating at your peak."

"If by 'devastating' you mean that you should fear for your life, then yeah. You're right." I jerked open the door. "Good night, Adrian."

"I'll see you soon."

"Not likely. I told you, I'm not into older guys."

I walked into the lodge. As the door closed, I just barely heard him call behind me, "Sure, you aren't." —page 142

The next morning, Rose finds Lissa with Christian . . . *and* Tasha. So much for avoiding the woman determined to steal Dimitri from her.

Tasha is teaching Christian how to use his fire magic as a weapon. This is totally forbidden among Moroi, and Rose—if she was feeling *really* spiteful—could get Tasha in serious trouble for this. However, she has to admit she agrees with Tasha's unorthodox methods. A Moroi using their magic alongside their guardian to take down a Strigoi makes total sense. More weapons against the murderous monsters is a good thing, right?

But just because she agrees doesn't mean she likes Tasha. At all. Lissa—who still knows nothing about Rose's feelings toward Dimitri—doesn't understand why Rose is being such a bitch. Rose brushes it off as her being grumpy from lack of sleep.

Mason meets up with them, and he's also grouchy because he's heard a rumor that Rose and Adrian got drunk together last night. *Gee, wherever could that have come from?* Looks like Mia, once again, is trying to make trouble for her.

She assures him that nothing is going on with her and Adrian. She and Mason go skiing again so they can spend more time together . . . he insists his ankle is just fine. He does a great job too, although he's not taking quite as many risks this time. Since Rose is upset and hurt by Dimitri and Tasha's romance, at the end of their ski date, she decides to encourage Mason's interest in her with a kiss. It's pretty good . . . but it isn't *nearly* as earth-shattering as the one she'd had with Dimitri. Still, it's sweet and nice and could possibly turn into more between them.

But instead of dreaming of Mason that night or even Dimitri— she dreams about *Adrian*. He notices something strange about her.

"Why do you have so much darkness around you?"

I frowned. "What?"

"You're surrounded in blackness." His eyes studied me shrewdly, but not in a checking-me-out sort of way. "I've never seen anyone like you. Shadows everywhere. I never would have guessed it. Even while you're standing here, the shadows keep growing."

I looked down at my hands but saw nothing out of the ordinary. I glanced back up. "I'm shadow-kissed . . ."

"What's that mean?"

"I died once." I'd never talked to anyone other than Lissa and Victor Dashkov about that, but this was a dream. It didn't matter. "And I came back." —*pages 154–155*

Later, Rose learns that this is the kind of dream that definitely *does* matter.

Rose is pulled out of the dream when Lissa shakes her awake to tell her some bad news. There's been another Strigoi attack!

Even though Rose isn't thrilled with either of them right now, she knows she can get more information from Dimitri or her mother. In a makeshift guardian headquarters, located in her mother's room, Rose learns more details about the attack, which was identical to the Badica massacre. This time, members of the Drozdov family and their guardians were killed in California, along with some of their staff—a list that Rose realizes with dismay includes Mia's mother.

Janine is incredibly levelheaded during this crisis and is leading the investigation with clearheaded authority. Rose might have problems with Janine, but seeing her mother work with such control in a time of chaos shows she's a true leader and one to be admired.

It is obvious that the threat of Strigoi attack is growing. The Moroi currently staying at the ski lodge hold a meeting in the large banquet hall to try to figure out what to do to keep themselves safe. There are simply not enough guardians available to protect everyone—some Moroi don't even have assigned guardians, since precedence goes to those in royal families. Several suggestions are shouted out, including one that will become a major topic of debate in the future—allowing novice guardians to graduate at sixteen instead of eighteen.

Tasha believes she has a better plan, and it's one she's believed in for quite some time. Moroi have their own special weapon that no one else has: their elemental magic. They should use that magic to fight with guardians against the Strigoi—even to go *after* the Strigoi rather than waiting till they attack.

To demonstrate her ability to defend herself, she lights something on fire. Chaos immediately breaks out at this forbidden act—and Tasha is considered crazy for even suggesting something so extreme. Moroi consider their magic to be peaceful and it should only be used in a benevolent way. To use it in such a violent manner goes against everything they've been led to believe.

With the adults up in arms over Tasha's ill-advised display, Dimitri quickly ushers the novices out of the meeting. In the hall outside, out of earshot of her friends, Rose finally has a chance to confront him about becoming Tasha's guardian . . . with benefits. He crisply tells her that whatever happens between him and Tasha is none of her business.

"Well, I'm sure you guys'll be happy together. She's just your type, too—I know how much you like women who aren't your own age. I mean, she's what, six years older than you? Seven? And I'm seven years younger than you."

"Yes," he said after several moments of silence. "You are. And every second this conversation goes on, you only prove how young you really are."

Whoa. My jaw almost hit the floor. Not even my mother punching me had hurt as badly as that. —pages 172–173

Just then, Adrian strolls by, giving Rose the perfect exit opportunity. If Dimitri is going to pretend he's too mature for her, then fine: she'll find another hot guy.

She turns her back on Dimitri and walks away with Adrian.

When they met, Rose told Adrian she's not into older guys, but based on the heated exchange he's just witnessed, Adrian wonders if there's something between her and Dimitri. Rose assures him that he's just imagining things.

Clearly smitten—and amused—by the beautiful Rose, Adrian offers to take her and Lissa to a special spa area of the resort, one used by the most elite Moroi. However, instead of just getting the two girls, he gets the two girls *and* all their friends when Rose takes the liberty to invite Mason, Mason's best friend, Eddie, and Christian along. Adrian's easygoing so it doesn't bother him. Mia is also included in their group. Despite their nasty history, Lissa doesn't want the girl to be alone now that she's grieving the death of her mother, and Rose has to agree.

While they all hang out in a hot tub, Mason lets it be known that he agrees wholeheartedly with Tasha's plan to go after the Strigoi. In fact, he thinks they should start fighting *now*.

Rose is suddenly the voice of reason, strangely enough, and she doesn't think they're ready to face Strigoi. Christian, on the other hand, stands by the idea that dhampirs should help Moroi learn to defend themselves with their magic. Mia is quick to agree with him after her personal loss.

As this debate is raging, Rose has a few drinks—*alcoholic* ones. When she gets up to grab another drink, the world starts spinning. But this is Rose—when alcohol mixes with her natural killer instinct, watch out. In her drunken haze, she notices that a fight has erupted in a nearby room between two Moroi. And she's just inebriated enough to think that jumping in is a good idea. Rose leaps between the guys to try to break things up, but when she gets caught in the crossfire, Mason is there to defend her. When the fight finally dissipates, Rose drunkenly scolds Mason for getting involved. Doesn't he know that she had it covered?

"Are you out of your mind?"

"Huh?" he asked.

"Jumping into the middle of that!"

"You jumped in too," he said.

I started to argue, then realized he was right. "It's different," *I grumbled.*

He leaned forward. "Are you drunk?"

"No. Of course not. I'm just trying to keep you from doing some-

thing stupid. Just because you have delusions of being able to kill

Strigoi doesn't mean you have to take it out on everyone else."

"Delusions?" he asked stiffly. —*pages 185–186*

Feeling nauseous, Rose leaves Mason behind and, while her head spins unpleasantly from alcohol, she wanders into a side room hoping to find some food to help sober her up. Instead, she finds herself in a feeder room where Moroi guys are drinking the blood of attractive human girls. It seems pretty sexy, actually. Rose can't help but be reminded of how good it feels to experience the bite.

"Want to volunteer?"

Light fingertips brushed my neck, and I jumped. I turned around and saw Adrian's green eyes and knowing smirk.

"Don't do that," I told him, knocking his hand away.

"Then what are you doing in here?" he asked.

I gestured around me. "I'm lost."

He peered at me. "Are you drunk?"

"No. Of course not . . . but . . ." The nausea had settled a little, but I still didn't feel right. "I think I should sit down."

He took my arm. "Well, don't do it in here. Someone might get the wrong idea." —*page 187*

Adrian works hard to be snarky and flirtatious on the outside, but on the inside he does care deeply about others, especially when they're putting themselves in harm's way. He directs Rose into the massage area of the spa and fetches her a glass of water. Conversation between them again turns to Lissa, although Adrian assures Rose he isn't interested in her friend the same way he's interested in her.

While his arrogant manner *does* annoy her . . . Rose really can't help but like being around him. There's something about Adrian that's incredibly hard to resist.

Lissa's been searching for her friend and is relieved to find her safe and sound. Alcohol numbed the bond, and Rose knows it was stupid of her to take such a stupid chance tonight. What if Lissa had been in danger?

Adrian surprises the girls by asking if it was their psychic bond that enabled Lissa to locate Rose. How does he know about their bond? It's a secret. He's extremely curious about which power Lissa specializes in, but the girls say nothing more. That's another secret they don't want to reveal to him—not a lot of people know that it's *spirit*. Rose is confused by the major interest Adrian is showing in Lissa. *Is he hitting on her?*

Lissa already has a boyfriend. And, for that matter, so does Rose if she's really interested in giving Mason a chance. When they leave the spa area, Mason is annoyed and hurt that Rose continues to spend so much time with Adrian, so she reassures him that there's nothing going on with the Moroi guy. When the others take off, they kiss, but when she wants to go further, Mason puts the brakes on. Rose is still drunk right now. If she still wants him when she's sobered up, they'll talk.

AMOR AMOR

The next morning, Adrian sends a gift to Rose's room—thirty little bottles of perfume. Since she really doesn't want to encourage his romantic attention, she returns them. Except for one, a scent called Amor Amor, which seems fitting, given her romantic woes of late.

When Rose brings the bottles back to Adrian, she's surprised to see that he already has a guest in his room: Lissa. What's *she* doing there?

Before she can bring herself to ask that very question, though, Dimitri suddenly appears in the hallway. And he's not happy. His *alleged* reason? Male and female students aren't supposed to be in each other's rooms.

"I'm sure you know the rules at St. Vladimir's."

Adrian shrugged. "Yeah, but I don't have to follow any school's stupid rules."

"Perhaps not," said Dimitri coldly. "But I would have thought you'd still respect those rules."

Adrian rolled his eyes. "I'm kind of surprised to find you lecturing about underage girls."

—*page 202*

However, just as soon as Adrian's gotten a nice zinger in, he launches into a rambling and disjointed speech. Everyone is confused—he sounds crazy. And then, the next moment, he's back to normal. They all leave his room puzzled by his strange turn. Once they reach the lobby, Lissa takes off when Dimitri asks to speak with Rose alone.

Rose jealously assumed Dimitri was on this side of the lodge to find Tasha, but she's wrong. He actually had been visiting Janine to go over more details about the Moroi attacks and fills Rose in on the details. While Dimitri is stiff in talking to Rose after their previous quarrel, he feels she has a right to know what he's learned. The guardians believe the Strigoi are in Spokane, Washington. There's a shopping plaza with underground tunnels and Strigoi sightings. However, despite having this valuable information, no offensive attack is being sent until they're given permission from higher up.

Dimitri admits that he's said some insulting things to Rose lately about her age, so he's telling her this info because he's confident she has the maturity to handle it. It's a sign of respect that warms her heart and brightens her mood. However, he cautions that what he's told her needs to stay confidential.

It feels like a special moment between them . . . until Tasha ruins it by showing up, wondering when Dimitri's shift ends. Rose feels sick and jealous at the reminder he might be Tasha's guardian—and *more*—very soon.

Dimitri just told Rose something in confidence, but he *really* shouldn't have. Rose is so angry at Dimitri that she shares this info about the Strigoi sightings with Mason almost immediately afterward. Serves Dimitri right!

But Mason's reaction is a bit more intense than Rose anticipated. He doesn't understand why the guardians aren't acting on this info right away. They should go to Spokane and take care of the threat themselves! Rose disagrees. They'd need more people, planning, and info before it would even be a possibility.

Mason thinks she acts like Dimitri now, after being tutored by him. She's gotten all serious and isn't as much of a risk taker anymore—not like him.

Talking about the man she really desires but can't be with is the last thing Rose wants right now, and it's *totally* spoiling the mood. Before it's spoiled *too* much, Mason shifts from discussing battle strategy to kissing her—definitely better, in Rose's opinion. She channels her bad mood into passion and kisses him back—hard.

This is the distraction she needs. Attention from a guy who makes her feel amazing and desirable. Someone who isn't wandering off to be with someone else just so he doesn't break any stupid rules.

But despite herself, Rose finds herself thinking longingly about the time she and Dimitri almost went all the way. Sure, it was only thanks to Victor Dashkov's charmed necklace, but still, she knows deep down there was something more there. Mason doesn't understand when she pulls away, but she knows she can't go further with him while desperately wishing she was with someone else.

ROYAL BANQUET

Later that day, Lissa invites Rose along to the royal banquet being held at the lodge that night. Rose doesn't understand why she wouldn't take Christian. You know, her *boyfriend?* The truth is, Christian's currently not speaking to Lissa. He's jealous she hung out in the gorgeous Adrian's room that morning, falsely believing it to be more than a "just friends" situation—so Lissa needs someone else to accompany her while he cools off. And there's clearly only one choice: Rose. Even though Rose hates formal Moroi events, she reluctantly agrees to go. When she's Lissa's official guardian, she'll be going to a lot of these!

After the meal, they mingle with the other royals. Lissa's in her element here: perfect, polished, and polite. A group of Moroi are discussing going on the offensive against the Strigoi: *Is it the right thing to do? Or is it a suicide mission?* Lissa raises the point that this isn't an all-or-nothing decision. Those who wish to learn and fight can. Those who don't want to don't have to. But there *should* be a choice. In her opinion, defense should be part of the Moroi school curriculum *right now*. Surprisingly, everyone seems pleased with the Dragomir princess's solution.

When Rose leaves Lissa to discuss Moroi politics with her fellow royals, she runs into Adrian. Even though the sexy and flirtatious guy annoys her on many levels, she feels an overwhelming urge to be near him. What's up with that?

Well, he *does* look better in a tuxedo than any other guy there. There's no question that Adrian would be extremely desirable to any girl—Moroi, dhampir, or human.

Unlike others at the party, Adrian's not too interested in discussing whether or not Moroi should use their magic to fight.

> *"I've got better things to do."*
>
> *"Like stalk me," I suggested. "And Lissa." I still wanted to know why she'd been in his room.*
>
> *He smiled again. "I told you, you're the one following me."*
>
> *"Yeah, yeah, I know. Five times—" I stopped. "Five times?"*
>
> *He nodded.*
>
> *"No, it's only been four." With my free hand, I ticked them off. "There was the first time, the night at the spa, then when I came to your room, and now tonight."*
>
> *The smile turned secretive. "If you say so."*
>
> —*pages 227–228*

The only other time Rose had spoken to Adrian was . . . in her dream—the one in which he'd mentioned the shadows all around her. She's tempted to mention it. Was it really only a simple dream . . . or something else?

Before Rose can decide whether to speak up, her mother storms up to them. Shame on Rose for making a spectacle of herself by wearing a tight dress and flirting with Adrian, a Moroi lord. Who does she think she is? Janine's accusation makes Rose mad, but she turns it around on her mother. Isn't that what she's *supposed* to do? Hook up with a Moroi in order to further her race? After all, that's what Janine did. But Janine isn't buying Rose's logic—Rose is too young to get pregnant.

Oh boy. *Not* a subject Rose wants to deal with right now. She feels the sudden urge to escape and swiftly flees to the rooftop patio. The door to the patio opens a few minutes later and Dimitri joins her. He followed her from the party—he'd been watching her when she'd had the argument with her mother.

It's clear to him that Janine's just worried about Rose and trying to be protective of her daughter. But perhaps she was being a bit *over*protective. And what she'd said about being too young to get pregnant . . . maybe that was aimed more at *herself* than at Rose.

Ah, Dimitri. So very insightful.

And suddenly, Rose realizes something important.

> *"We aren't fighting right now," I blurted out.*
>
> *He gave me a sidelong look. "Do you want to fight?"*
>
> *"No. I hate fighting with you. Verbally, I mean. I don't mind in the gym."*
>
> *I thought I detected the hint of a smile. Always a half-smile for me. Rarely a full one. "I don't like fighting with you either."*

Sitting next to him there, I marveled at the warm and happy emotions springing up inside of me. There was something about being around him that felt so good, that moved me in a way Mason couldn't. You can't force love, I realized. It's either there or it isn't. If it's not there, you've got to be able to admit it. If it's there, you've got to do whatever it takes to protect the ones you love. —pages 235–236

Rose decides that she wants Dimitri to be happy. He should take the position as Tasha's guardian—it's a great opportunity for him and a chance to have children. No matter what happens, she knows she'll always love him.

She also knows she has to talk to Mason—to apologize for how she's treated him and to end things with him once and for all.

But she can't find him anywhere.

MASON'S PLAN

It's not long before Rose comes to a sickening realization: the reason she can't find Mason is because he's no longer at the ski lodge. Mason, his friend Eddie, and Mia must have all gone to Spokane so that he could fulfill his crazy dream of killing Strigoi. And it's all Rose's fault! The only reason Mason knows they're in Spokane is because Rose told him.

She needs to stop them! She realizes that Mason, Eddie, and Mia must have used compulsion to get past the guards at the gates—but Rose, as a dhampir, doesn't have that ability. She needs to find a Moroi to assist her. Lissa's the obvious choice, but Rose does something surprising. She finds Christian instead and tells him everything. But even he knows Lissa's much better at compulsion than he is.

> *"I know. But I don't want to get her in trouble."*
>
> *He snorted. "But you don't mind if I do?"*
>
> *I shrugged. "Not really."*
>
> *"You're a piece of work, you know that?"*
>
> *"Yeah, I do, actually."* —*page 242*

Christian agrees to join Rose. They hitch a ride into town and head to the bus station, but there's no sign of Mason and the others—they've already headed to Spokane. *Crap.*

When Rose and Christian reach Spokane, Rose feels a tug on the bond. She slips into Lissa's head and sees that her friend is being questioned by Dimitri about Rose and the other students' whereabouts. Lissa is frustrated and afraid—and upset that she wasn't told about any plans to leave the lodge—but she has no idea where Rose is. She sadly reminds Dimitri that the bond only works one way. When Dimitri continues to press, Lissa snaps at him that she'd help if she could. But she can't. Dimitri's not the only one worried about Rose and the others.

The concern Rose sees in Dimitri's eyes through the bond eats her up inside.

When Rose and Christian reach the shopping center, they find the missing trio looking dejected in the food court. The trip's been a big fat failure, and Rose couldn't be more relieved that her friends are safe.

> *"Did you kill any Strigoi? Did you even find any?"*

"No," admitted Eddie.

"Good," I said. "You got lucky."

"Why are you so against killing Strigoi?" asked Mia hotly. "Isn't that what you train for?"

"I train for sane missions, not childish stunts like this."

"It isn't childish," she cried. "They killed my mother. And the guardians weren't doing anything. Even their information is bad. There weren't any Strigoi in the tunnels. Probably none in the whole city."

—page 250

While Mason, Eddie, and Mia didn't find any Strigoi in their search, they did find the underground tunnels that are connected to the mall. The thought of checking them out again while they wait for the next bus appeals to Christian. Since he usually spends a lot of time in a cramped attic, Rose isn't all that surprised that he'd think this would be fun.

Reluctantly, she agrees that they can take a peek. A quick one!

Rose and Christian follow the others to the far end of the mall and down a dirty, smelly set of stairs, leading into the tunnels below. Grime-caked cement, ugly fluorescent lights, boxes of cleaning and electrical supplies . . .

But no Strigoi.

It's kind of boring, really.

But then Rose spots some writing on the wall. It's a list of twelve letters with an *X* next to a couple of them. Mia dismisses it as nothing, but Rose keeps studying the list until it clicks. The letters are the initials of the twelve royal Moroi families . . .

Rose has just found a checklist of the attacks.

Strigoi *were* here—and they might be back soon. Rose doesn't share what she's figured out with the others. All she knows is they need to get out of there. Right now.

THE KIDNAPPING

Rose is relieved that it's still light out, which means they're safe from Strigoi for the moment, but she needs to get back to the lodge and report what she's found as soon as she can. Unfortunately, they get lost on their way back to the bus station.

And they're not alone—someone is after them.

A van screeches to a halt and three big guys get out. The novices fight back, and these humans might lack dhampir strength, but they've managed to corner Rose and her friends. When one of the humans grabs Mia and presses a gun to her neck, the others are forced to get into the van so she isn't killed.

Bound and scared, the five of them are taken to a house and put in a small room in the basement, tied to chairs. Their panic rises when a man and woman enter the room. They're unfamiliar, but one thing's for certain: they're Strigoi. Very possibly, they're the Strigoi that attacked and murdered the royal families.

The man's name is Isaiah and his companion is Elena. Isaiah knew Christian's parents, who had chosen to become Strigoi. He'd personally warned them not to go back to the Moroi world to reclaim their son so he could become Strigoi too. Christian's aunt Tasha had fought hard against them—it's how she was scarred—and guardians eventually killed Christian's parents.

Isaiah wants to "awaken" the Moroi he's just captured—both

Mia and Christian. This way, he's helping Christian's parents fulfill their dream of having him join the ranks of the Strigoi.

But Mia and Christian must willingly *choose* to be awakened. Isaiah wants to make a game out of it. It's big fun for him!

For Isaiah to grant Christian or Mia immortality, they need to kill one of their dhampir friends—something that they'd never agree to do. Not yet, anyway.

> *"Easy to be brave when you aren't hungry. Go a few days without any other sustenance . . . and yes, these three will start to look very good. And they are. Dhampirs are delicious. Some prefer them to Moroi, and while I myself have never shared such beliefs, I can certainly appreciate the variety.*
>
> *Christian scowled.*
>
> *"Don't believe me?" asked Isaiah. "Then let me prove it." He walked back over to my side of the room. I realized what he was going to do and spoke without fully thinking things through.*
>
> *"Use me," I blurted out. "Drink from me."* —page 270

Rose wants desperately to protect her friends. She's already experienced the bite—when she and Lissa had run away, her friend had regularly fed on her. Rose knows that it can be addictive and she's strong enough to handle that—but Eddie and Mason haven't. She wants to save them from having to experience that.

Isaiah disagrees. Why give her what she wants? He bites Eddie instead—cautioning that if the novice resists, he can make it very painful. Once Isaiah uses compulsion on Eddie, the dhampir offers up his neck freely.

Rose looks away—sickened that they're at the mercy of this Strigoi.

When Isaiah leaves, the group is bruised, hungry, and terrified of what will happen next.

During the second day of captivity, Rose falls asleep and dreams about Adrian again. This time, he admits that just like last time, this isn't a normal dream—it's a *shared* dream. They're both dreaming of the same place, and this is an actual conversation they're having. One in which Adrian makes an observation about Rose's shadow-kissed status that will come to be very important later.

> *"I need to know what you mean. About there being darkness around me. What does it mean?"*
>
> *"Honestly, I don't know. Everyone has light around them, except for you. You have shadows. You take them from Lissa."*

—page 275

Rose tries to tell him where she is so the group can be rescued. But the dream fades away and she wakes up when the Strigoi arrive to taunt the Moroi about their growing hunger. Isaiah is ready to bite Eddie again, who's become addicted to this act thanks to the drug-like endorphins in a Strigoi's saliva, but Rose offers to let Isaiah bite her instead.

She's very adamant and selfless about it—so much so that Isaiah guesses that she's done this before . . . and liked it. He thinks Rose might be a blood whore in the making. But he's not going to give her what she wants. He bites Eddie again and Rose feels *envy* this time instead of disgust. She hates to admit that part of her did become addicted to the bite. And yes, part of her does want to experience that again, even knowing the consequences.

Before he leaves, Isaiah sneeringly tells Christian that when the time comes, the Moroi will have a willing victim in Rose.

Later, Rose slips into Lissa's mind. Adrian thinks Lissa holds the key to finding Rose. He insists that as a spirit user, Lissa should also be able to talk to her in her dreams—just like he can—and that Rose and Lissa's connection would be stronger because of their bond. But Lissa's still on the medication that cuts her off from her magic, so he can't properly teach her to do this.

Rose finally understands why Adrian had so many questions for Lissa earlier. Suddenly, it all makes sense. Adrian's questions. The dreams. It's because he's a spirit user too!

> *He threw his arms up in the air. "How can I teach you to walk through dreams then? How else are we going to find Rose?"*
>
> *"Look," she said angrily, "I don't want to take the meds. But when I was off them . . . I did really crazy stuff. Dangerous stuff. That's what spirit does to you."*
>
> *"I don't take anything. I'm okay," he said.*
>
> *No, he wasn't, I realized. Lissa realized it too.*
>
> —pages 283–284

Still, despite her reservations, Lissa finds herself being tempted more and more by Adrian's offer. She wonders if she'd be okay—relatively speaking—if she went off her medication. Adrian can use spirit and seems fairly okay, other than some crazy talk now and then . . . (Although she'll later come to realize that he's far from okay. He self-medicates with cigarettes and alcohol.)

Rose reluctantly pulls out of Lissa's head and finds herself back in the basement, tied up with her friends. Everybody's in bad shape and things seem hopeless.

Suddenly, something occurs to her—the Moroi's elemental magic! They aren't *completely* helpless. But how can she let Christian know what she's thinking? She tries to give him a signal that she wants him to burn through her wrist bindings.

Instead, he asks the guards to untie him: he's ready to drink blood in order to save his own life, and he wants to drink from *Rose*. She's not sure if she should play along or not—is he being serious?

"Christian," I whispered, surprised at how easy it was to sound afraid. "Don't do this."

His lips twisted into one of the bitter smiles he produced so well. "You and I have never liked each other, Rose. If I've got to kill someone, it might as well be you." His words were icy, precise. Believable. "Besides, I thought you wanted this."

"Not this. Please, don't—"

One of the guards shoved Christian. "Get it over with or get back to your chair."

Still wearing that dark smile, Christian shrugged. "Sorry, Rose. You're going to die anyway. Why not do it for a good cause?" He brought his face down to my neck. "This is probably going to hurt," he added. —*pages 288–289*

Instantly, intense pain courses through Rose's body. But it doesn't start at her neck . . . There's a searing sensation at her wrists as he begins to burn through the plastic bindings that hold them together. Christian is on her side after all!

Rose breaks free and starts kicking butt. One guard has a gun, but Christian uses his magic to heat it up, so it's too hot to hold. Then he snips Mason's bindings so he can join the fight. After an intense battle, the three of them defeat the guards and release Eddie and Mia. Then they formulate their plan of escape. If they can get out of the house, the Strigoi won't be able to follow them— they burn up when they come into direct contact with the sunlight. The five friends head up the stairs into the main living area of the house, which has an aquarium in it, and Rose instructs Mason to get the others out of there if something bad happens to her.

Just as Rose feels they're going to make it out okay, Isaiah and Elena appear. Rose holds off the Strigoi while the others get to safety.

> *"Are you thinking you can take us both on by yourself?" He chuckled. Elena chuckled. I gritted my teeth.*
>
> *No, I didn't think I could take them both on. In fact, I was pretty sure I was going to die. But I was also pretty sure I could provide one hell of a distraction first.* —*pages 297-298*

The Strigoi drag Rose back into the shadows of the room as Mason gets the others outside just in time.

Isaiah is furious that his game has been ruined. To punish Rose, he plans to make her a real blood whore, since he's aware she's given blood before and enjoyed it. However, this time it won't be pleasant for her. He'll make it hurt every time she's bitten . . . until she finally dies.

It feels as if all is lost—Rose is going to die slowly and horribly at the hands—and fangs—of Strigoi.

But Rose isn't alone. She has friends who care about her fate, just as she cared about theirs.

"Let her go, or I'll kill you."

We all turned at the new voice, a voice dark and angry. Mason stood in the doorway, framed in light, holding my dropped gun. Isaiah studied him for a few moments.

"Sure," Isaiah finally said. He sounded bored. "Try it."

—*page 300*

Mason raises the gun and fires it into Isaiah's chest over and over . . . It doesn't do anything.

Isaiah releases Rose and grabs hold of Mason's head. Without warning, he twists sharply . . . and Rose hears a sickening crack.

Mason's eyes go wide . . . and then blank . . . as he collapses to the ground.

He's dead. The Strigoi killed him. Mason came back to save Rose's life and now he's gone forever.

Horror and shock crash over Rose. When Elena makes a move to feed on Mason's dead body, Rose stops feeling—she just acts. She couldn't stop this from happening, but she can protect Mason now. She screams for the Strigoi to stay away from Mason.

The *chotki* Lissa gave Rose for Christmas falls from her pocket and Isaiah picks it up, intrigued by the Dragomir symbol on it.

He'd really love to kill a Dragomir—

The aquarium suddenly bursts apart. The water magically coalesces in the air and moves forward to wrap around Isaiah's face, giving Rose a chance to grab a piece of the broken aquarium glass. She plunges it into the vampire's chest—aiming for the heart. He's still alive, but he blacks out from the pain. Rose then grabs a sword that's mounted on the wall and, taking everything she's learned from both Dimitri and her mother, attacks Elena. It isn't easy with a dull blade, but her rage gives her the strength to decapitate the Strigoi.

Mia's at the doorway, looking ill at the violent scene before her. It was her water magic that broke the aquarium and suffocated Isaiah. The girl Rose previously considered her nemesis had come through for her when it counted the most—tough times forge strong bonds and can turn enemies into allies . . . and friends.

When Isaiah tries to rise to his feet, Rose is on him. Hacking and hacking, she finally manages to detach his head from his body, eliminating the immediate Strigoi threat.

She's killed her first two Strigoi today—a huge accomplishment for a novice guardian. She should feel proud. This is everything she trained for! But it doesn't seem to matter—Mason is dead. Grief-stricken, Rose doesn't want to leave his body. Not for any reason.

Others finally arrive, but a dazed and in-shock Rose ignores them, blind to anything but her need to protect Mason's body. But then Dimitri is there at her side, softly urging her to put down the sword. He soothes Rose, telling her that everything is okay now. She's still driven to protect her friend, but Dimitri assures her she's done that.

The sword drops from her hands and clatters to the ground. Rose collapses—she wants to cry, but she can't. Dimitri wraps his arms around her and helps her to her feet.

Others are there, too. People Rose knows and trusts, but she can't concentrate enough to tell who they are. She just clings to Dimitri, unable to move from the spot where her friend was killed.

Janine's there—although Rose doesn't register anything other than a voice telling Dimitri to get Rose out of the house. Her mind refuses to process what happened, and all she can really do right now is follow simple directions, aided by Dimitri. His presence and strength is all that's helping to get her through this.

She eventually finds herself on an Academy jet on its way back to St. Vladimir's, with Janine by her side. She wants to know what she can do for her daughter, but Rose doesn't answer. As the tears finally come, all she can do right now is cry over the death of her friend.

MARKED BY DEATH

Having successfully killed two Strigoi, Rose is honored in a *molnija* ceremony. Before, she'd looked at the marks—like those her mother has—as badges of honor, but now they represent something she wants to forget. After the back of her neck is tattooed, she's greeted into the ranks of the guardians.

> *And then when my mother came up to me, I couldn't help the tear that ran down my cheek. She wiped it away and then brushed her fingers against the back of my neck. "Don't ever forget," she told me.*
>
> *Nobody said, "Congratulations," and I was glad. Death wasn't anything to get excited about.* —*pages 314-315*

Something very small has shifted in Rose and Janine's relation-

POP QUIZ:
Frostbite

1. Rose is scheduled for an important interview at the beginning of *Frostbite* to determine her commitment to being a guardian. What is this interview called?
2. Before he'll teach her to use a silver stake, Dimitri insists that Rose learn the location of what?
3. A "hat trick" for a guardian would be to kill three Strigoi by staking, _____, and burning.
4. What does Tasha Ozera teach?
5. What is Adrian Ivashkov's royal title?
6. Whose mother is killed during the Strigoi attack on the Drozdov family?
7. True or false? Tasha suggests to everyone that they should lower the graduation age of dhampirs so there will be more guardians to protect Moroi.
8. Where do the guardians pinpoint the location of the Strigoi they're searching for?
9. Who makes up the trio that originally leaves the ski lodge to hunt Strigoi?
10. What does Mia explode with her magic to help Rose when she fights the Strigoi?

* For quiz answers, see p.299.

ship. They aren't friends, but they're not enemies anymore either. They both bear the marks of death—as well as the inner scars. And that forges something between them that is strong enough to start to erase past hurts.

After the ceremony, flowers are delivered to Rose from Adrian—and Lissa fills her in on the details about the other spirit user. He's going to take the semester off from college and hang out at St. Vlad's with them. His plan is to work with Lissa on how to use spirit—but he wouldn't mind spending more time with Rose, either.

Dimitri lets Rose know there's no practice today because she needs to recover. Taking a life, even a Strigoi's, is a lot to come to terms with. Rose blames herself for Mason's death, but Dimitri tells her not to. Rose has made some bad decisions lately, but Mason was responsible for his own decisions. It wasn't Rose's fault.

Speaking of decisions, Dimitri's

made one of his own lately.

> *"I told her no. Tasha."*
>
> *"I . . ." I shut my mouth before my jaw hit the floor. "But . . . why? That was a once-in-a-lifetime thing. You could have a baby. And she . . . she was, you know, into you . . ."*
>
> *The ghost of a smile flickered on his face. "Yes, she was. Is. And that's why I had to say no. I couldn't return that . . .couldn't give her what she wanted. Not when . . ." He took a few steps toward me. "Not when my heart is somewhere else."*
>
> *I almost started crying again. "But you seemed so into her. And you kept going on about how young I acted."*
>
> *"You act young," he said, "Because you are young. But you know things, Roza. Things people older than you don't even know. That day . . ." I knew instantly which day he referred to. The one up against the wall. "You were right, about how I fight to stay in control. No one else has ever figured that out— and it scared me. You scare me."* —*pages 325-326*

They know they still can't be together—not really. Between the age thing and being Lissa's guardians, there's too much working against them. However . . . they're not Lissa's guardians *yet*.

Dimitri kisses Rose passionately, which fills her with hope and happiness, and then says he'll see her at their next training session. After all, he still has things to teach her. Lots of things.

CHAPTER 3

Shadow Kiss

RICHELLE ON *SHADOW KISS*

If readers thought the ending to *Frostbite* was harsh, it was nothing compared to this one. *Frostbite* was just the warm-up act! Again, I'd known from day one that the series was going to go in this direction, so the ending to this book wasn't that difficult for me to write. In fact, it's probably one of my favorite things that I've ever written! No author wants to be cruel, but we all really want to create something that has an impact on readers, and *Shadow Kiss's* ending certainly delivered. This book's publication was also kind of a wake-up call for me about how much of a following the series now had. The first book had done well, but it certainly wasn't an overnight blockbuster. The series' popularity had been growing steadily but gradually, and it wasn't obvious to me, the author, how big the fan base was getting. Both *Shadow Kiss* and the previous book had made the *New York Times* Bestseller list, but the impact of what that truly meant didn't hit me until, immediately after *Shadow Kiss's* publication, my inbox began getting filled with distraught e-mails from readers devastated by the ending. I was flooded with comments from those who couldn't believe I'd done something so mean to the characters. An astonishing amount of people told me that they'd thrown the book across the room in outrage—but then they'd add that they were eager to read the next book. What probably shocked me the most was that there was a handful of people who believed this was a trilogy and that I actually ended the series this way! Now *that* would've been mean.

First line: His fingertips slid along my back, applying hardly any pressure, yet sending shock waves over my flesh.

GHOST FROM THE PAST

Rose is having a very sexy dream, but it's not Dimitri who's the object of her affection; it's . . . *Christian?*

Oh no. It's happening again. Rose slipped into Lissa's mind by accident, something that's easier to control when she's awake. Luckily, she's able to pull herself out of her friend's romantic encounter with her boyfriend.

But now she's extremely cranky since it's only another reminder that Lissa can have the perfect relationship out in the open, but Rose's feelings toward Dimitri need to be bottled up and kept a secret. *So* not fair.

She doesn't want to go back to sleep and risk facing the couple again, so she decides to get some fresh air. Maybe a walk through the campus will help take her mind off her own troubles . . .

But her "troubles"—aka Dimitri—are currently out on patrol. She plays it off like her being out in the middle of the night (which in the vampire world is actually *day*) is no big deal.

"Rose—" Dimitri's hand caught my arm, and despite all the wind and chill and slush, a flash of heat shot through me. He released me with a start, as though he too had been burned. "What are you really doing out here?"

He was using the stop fooling around *voice, so I gave him as truthful an answer as I could. "I had a bad dream. I wanted some air."*

"And so you just rushed out. Breaking the rules didn't even cross your mind—and neither did putting on a coat."

"Yeah," I said "That pretty much sums it up."

"Rose, Rose." This time it was his exasperated voice. "You never change." —page 7

But she *has* changed. What happened in Spokane—losing Mason and singlehandedly killing two Strigoi—has given Rose a darker outlook on life. And Dimitri knows it.

When Alberta, the captain of the school guardians, draws near, Dimitri tells Rose to stay out of sight. But from her hiding place, she ends up hearing something shocking. Dimitri is scheduled to testify at Victor Dashkov's upcoming trial for kidnapping Lissa. Victor had wanted her to use her spirit ability to heal his debilitating disease and didn't hesitate in killing anyone who got in his way. Now he's being judged. But this doesn't make any sense to Rose . . . why aren't she and Lissa testifying on their own behalf? They were both involved in the incident.

Alberta leaves and Rose comes out of her hiding spot to grill Dimitri about this. Victor is one of the highest-ranking royals, very close to the throne, and Dimitri says that those who know about the trial would prefer things stay quiet. He assures her that there's more than enough evidence to put Victor behind bars without Rose or Lissa attending the trial. While Dimitri is sorry and understands why she'd be upset about this—Rose would love to help convict the man who very nearly destroyed her and Lissa's lives—it wasn't his decision.

They part ways and an annoyed Rose heads back to her dorm. But someone is watching her. Someone familiar.

Stunned, she realizes that it's Mason.

But that's impossible. He was killed three weeks ago!

He beckons to her, a sad, grim expression on his face. Terrified, she runs away. When she looks back, he's gone. Maybe it was just her imagination.

GETTING EXPERIENCED

The next day is the exciting start of the novices' field experience. For the next six weeks, Rose—even though she has two *molnija* marks, she's still a novice guardian—and the other seniors in her class will be assigned a Moroi student. Each of them will protect their Moroi from fake Strigoi attacks, instigated by guardians, to test what they've learned so far. Rose thinks it's a done deal that she'll be assigned to Lissa. The two of them will ace this assignment. Piece of cake.

But she isn't. She's shocked when Eddie gets Lissa. And Rose gets . . . *Christian.*

This seriously can't be happening. She's supposed to get *Lissa*—her *best friend*. The girl she protected for two years when they were out on their own. The one she will be protecting full-time once they graduate. Somebody must have made a huge mistake!

An angry and indignant Rose confronts Alberta and Dimitri and insist they see reason and reassign her to Lissa. Instead, she's told that this is a lesson for her. In real life guardians don't have a choice: whoever they're assigned to is who they get. Bottom line: she'll need to suck it up or she'll fail this very important assignment.

Fine. But she's not going to be happy about it.

Meanwhile, ever since they got back from Spokane, Adrian's been hanging out at the school to learn more about the spirit ability he and Lissa share. But it's not Lissa who he has a thing for. It's the pretty girl he likes to call "little dhampir."

"Look, Rose. You don't have to keep up with the hard-to-get thing. You've already got me."

Adrian knew perfectly well I wasn't playing hard to get, but he always took a particular delight in teasing me. "I'm really not in the mood for your so-called charm today."

"What happened, then? You're stomping through every puddle you can find and look like you're going to punch the first person you see."

"Why are you hanging around, then? Aren't you worried about getting hit?"

"Aw, you'd never hurt me. My face is too pretty."

pages 34–35

But his flirtation is lost on her in her current dark mood. He notices that it's not just her mood, but her aura that's also edged in darkness. It's like there's always a shadow following her. Something about how he says it makes her shiver. Once before, Adrian mentioned that Rose "takes shadows" from Lissa. But Rose doesn't know what this means. For now, it simply feels like a permanently bad mood.

Lissa has been officially granted permission to go off her depression meds and is able to use her magic again so that she and Adrian can get deeper into learning spirit. This worries Rose, who's seen her friend slide into darkness before because of her power. She asks Eddie, who'll be working closely with Lissa during the tests, to keep an eye on her.

As the field experience begins, Rose needs to tag along with Christian—who she's *still* not overly fond of despite their shared traumatic experience in Spokane—wherever he goes. Before the end of day one, they're presented with their first "attack," and Dimitri is playing one of the Strigoi. Eddie—also part of the kidnapping by Strigoi—fights them off and gets Rose to hang back and "protect" the Moroi. It goes fairly perfectly, even though Rose would prefer to play a bigger role in the scuffle. Still, not bad for a first day's work. Also, as she spends some time with Christian, things get friendlier between the two. She begins to think the next six weeks won't be so bad after all.

While accompanying Christian back to his dorm, Brandon Lazar, a friendly Moroi student who also lives there, falls into step with them. Rose is surprised to see that his face is bruised, which makes her wonder if he too has been fighting guardians lately. She questions him about this, and the kid shrugs it off as nothing, firmly telling the inquisitive Rose to let it go. But that's not something Rose does very easily, not when her curiosity—and concern—has been piqued. She's going to press for more information, but suddenly, they're attacked again!

Finally, Rose has a chance to kick some butt and show everybody that she's got what it takes to be a guardian. She puts herself in between Brandon and Christian and faces off with Stan, an instructor who's given her a hard time ever since she returned to the school.

But when a vision of Mason appears again, it's enough to make Rose completely lose her focus, and she gets taken down hard, failing the assignment very badly. After all of her complaints and attitude about being assigned to Christian rather than Lissa, Stan assumes she's trying to rebel against the test.

Rose is dragged before a disciplinary committee and reprimanded, but she can't exactly tell them the truth. To say she's seeing ghosts would make her look crazy and possibly get her kicked out of school— or worse. But to say nothing makes her look incompetent—someone not capable of guarding a royal like Lissa. It's a lose-lose situation.

Just when her fate is looking bleak, Dimitri jumps to her defense. Rose is given another chance but put on probation. Plus, one day a week she'll be required to do community service as punishment. Could be worse.

Later, when another novice guardian taunts Rose for her abysmal performance, her temper boils over, and she gets him back by putting his Moroi charge in immediate danger—from *her*. It actually takes Adrian and his strong compulsion to make Rose let the girl go. Rose is dealing with some *major* anger issues. Maybe Mason's ghost stirred up some deep feelings in her.

Lissa's angry too, since she incorrectly assumes that Rose purposefully screwed up with Christian all because she doesn't like him. Rose can't believe that her best friend would immediately think the worst of her.

> *"Do you really think I'd do this? Abandon Christian and make myself look stupid on purpose just to get back at my teachers?"*
>
> *"No," she said finally. "You'd probably do it in a way where*

you wouldn't get caught."

"Dimitri said the same thing," I grumbled. "I'm glad every-one has so much faith in me."

"We do," she countered. "That's why all of this is so weird."

"Even I make mistakes." I put on my brash, overconfident face. "I know it's hard to believe—kind of surprises me myself— but I guess it has to happen. It's probably some kind of karmic way to balance out the universe. Otherwise, it wouldn't be fair to have one person so full of awesomeness."   —*page 80*

Rose knows she has to tell Lissa and the others about the Victor Dashkov trial they're not invited to. And just as she expected, Lissa's freaked by the very mention of his name. As Lissa struggles to get control over her emotions, Rose finds she's *losing* control over her own. Her now-familiar black mood has seized her again, and she wants to let it out by ranting and raving about how mad she is that they can't go to Victor's trial.

But her first duty is to protect Moroi, not to give in to her own impulses. It's the guardian mantra: *They come first.*

Those words are starting to annoy her.

That night, while Rose is camped out on Christian's bedroom floor—being a guardian is a twenty-four-hour-a-day job—she's drawn into one of Adrian's spirit dreams. And he's not exactly the sanest she's ever seen him.

> *"Rose is in red*
> *But never in blue*

Sharp as a thorn

Fights like one too."

Adrian dropped his arms and looked at me expectantly.

"How can a thorn fight?" I asked.

He shook his head. "Art doesn't have to make sense, little dhampir. Besides, I'm supposed to be crazy, right?"

"Not the craziest I've ever seen."

"Well," he said, pacing over to study some hydrangeas. "I'll work on that." —*pages 91-92*

Rose takes Adrian's craziness in stride—it seems to simply be a part of who he is. She's been feeling pretty crazy lately, too, but Adrian points out that truly crazy people rarely question whether or not they're crazy. Good point. It makes her feel just a little bit better.

Adrian lets Rose know that he's tired of her giving him the brush-off whenever he shows interest in her. He knows she's into Dimitri, but come on, the guy isn't perfect. *He* can't get Rose into Victor Dashkov's trial, but Adrian, on the other hand . . . well, he just *might*. He suggests she start being nicer to him.

When Christian and Rose meet up with Lissa and Eddie after class one day, they're "attacked." Eddie and Rose fight together to take down the "Strigoi" threat. Rose is so determined to kick butt that she forgets that being a guardian isn't just about the glory of the fight. Eddie's praised and Rose is chastised for not protecting the Moroi and instead looking for a chance to redeem herself. She really can't win lately.

To make matters worse, Eddie got his face scraped in the scuffle, and Lissa can't resist healing him with spirit. Adrian's amazed by this use of their ability and scratches himself purposefully to get her to do it again so he can learn from it.

Rose's mood drops further.

So does Christian's, although not for the same reasons. He's growing increasingly jealous at how much time Lissa and Adrian are spending together. Bottom line: Christian doesn't feel that he's good enough to be with Lissa. And Adrian . . . well, he's the queen's gorgeous, rich grand-nephew.

Rose assures Christian that he has nothing to worry about—Lissa's crazy about him. But Christian isn't convinced . . .

However, he is hungry. Rose accompanies Christian to the on-campus feeder room located near the cafeteria so he can get some blood. There, Jesse and Ralf, two Moroi guys that Rose hates, approach him with an offer to join a secret group they've recently formed, but Christian turns them down flat. While he'd like to be more accepted around school, even *he* has standards. Still, he wonders what kind of group it is . . .

ALMOST A DATE

Dimitri volunteers to help Rose with her community service, which surprises her. This is supposed to be his day off; why would he want to spend it cleaning the chapel?

As they clean, Rose is still plagued by her Mason sightings. This seems like as good a place as any to find answers, so she decides to ask the priest about ghosts. But what the priest tells her isn't exactly what she wants to hear: some believe that those who die young and violently will wander the earth for a time after their deaths. Could Mason really be a ghost—and is he haunting *her*?

Rose still feels chilled by her conversation with the priest as she and Dimitri take some boxes across campus to the elementary dorm. Rose waits outside while Dimitri brings the boxes in, and that's where she meets Jill Mastrano—a fourteen-year-old who's totally starstruck by the infamous Rose Hathaway. Jill's a young, super-enthusiastic Moroi who tells her she wants to learn to use her magic defensively—and *also* learn to throw a punch. Maybe Rose can teach her some moves some time? Moroi students are getting beaten up lately by "some psycho," and Jill wants to know how to properly defend herself.

This makes Rose remember Brandon's bruises from the other day. What is going on at St. Vlad's and who is beating kids up?

Before Rose can show Jill any fighting techniques, Dimitri shows up. Jill is tongue-tied around the handsome Russian and scurries off. Rose is still surprised the girl would want help from her, but Dimitri's not. Rose is outgoing and dedicated, and she excels at everything she does—she's definitely earned a lot of respect.

Not enough to get an invite to the trial, though, she reminds him. She wants to know if he can do anything to help, but he can't. He just doesn't have as much influence as Rose might think.

To Rose, Dimitri should be able to do *anything*. Why not this when she wants it so much? She refuses to accept that there's nothing he can do to help. And if he's so disinterested in her, why did he even bother helping her clean the chapel today? Is he spying on her? Trying to keep her out of trouble?

"Why does there have to be some ulterior motive?"

I wanted to blurt out a hundred different things. Like, if there wasn't a motive, then that meant he just wanted to spend time with me. And that made no sense, because we both knew we were only supposed to have a teacher-student relationship. He of all people should know that. He was the one who'd told me.

"Because everyone has motives."

"Yes. But not always the motives you think." He pushed open the door. "I'll see you later."

I watched him go, my feelings a tangle of confusion and anger. If the situation hadn't been so strange, I would have almost said it was like we'd just gone on a date. —*page 133*

OFF TO COURT

Turns out Rose shouldn't have spent so much time worrying—Lissa has exciting news: they're going to Victor's trial! Somehow, Rose, Lissa, and Christian are now set to testify, and Eddie will come along too—the field experience doesn't stop just because Lissa's going off campus. A happy Rose apologizes to Dimitri—obviously he came through and got them invited. But it wasn't him. Huh? But if it wasn't him, then how did they get the opportunity to testify and the chance to do their part to send Victor Dashkov to prison?

On the flight to the Moroi Royal Court, Rose isn't feeling so good. She has a massive headache, her mood is nasty, and she sees shadows darting through the plane. Adrian notes her aura is black . . . *very* black. Lissa tries to heal her headache with spirit, but it doesn't do any good. Once at Court, though, Rose feels a bit better—but she's still troubled by the memory of the shadows.

Lissa is called before Queen Tatiana. In the past, the queen has made it quite clear that Lissa shamed her family name by running away from St. Vlad's, and Lissa is nervous about what she might say this time. She asks Rose to watch through the bond for moral support. Even if she can't be there in person, Lissa will still feel better knowing she's there in spirit.

Today, Tatiana is a bit more gracious and curious about seeing Lissa's spirit ability in action. Since Victor's on trial for forcing Lissa to use her rare ability to help heal his disease, her previously secret abilities are no longer secret. Queen Tatiana has Lissa demonstrate her mysterious and intriguing magic by bringing a plant back to life—and is very impressed by what she sees. Impressing the queen is *not* an easy feat, and Lissa (and Rose, through the bond) is thrilled.

Feeling that Lissa is doing just fine on her own, Rose breaks the bond and decides to go out exploring the grounds. She meets up with Eddie and Christian, who are with a familiar face—her former nemesis, Mia Rinaldi. After their traumatic experience in Spokane, as well as losing her mother, Mia left St. Vlad's and moved to Court to be with her father. Mia's since made friends with guardians here and is learning to fight in hand-to-hand combat. Since the kidnapping, Rose thinks Mia has changed for the better. However, she can't say the same for herself. Rose feels that she's worse off now than she was before—to her, the constant dark moods seem to be proof of this.

The four of them being together after all they experienced is not easy—it only makes them think of Mason.

Soon, they're joined by Lissa and Adrian. Christian asks if the meeting with the queen helped clue her in on who got them the invite to the trial.

It certainly did. It was Adrian. As Tatiana's favorite great-nephew, he was able to convince the queen that they needed to be there. And he didn't do it for Lissa . . . he did it for Rose. This generous gesture surprises her deeply.

> *"I just thought . . ."*
>
> *I couldn't finish. I'd thought Dimitri would be the one who came through for me, the one who—despite what he said—could make almost anything happen. But he hadn't.*
>
> *"Thought what?" Adrian prompted.*
>
> *"Nothing." With much effort, I managed to utter the next words. "Thank you for helping us."*
>
> *"Oh my God," he said. "A kind word from Rose Hathaway. I can die a happy man."*
>
> —*page 174*

Mia gives Rose a note she was told to deliver. It's from Victor Dashkov, and it's a taunt that he intends to share stories of Rose and Dimitri's forbidden romantic escapades, thanks to his lust-charmed necklace, in court—something that would get both of them in *serious* trouble.

She shares this unsettling news with Dimitri. He makes a quick phone call to a contact who he knows will be able to get them in to see Victor.

When they arrive at the Court's prison facilities, seeing Victor for the first time since he was imprisoned at St. Vlad's after Lissa's kidnapping makes Rose's skin crawl.

Compared to how sickly he'd looked before, now he appears

young and healthy—but it's unlikely to last. Frequent healings from Lissa would have been required to keep his disease permanently at bay. For now, though, he's in good health to face his trial.

Victor is delighted at the chance to taunt Rose and Dimitri in person. The question is, what does he want from them? But Victor really isn't interested in petty things like revenge. He has his sights set on higher aspirations: revolution. There's been a lot of unrest building in the Moroi community, with people clamoring for a more forward-thinking government. And Victor would think that Rose of all people would be interested in overthrowing a government that holds on to archaic traditions like the virtual enslavement of the dhampir race. He even believes there's someone she knows who would be the perfect person to spearhead this revolution—Lissa. With her compulsion and spirit magic, nothing would be impossible if she was in a position of power.

The conversation ends when Victor threatens to discuss Dimitri and Rose's relationship, especially pertaining to the lust charm, and the normally controlled Dimitri offers up his own veiled threats. If Victor tries to ruin Rose, he's ruining his chance to get Lissa to help him with his rebellion fantasies.

> *"And it'll all be pointless anyway, because you won't stay alive long enough in prison to stage your grand plans. You aren't the only one with connections."*
>
> *My breath caught a little. Dimitri brought so many things to my life: love, comfort, and instruction. I got so used to him sometimes that I forgot just how dangerous he could be. As he*

stood there, tall and threatening while he glared down at Victor, I felt a chill run down my spine. I remembered how when I had first come to the Academy, people had said Dimitri was a god. In this moment, he looked it. —*page 188*

When they leave, Dimitri seems shaken by the confrontation. Rose wonders if he meant what he said. Would he really have Victor killed?

"I'd do a lot of things to protect you, Roza."
My heart pounded. He only used "Roza" when he was feeling particularly affectionate toward me. —*page 189*

THE TRIAL

When Victor is brought into the courtroom the next day, Rose can feel Lissa's fear through the bond. It's the first time her friend has seen the man since he kidnapped her and forced her to heal him with spirit.

Witnesses are called to testify against Victor, including Dimitri. The tense part is when he speaks about the lust charm—after all, he can't exactly admit the *lust* part. Instead, he says the charm made Rose attack him (not *that* far from the truth, really), which delayed them from getting help for Lissa. It's obvious to Rose that lying on the stand is difficult for Dimitri, but there's no way around it.

After Christian testifies, it's Rose's turn. She does her best to brush over the "attack" charm and tries to ignore Victor's knowing smirk.

Lissa's account as Victor's victim is the most moving—and she even works in a little spirit-induced charisma to gain everyone's sympathy as she painfully relates how she was tortured by Victor's henchman.

Victor takes the stand as if he doesn't have a care in the world. His defense is that he was dying and felt he had no choice but to use Lissa's magic to heal him. Worst of all, he takes no responsibility for convincing his own daughter Natalie to turn Strigoi to rescue him. As he says, Natalie made her own decisions, ones that ultimately led to her death.

> *"Can you say that about everyone you used to meet your ends? Guardian Belikov and Miss Hathaway had no say in what you made them do."*
>
> *Victor chuckled. "Well, that's a matter of opinion. I honestly don't think they minded. But if you have time after this case, Your Honor, you might want to consider trying a statutory rape case."*

page 199

Rose is stunned, but luckily, no one believes him, thinking he's just trying to shift focus off himself. Looks like he'd just wanted to tease them. Evil jerk.

The queen delivers her verdict: Victor's found guilty and sentenced to life in prison. Finally, Lissa can move on from her ordeal and feel safe again.

Adrian gives Rose a congratulatory hug in public (one that will lead the queen to want to chat with her later). But first, Tatiana wants to see Lissa and offer the last Dragomir a chance to come to live at Court after graduation and attend the nearby Lehigh University. Lissa graciously accepts the generous offer.

Then it's Rose's turn. She expects that she'll be told, as Lissa's future guardian, that she'll have to be extra careful of the princess at the university, but that's not the subject at hand. The queen wants Rose to stop the affair she's having with Adrian.

Say what?

> *"Um, Your Majesty . . . there's some kind of mistake. There's*
> *nothing going on between Adrian and me."*
> *"Do you think I'm an idiot?" she asked.*
> *Wow. That was an opening.*
> *"No, Your Majesty."*   —*page 207*

The queen assumes Rose is a "cheap dhampir girl" looking to run off with a rich Moroi lord. And Rose's former party-girl reputation doesn't exactly help matters. Tatiana even brings up Rose's mother, Janine, who was once involved with a Moroi named Ibrahim—but even *she* learned that Moroi men don't marry dhampir girls. They just play with them. That's when the queen unleashes the greatest threat in her arsenal: if Rose doesn't end things with Adrian, Tatiana will ensure that she isn't assigned as Lissa's guardian after graduation.

The queen's plans are very clear. She wants Adrian and Lissa to have an arranged marriage that will help further the Dragomir line. The princess's current relationship with Christian is unacceptable. Thanks to his parents' decision to become Strigoi, his being a royal is irrelevant.

Wow. This is info Rose definitely isn't ready to share with the others, not until she has time to process it herself.

A GLIMPSE AT THE FUTURE

While they're waiting for the flight back to St. Vlad's, Lissa takes Rose to the spa. Since Rose uses her hands so much to punch things, a manicure sounds like total luxury. While there, Rose meets Ambrose, a to-die-for hot guy who sure isn't like any other dhampir she's ever met—by the bite marks on his neck, it's obvious he's a male blood whore. That is *so* not normal. But Ambrose is very happy with his choices—and they *are* choices, unlike Rose, who really never had a say in what she's become and where her future will lead.

Speaking of the future, Ambrose, who's also rumored to be the queen's secret lover, takes the girls to see his fortune-telling aunt, Rhonda, so they can get a tarot-card reading.

Lissa's told her life is about to change in ways that, while difficult, will *"ultimately illuminate the world."* Sounds pretty cool.

Rose is told that she will *"destroy that which is undead."*

Lame. She already knows that. She's training to be a guardian, after all. What a stupid fortune!

When Dimitri comes to retrieve the girls for the flight, he too is given a little insight on his future. He's told: *"You will lose what you value most, so treasure it while you can."*

It's an ominous reading, and one that will prove true all too soon ...

DESCENDING DARKNESS

On the flight back to the Academy, Rose is again plagued by a headache and shadowy forms. Due to inclement weather, the plane is diverted to a nearby airport. When they land, Rose's world explodes. The pain in her head becomes so intense, it feels like her skull is being ripped open.

She sees ghostly faces—many of whom she recognizes as victims of Strigoi massacres—and they're reaching out to her with pale, shining hands. They want something from her. They're trying to tell her what it is, but they can't speak. There's a growing patch of blackness, and Rose instinctively knows it's the entrance to the world of death—she died in the car crash, but Lissa brought her back. She shouldn't be alive. This—*this* is where she's supposed to go.

She starts screaming and screaming. Mason appears, and she begs him to make the others leave her alone. She can't get away—they're everywhere and they're reaching for her. Finally, Rose can't take it anymore, and she passes out from the fear and pain.

When she wakes, she's in the school's clinic, and everybody's worried about her. Finally she tells them the truth: she's been seeing ghosts, including Mason.

As predicted, no one—her friends or the school officials—believes her. It seems clear to the school doctor that her visions are a result of post-traumatic stress. Witnessing Mason's murder and then killing the Strigoi responsible must have taken their toll on her. Obviously, her recovery has been hindered by fighting the "fake" Strigoi during the field experience sessions.

It's suggested that she drop the field experience entirely, but Rose doesn't like this suggestion at all—she needs to pass to graduate. Dimitri, deeply concerned with Rose's well-being but also familiar with her stubborn streak, suggests she take part in the testing part-time. She's also to see a counselor.

Rose is grateful Dimitri stepped in and helped, but she doesn't realize quite how upset he was to see her in such distress.

"Rose," he said, the pain in his voice making my heart stop, "this shouldn't have been the first time I heard about this! Why didn't you tell me? Do you know what it was like? Do you know what it was like for me to see you like that and not know what was happening? Do you know how scared I was?"

I was stunned, both from his outburst and our proximity. I swallowed, unable to speak at first. There was so much on his face, so many emotions. I couldn't recall the last time I'd seen that much of him on display. It was wonderful and frightening at the same time. I then said the stupidest thing possible.

"You're not scared of anything."

"I'm scared of lots of things. I was scared for you." He released me, and I stepped back. There was still passion and worry written all over him. —————pages 253-254

She didn't tell him about the ghosts because he wouldn't have believed her. He *still* doesn't believe her. But it makes sense to her that she's the only one who can see the ghostly visions—she's *shadow-kissed*. Because she died, she has a connection to the world of the dead. Killing the Strigoi has strengthened that connection.

And this experience has strengthened Rose and Dimitri's relationship. This has shown Rose how much he cares about her—and it's not just the concern of a tutor for his student. It's way deeper and more powerful than that.

When they part, Rose realizes she forgot her overnight bag and heads back to the clinic to retrieve it. There, she spots another Moroi student, Abby Badica, who's been beaten up by the mysterious school bully. To get to the truth, Rose pretends she already knows what's going on, and Abby begs Rose to "keep things quiet until everything's set." If the rest of the "Mână" find out she's at the clinic for medical attention, she'll get in trouble. She tells Rose that she wants the chance to "try again."

When the doctor arrives, Rose is blocked from getting more information, but now she definitely has a clue who's behind the recent royal-bashing—they're called the Mânâ.

Rose starts to guard Christian again as she heads to class—and Adrian's hanging around, too. While Christian continues to fight his jealousy, Lissa teaches Adrian how to bring plants back to life. Adrian also shares what he's learned about their mysterious mutual ability. There are stories about "super compulsion" being used to make others live through their worst nightmares, kind of like a vivid hallucination. Sounds pretty scary, actually.

As they walk back to their dorms, Rose suggests to Adrian that he be careful of Christian's rising jealousy toward him and Lissa.

> *"What?" he asked in mock astonishment. "Doesn't he know my heart belongs to you?"*
>
> *"It does not. And no, he's still worried about it, despite what I've told him."*
>
> *"You know, I bet if we started making out right now, it would make him feel better."*
>
> *"If you touch me," I said pleasantly, "I'll provide you with the opportunity to see if you can heal yourself."* —page 270

Adrian confides that he saw something weird earlier when Lissa used her magic to demonstrate bringing the plant back to life—something only he, as a spirit user, could see. Her aura dimmed. But then that darkness didn't just disappear . . . it went into Rose. Lissa isn't having side effects from her magic anymore because

Rose is absorbing her darkness! *And* her madness, which, to Adrian, could easily explain the ghosts.

It makes a strange sort of sense and makes Rose think of St. Vladimir and his shadow-kissed guardian, Anna. Rose goes to the chapel to ask the priest what ultimately happened to Anna so she can get a sense of what she might expect. The answer isn't very reassuring: Anna committed suicide.

When Mason appears before Rose again, she has to ask him directly: Is she really going crazy? Or is he really there?

All she can get him to confirm—he's only able to communicate with nods or shakes of his head—is she's *not* going crazy, he's not looking for revenge, and he's having trouble finding peace. There's another reason he's there, but he can't get the information across to Rose no matter how hard he tries. And then he disappears again.

Counseling sessions don't help much. Rose tells the counselor about the problems with her mother, the guilt over Mason's death, and her fixation on unattainable guys. (This subject is one of the counselor's favorites. Does she only pick guys she can't have so it will always ensure she'll stay dedicated to Lissa? This is *so* not helpful.)

Rose definitely has issues—she doesn't need a counselor to tell her *that*.

Trying to focus on something else, Rose questions Adrian about the *Mână*. She learns the word is Romanian for "the hand," and it's a secret society found at a lot of schools. Apparently, its membership consists of royals who band together to feel special and exclusive. Rose remembers Jesse and Ralf inviting Christian to their group. Could this be related?

Rose is still disturbed by the counselor's insistence that she intentionally falls for guys who are unattainable as a way to ensure she'll always be around to protect Lissa. Adrian's pretty unattainable since it's obvious to her he just wants her body, not a real relationship. She decides to test the theory on him and see just how interested in him she could get.

"Use compulsion to make me want to kiss you—except you have to promise not to actually kiss me."

"That's pretty weird—and when I say something's weird, you know it's serious."

"Please."

He sighed and then focused his eyes right on me. It was like drowning, drowning in seas of green. There was nothing in the world except for those eyes.

"I want to kiss you, Rose," he said softly. "And I want you to want me too."

Every aspect of his body—his lips, his hands, his scent—suddenly overpowered me. I felt warm all over. I wanted him to kiss me with every ounce of my being. There was nothing in life I wanted more than that kiss. I tilted my face up toward his, and he leaned down. I could practically taste his lips.

"Do you want to?" he asked, voice still like velvet.

Did I ever. Everything around me had blurred. Only his lips were in focus.

"Yes."
—pages 291–292

Holding true to her request, he doesn't actually kiss her. And she's proven something very important to herself—she's definitely in love.

With *Dimitri*.

Adrian is incredibly sexy and charming. There's no doubt that Rose is attracted to him. But even under compulsion, it hadn't been the electric, all-encompassing feeling she had had with Dimitri—that feeling like they were bound together by forces way bigger than both of them combined.

With Dimitri, it's really love, not just a trick her mind is playing on her.

But in her heart, she already knew that.

Rose takes Christian to another feeding session. The human feeder is definitely crazy—giving so much blood to a vampire will do that to a person—but her insights are surprisingly helpful. She thinks if Rose has seen a ghost on campus, then there must be something wrong with the wards—the magical barrier that surrounds the school is designed to keep Strigoi out, which means that they should also fend off the dead.

It suddenly makes sense. It's why she didn't have a ghost problem at Court. The wards there are very strong. But on the plane and at the other airport, there were *no* wards—which could explain the onslaught of ghosts. If this is true, if there's something wrong with the wards at school, then Rose isn't the only one in danger.

Rose approaches Dimitri with this disturbing info, but he assures her the wards are checked daily and guardians would notice a problem.

Maybe she just has to face facts: the only one who believes her is a demented human feeder. She's going crazy. For real.

She shares what she's learned about Anna and how she's scared that she'll suffer a similar fate. All Dimitri can do is reassure her that she's going to be okay. She's wild and impulsive, but she's strong. He's certain she and Anna won't share the same fate.

This moment between them only intensifies their feelings for each other. If they're trying to avoid the many complications of their forbidden relationship, they're not helping matters right now. But it just feels so right.

THE HAND

Through the bond, Rose gets the confirmation about the *Mânǎ* she's been looking for when she sees Jesse and Ralf approach Lissa about joining. They want every royal Moroi name represented, and Lissa is the last Dragomir. Lissa really doesn't like the sound of the elite club, though. Sounds snobby to her. They explain it's more important than that; it's to help get their voices out politically—keeping the government from making "stupid" decisions and making the queen and everyone else see the *Mânǎ*'s way, no matter what.

Sounds kind of like compulsion. And compulsion is supposed to be forbidden. While Lissa will use it when absolutely necessary, manipulating the minds of others against their will is morally wrong.

Jesse and Ralf disagree. Also, it's not like Lissa is one to talk. They've heard rumors that she is particularly good at compelling people—how else could she have gotten away with so much? The boys don't back off until Eddie steps in as Lissa's guardian. Eddie's not afraid of kicking a little Moroi butt, and Rose is totally okay with that.

Speaking of kicking butt, Rose finally gets to do it when they're "attacked" again. She's doing great, taking down two guardians with her practice stake. Even though she's only been allowed to practice part-time—and she's being gently eased back into things after her breakdown on the plane—the "Strigoi" are no match for

Rose. That is, until she sees the third "Strigoi": Dimitri.

Rose hesitates. This is the guy she loves standing in front of her. Can she fight him? Can she win? After a momentary hesitation, she rushes toward him. Even though they're very evenly matched after all their practice sessions, Rose manages to "stake" him successfully.

> *Behind me, people were clapping, but all I noticed was Dimitri. Our gazes were locked. I was still straddling him, my hands pressed against his chest. Both of us were sweaty and breathing heavily. His eyes looked at me with pride—and a hell of a lot more.*
>
> *—page 326*

Luckily, no one else notices the intense heat between the two. Rose is praised for passing the test perfectly.

Feeling good, she cleans up and heads to the cafeteria . . . where there's a *big* problem escalating. Somebody has told Christian about Adrian and Lissa's "arranged marriage," and he assumes it's been Adrian's plan all along to steal Lissa away from him.

Christian is hurt and insane with jealousy. He wants to cause some pain of his own—and he's got the fire magic to help back him up. Somebody's going to be seriously injured if Rose can't get this situation under control. She has Adrian use compulsion to calm Christian down and, luckily, it works.

Why didn't Lissa stop this confrontation from happening? Where is she? Rose checks the bond and finds that Lissa is in great distress. She's in pain—and screaming.

On the other side of campus, members of the *Mână*, led by Jesse and Ralf, are forcibly subjecting Lissa to their initiation test. She is to use her compulsion to stop her attackers, who are using their own powers to throw rocks at her, attempt to drown her, and—just like Victor's henchman did—use air magic to try to suffocate her.

Rose races there and starts kicking ass, furious at the group of spoiled Moroi students. Most of them scatter at the sight of her.

But it's Lissa who the remaining *Mânâ* members should be worried about. Now unhinged by the torture and reminded of what Victor's henchmen did to her, Lissa turns her attention to Jesse. He should be careful what he wished for. He wanted to see Lissa's compulsion at work? How about some super-compulsion? She traps him in a nightmare where spiders are crawling on him. Lissa's overwhelmed by darkness, unable to stop herself from hurting Jesse.

Rose knows what she has to do: absorb some of that darkness into herself. But when she does, the darkness manifests itself as uncontrollable rage. She starts to beat the life out of Jesse, and it takes Eddie pulling her back to stop her from accidentally killing him.

When other guardians arrive to get everything under control, Dimitri takes a still enraged Rose away from the scene before she can cause any more damage. They go to the cabin in the woods where her dark mood can be dealt with privately.

He's desperately worried about her—this looks pretty bad. But slowly she's able to pull herself out of the darkness, leaving her with the horrible fear that she's destined for the same fate as Anna.

"It won't happen to you. You're too strong. You'll fight it, just like you did this time."

"I only did because you were here." He wrapped his arms

around me, and I buried my face in his chest. "I can't do it by
myself," I whispered.

"You can," he said. There was a tremulous note in his voice.
"You're strong—you're so, so strong. It's why I love you."

—*page 348*

Their feelings for each other, which have been building steadily
to this point, finally spill over. There's nothing they can do but give
in to it. They kiss, and this time there's no pulling back. When they
make love, Rose knows it's right—it's perfect—because they're in
love with each other.

Afterward, Dimitri assures her that he won't let anything bad
happen to her. His words are both wonderful and dangerous, but
she makes him the same promises. They're in love, and the world
seems golden and wonderful.

But it's not to last.

MASON'S WARNING

Mason's ghost appears to Rose as they head back to the school.
He has a message, and this time he's finally able to put it into
words: *"They're . . . coming . . ."*

It's Strigoi. They've breached the wards.

Rose and Dimitri are attacked, but Dimitri's able to stake the
Strigoi. He sends Rose back to campus with a message for the
other guardians: *buria.*

She doesn't argue. She runs, scared to death that Dimitri's going to
get killed. She relays the message Dimitri gave her: *Buria.* Russian for

"storm," it's a signal of a Strigoi attack. The guardians don't hesitate.

Because of the field experience, Lissa's dorm is mostly protected, but the same can't be said for the elementary dorm, where Jill lives. The campus is under immediate lockdown. Rose is given a stake and told to watch over the kids.

She checks in on Lissa through the bond—she's safe, at least, and with Eddie and Adrian. But where's Christian? Even though she's defying orders, she heads out to make sure he's okay. When she finds him, she senses Strigoi nearby—she can sense them now too, just as she can ghosts.

Rose fights hard and stakes one. But another gets the upper hand and she's certain she'll die—but then he bursts into flames. Thank you, Christian!

Christian thinks that the two of them make a good team. They could fight the Strigoi together and help protect the school. It goes against everything she's been taught about keeping Moroi safe, but it makes total sense. Together they kick Strigoi butt on the way back to the elementary campus. Total badasses!

One blond Strigoi seems to know her. He's familiar with Lissa too. He'd love to be the one to take down the last Dragomir. He slips away before she manages to stake him—it's one kill she'll later have wished she'd made.

Rose is beyond relieved when Dimitri returns battered but not dead. They survived! But the bad news comes quickly. The Strigoi killed many in their attack, and they also carried some away. And one of those kidnapped is Eddie.

No . . . it's not possible. Rose lost Mason; she can't lose Eddie too.

The wards around the school are reinforced, and more guardians have been called in to help deal with the aftermath of the attack. One is

Rose's mother. Rose tries to get her plan across to Janine—and she does have a plan. In order to rescue the Moroi, they need to know where they are—and Rose thinks she knows how they can get that information.

She takes Dimitri with her to the school's gates. Since the wards have been strengthened, Mason's ghost is stuck outside now. Dimitri's skeptical since he can't see anything, but he's willing to trust Rose's instincts.

Outside the gates, Mason appears to Rose. Using a map, he helps pinpoint where the Strigoi have taken their victims—caves five miles away. Since it's now daylight, the Strigoi are trapped, which means there's still a chance to get to them and rescue the others.

It's good enough information to launch a rescue mission.

Dimitri takes Rose for a walk to try to calm her down while they wait for everything to be organized. She's certain he's going to lecture her on how their being together was wrong and how it can't happen again. But he most definitely doesn't feel that way.

"Even before the Strigoi attack, as I watched all the problems you were struggling with, I realized how much you meant to me. It changed everything. I was worried about you—so worried. You have no idea. And it became useless to try to act like I could ever put any Moroi life above yours. It's not going to happen, no matter how wrong others say it is. And so I decided that's something I have to deal with. Once I made that decision . . . there was nothing to hold us back." He hesitated, seeming to replay his words as he brushed my hair from my face. "Well, to hold me back. I'm speaking for myself. I don't mean to

act like I know exactly why you did it."

"I did it because I love you," I said, like it was the most obvious thing in the world. And really, it was. —page 398

He wants to be with her after graduation and will do anything to make that happen.

In the middle of the rescue mission and all this chaos, Rose has a glimmer of hope for the future. For a minute, she lets herself think it might all work out perfectly. Rose can have Dimitri *and* Lissa in her life. She doesn't have to give up one or the other. It's everything she wanted.

RESCUE AND LOSS

A large team of fifty guardians, novices, and Moroi travel to the caves. Dimitri and Janine are part of the first team to go inside.

It's not long before sounds of fighting reach those waiting tensely outside. Some rescued Moroi and dhampirs emerge, but Dimitri's team gets trapped!

Reinforcements have to go in to help. Rose is among them, and her ability to sense Strigoi proves extremely helpful. She fights with everything she's got on her way to where Dimitri and the others are trapped behind a collapsed wall.

With Rose helping to fight off the Strigoi—which distracts them—those trapped, including Dimitri, are able to free themselves from their position. Together they head out of the caves. It's a huge maze, with Strigoi hiding behind every corner. Overwhelmed and outnumbered, they decide to retreat and head back behind the wards since the sun is setting, which will mean the

Strigoi can emerge from their dark, protective caves. But there's good news for Rose: Eddie's among those successfully rescued.

Just before they can get out, another group of Strigoi attack and Dimitri is taken by surprise. It's an attack that will change everything.

It was the blond Strigoi. The one who had spoken to me in the battle.

He grabbed Dimitri and pulled him to the ground. They grappled, strength against strength, and then I saw those fangs sink into Dimitri's neck. The red eyes flicked up and made contact with my own.

I heard another scream—this time it was my own.

page 413

Rose is forced to flee the caves in the ensuing chaos. But the second she emerges, she's desperate to go back to Dimitri, to save him, to be near him, to do anything but stand helpless while the man she loves more than anything in the world is only a few hundred feet away. Her mother tells her it's too late—Dimitri's dead.

AFTERMATH

It's torture waiting for the chance to go back to check the caves. Rose's relentless grief is enough to clue Lissa in to something she should have recognized a long time ago: Rose and Dimitri are in love.

When they finally head back to retrieve the dead, Dimitri's body isn't among them. That can only mean a couple of things, but none are good.

Rose crosses the wards once more so she can speak to Mason's ghost. What she learns shatters her world. Dimitri is neither alive nor dead now.

He's been turned into a Strigoi.

Rose's heart and her world shatter.

Dimitri's tarot card reading from Rhonda was that he "will lose what you value most."

Rose thought it might be *her* . . . or it might be Dimitri's *life* . . .

But it was his *soul* that he lost. He's not dead, but he's gone, replaced by a monster. It's the last thing Dimitri ever would have wanted.

A week passes, and there have been no classes since the attack. The school is in deep mourning for those lost in the attack. After the memorial services, Rose seeks Adrian out—she needs to talk to him about something very important.

She needs money—a lot of it. She's leaving the Academy. She has things she needs to do, and graduating isn't one of them anymore. She isn't willing to go into further detail about her plans than that.

When she flirts to get what she wants, Adrian's hurt that she'd play on his feelings for her. It's not fair. He knows that she's in love with Dimitri, not him.

She presses for the money—she doesn't want to talk about Dimitri; it hurts too much. Adrian decides that it might be good if Rose leaves. Maybe that's the only way she'll be able to get over Dimitri. Maybe if she's away from Lissa's aura, Rose can find a way to be happier . . . and stop seeing ghosts.

Fine. He's willing to give her the money she needs—but with one condition. When she returns, she has to agree to give him a chance romantically. Looks like Rose was wrong about him. Adrian isn't only interested in her body; he's interested in *her*.

She agrees, although right now she's only saying what it takes

POP QUIZ:
Shadow Kiss

1. Rose and Lissa weren't invited—or even told—about whose upcoming trial?
2. Who is assigned to be Lissa's guardian during the novices' field experience?
3. Where is the trial taking place?
4. How does Queen Tatiana want Lissa to demonstrate her spirit magic?
5. Deeming Lissa's relationship with Christian unacceptable, the queen wishes to arrange a marriage between the Dragomir princess and who?
6. Fill in the blank: *"You will lose what you value most, so _____ it while you can."*
7. How did St. Vladimir's shadow-kissed guardian, Anna, die?
8. What is the name of the royal student secret society formed by Jesse and Ralf at St. Vlad's?
9. What word does Dimitri give Rose to tell the guardians to warn of a Strigoi attack?
10. Fill in the blank: *"I set off, off to kill the man I _____."*

* For quiz answers, see p.299.

to get what she wants. After all she's lost, the last thing she can even think about is dating somebody else.

It's Rose's eighteenth birthday today, an important day—but one she doesn't meet with celebration. Being officially an adult means that she has the legal right to drop out of St. Vladimir's no matter what anyone else says. And that's exactly what she does.

As she's leaving through the Academy's gates, Lissa catches up to her, desperately trying to convince her friend not to leave. She knows what Rose is planning to do now—Lissa was present in the van during the shopping trip when Rose and Dimitri made the promise to each other if either was ever turned into a Strigoi. Rose is leaving St. Vlad's to find him . . . and kill him.

Even though it means leaving her best friend in the world, Rose tells her that this is something she has to do. She never wanted to have to choose between them, but it's come down to this.

Mason appears briefly to her once more, before he finally is able to leave forever. He's found his peace. Rose needs to do the same.

For the first time since his death, thinking about Mason no longer devastated me. I was sad and I really would miss him, but I knew he'd moved on to something good—something really good. I no longer felt guilty.

Turning away, I stared at the long road winding off ahead of me. I sighed. This trip might take a while.

"Then start walking, Rose," I muttered to myself.

I set off, off to kill the man I loved. —page 443

CHAPTER 4

Blood Promise

RICHELLE ON *BLOOD PROMISE*

Blood Promise stands out to me for a few different reasons. It was the first book to really deviate from the kids-in-school format and thrust Rose out into the real world. That certainly required a shift in my mindset while writing it, particularly since I also had to contend with an entirely foreign culture and language! A visit to Russia was out of the question for me, but the digital age we live in put all sorts of resources at my fingertips. I think one of my very favorite things that I found was a website that had virtual tours of the Trans-Siberian Railway cars. You could "walk" around the sleeping compartments and dining car and see all the features and décor. This was an amazing asset to have and really added a richness to the book. Still, I was concerned that some readers wouldn't accept the change in story location and style, and my anxiety increased when we ended up accelerating this novel's publication schedule. Amazingly, it all came together, and readers really enjoyed it. This book vies with *Shadow Kiss* as my favorite in the series.

First line: I was being followed.

ROZA DOES RUSSIA

Rose has traveled across the world to Russia with one important but heartbreaking goal: to find and kill Dimitri. It was a promise they once made to each other if either was turned into a Strigoi, and she's determined to hold true to it.

She loves him so much—the only thing she can do to prove that now is to keep that promise.

She's been staking out a Moroi nightclub in St. Petersburg for information that could lead her to a dhampir commune. Her ultimate destination is Dimitri's hometown—she thinks he might have returned there. But finding it is harder than she'd expected, especially since she doesn't know the name of it; she's mostly met with brick walls and the assumption that she's looking for such a village because she's an aspiring blood whore.

Outside the club, she senses she's being followed. When she confronts her pursuer—*not* a Strigoi—she meets Sydney Sage, an eighteen-year-old Alchemist, who's pretty mad at Rose for leaving a path of dead Strigoi bodies behind her since her arrival in Russia.

Speaking of Strigoi, one attacks them at that very moment. Fortunately, Rose manages to stake it. Sydney is shocked—she's never seen a staking before—but she manages to compose herself enough to demonstrate one of her many responsibilities as an Alchemist. She sprinkles something on the body that makes it disintegrate, leaving only dust behind.

Sydney fills Rose in on the info she needs: Alchemists are a group of humans who help the Moroi hide their existence from the rest of the human world. Rose would have been told about them if she'd stuck around St. Vlad's long enough to graduate.

Rose can't help but notice the intricate design of flowers and leaves that Sydney has tattooed on her face. All Alchemists have this mark. It's made from a mixture of gold, Moroi blood, and earth and water magic—which gives them long life and good health. It also prevents them from speaking of their jobs with other humans. Despite their job requirements, Alchemists consider all vampires—including half-Moroi dhampirs—to be evil creatures of the night.

> *"We're not like Strigoi!" I snapped.*
>
> *Her face stayed bland. "Moroi drink blood. Dhampirs are the unnatural offspring of them and humans."*
>
> *No one had ever called me unnatural before, except for the time I put ketchup on a taco. But seriously, we'd been out of salsa, so what else was I supposed to do? "Moroi and dhampirs are not evil," I told Sydney. "Not like Strigoi."*
>
> *"That's true," she conceded. "Strigoi are* more *evil."* —*page 38*

Okay, so maybe Rose hasn't found a new BFF, but she's definitely found someone who knows about local vampires. Rose asks about the village she's looking for, but instead of offering up an answer, Sydney makes a phone call to get her orders. She's told to take Rose to the village personally. Sydney obliges, but she doesn't seem all that happy about spending more time with an evil creature of the night.

Their train for Moscow leaves late the next morning to take them on their first leg of the journey, and it gives Rose a lot of time to think. The real possibility that she'll be facing Dimitri in a few short days weighs heavy on Rose. She gave up a lot to travel to Russia, forfeiting her education and bruising her friendship with Lissa in the process. But it's the second issue that most troubles Rose, the fact that Lissa felt abandoned when Rose left school. Rose still has the bond, though, and checks in with her friend to see how everything is.

And Lissa's frustrated. Ever since she agreed to move to Court after graduation and attend Lehigh University, it feels as if the queen's trying to dictate her life. At Tatiana's "request," she has to go greet two newcomers to the school. Eugene Lazar, who's from one of the royal families, is taking over as headmaster, and he's bringing his daughter, Avery, with him. Also joining them are her brother, Reed, and her guardian, Simon. Rose thinks that putting a royal in the head-of-school position is likely a decision the queen made to ease parents' minds after the recent Strigoi attacks. Good for the parents—but bad for Lissa.

Now she has to show Avery around campus—and Lissa doesn't know why, but the whole thing feels suspicious to her. Was Avery sent here to keep an eye on Lissa and report back to the queen? Lissa decides to do the bare minimum of showing Avery around—and definitely won't take the girl into her confidences. No way.

This apprehension is cool with Rose. At least Lissa isn't jumping at the first chance to replace her as a friend.

After a short stop in Moscow, Rose and Sydney catch their next train, which will take them to Siberia. They're sharing first-class accommodations on board, and the girls are able to get some sleep in their private room. As Rose dozes off, she has a spirit dream starring Adrian—a regular occurrence since she left. While she doesn't appreciate the intrusion, she knows he means well.

"I suppose I should be grateful you only show up about once a week."

He grinned and sat down backward in one of the slatted wood-

en chairs. He was tall, like most Moroi, with a leanly muscled build. Moroi guys never got too bulky. "Absence makes the heart grow fonder, Rose. Don't want you to take me for granted."

"We're in no danger of that; don't worry." —page 64

JOURNEY TO BAIA

Sydney seems uncomfortable traveling with Rose, but they manage to form a decent relationship—if not *quite* a friendship—over the next few days. After a long train ride on the Trans-Siberian, Sydney happily buys a car (she's a car nut). They'll have to drive the rest of the way on a remote road. And to add to the fun, the threat of Strigoi makes it dangerous on the roads at night. Harder to see what's coming—and what's coming could kill you.

In a way, Rose almost wishes she'll never find Dimitri. Then she'll never have to face what he's become—or what she has to do. During the long stretches of travel time, memories of the man she fell in love with haunt her constantly.

How can she kill someone she loved so much?

But that's exactly the point. That man is gone forever, replaced by a monster.

Back at St. Vlad's, Adrian and Lissa are practicing spirit and discussing the very same issue: Rose and Dimitri. Rose listens in through the bond.

"Do you think she can kill Dimitri?"

Adrian took a long time in answering. "I think she can. The question will be if it kills her in the process."

Lissa flinched, and I was a bit surprised. The answer was as blunt as one Christian might give. "God, I wish she hadn't decided to go after him."

"Wishing's useless now. Rose has got to do this. It's the only way we can get her back." He paused. "It's the only way she'll be able to move on." —*page 82*

He's right about that. Rose is surprised by how well Adrian seems to understand her.

When Lissa leaves Adrian, she overhears an argument between Avery and her father. Avery is obviously drunk, and her father is ashamed of her behavior. Despite herself, Lissa finds that she feels sorry for the girl, who obviously isn't happy about being stuck at the Academy. The next day, Lissa decides to invite her to lunch. Why not be friendly? It's not going to kill her—and maybe they *will* become friends after all . . .

SPIRITS VS. STRIGOI

Sydney and Rose reach a house owned by people connected with the Alchemists where they'll be spending the night and get some rest.

But suddenly Rose feels nauseous . . . and she knows what that means. There are Strigoi nearby.

She slips out of the house to investigate, stake in hand. A pair of Strigoi ambush her, and she's hurt badly. Injured and at an extreme disadvantage, she's about to be killed by Strigoi—when suddenly ghosts appear from everywhere. Since Rose is shadow-kissed, she can see ghosts, which is how she saw Mason back at St. Vladimir's.

She's worked hard to build up barriers to block her from the spirit world, and her out-of-control emotions must have messed with that. But it turns out, she's not the ghosts' target. Instead, they swarm the Strigoi.

It gives her enough of an advantage to stake the two vampires before she puts her barriers back up and the ghosts fade away.

Sydney runs toward her just as Rose succumbs to her injuries and passes out cold.

She has a good dream—one about taking care of one of Dimitri's injuries back when they were fighting their desire for each other.

> My fingertips touching his skin had sent shock waves through me, and he'd felt them too. He caught hold of my hand and pulled it away.
>
> "Enough," he said, voice husky. "I'm fine."
>
> "Are you sure?" I asked. He hadn't released my hand. We were so, so close. The small bathroom seemed ready to burst with the electricity building between us. I knew this couldn't last but hated to let go of him. God, it was hard being responsible sometimes.
>
> "Yes," he said. His voice was soft, and I knew he wasn't mad at me. He was afraid, afraid of how little it would take to ignite a fire between us. —page 96

Later, she'll learn she said Dimitri's last name aloud in her sleep and that Sydney used it as a clue to get them where they needed to go. She'll also learn that a mysterious Moroi named Abe Mazur helped too.

When she wakes up, it takes her some time to realize that she's exactly where she wanted to be. Dimitri's hometown. In fact, she's in Dimitri's family's house—and his mother, Olena, is helping to nurse her back to health!

A surprised Rose meets the rest of Dimitri's family, including Dimitri's sisters Karolina and Viktoria and his grandmother, Yeva. Later, she'll also meet the third sister, Sonja, who's currently pregnant. The Belikovs don't yet know who Rose is or that she's connected to Dimitri, only that she's a dhampir traveling with an Alchemist who needed help. The wise and witchy Yeva believes that Rose has ulterior motives for being in town—and she's right. But Rose isn't ready to break the news about Dimitri to his warm and generous family yet—a family who have generously welcomed her into their home without even knowing who she is.

Viktoria takes Rose on a tour of the small town, and she's surprised to discover that it's way more normal than she ever would have guessed. It even has a large human population. Rose and Viktoria meet up with a friend of Viktoria's, a cute dhampir guy who obviously has a big crush on Dimitri's youngest sister. Too bad it doesn't seem to be mutual.

The subject of the *unpromised* comes up—dhampirs who never completed their training but who kill Strigoi. That's what Rose is now since she's a St. Vlad's drop-out.

When Viktoria speaks glowingly of her brother, Rose feels horribly guilty for keeping the truth from his family—the truth about who she really is and what has happened to Dimitri. It's not fair to anyone. Back at the house, Rose gathers everyone together and breaks the horrible news to them: Dimitri is now a Strigoi.

His family is stunned by the news, but despite their overwhelming grief, it doesn't take long before they begin to plan his memorial service. Sydney helps Rose understand why this is.

> *"But he's not dead—"*
>
> *"Shh." She cut me off with a sharp gesture and glanced warily at the others as they hustled around. "Don't say that."*
>
> *"But it's true," I hissed back.*
>
> *She shook her head. "Not to them. Out here... out in these villages... there's no in-between state. You're alive or you're dead. They aren't going to acknowledge him being one of... those."*
>
> *She couldn't keep the disgust out of her voice. "For all intents and purposes, he is dead to them. They'll mourn him and move on. So should you."* —page 117

But Rose is far from ready to move on.

Sydney wonders if Rose has had the chance to meet Abe Mazur yet, a guy who helped get her here to Baia in the first place. He's a Moroi with a lot of influence and power but not a royal. His nickname is *Zmey*, which is Russian for "serpent." He sounds like trouble to Rose, especially when she learns that he's been specifically searching for her on behalf of someone. Who's he working for? A friend or a foe?

IN MEMORIAM

Dimitri's memorial service comes together quickly. The service is held at the Belikovs' house, and from the turnout, it's clear that Dimitri was well loved by all in the village. The emotion is over-

118

whelming for Rose, and she needs to get some fresh air. Outside, she finally meets Abe. He's flamboyant and dangerous . . . the kind of guy who might break kneecaps for a living. She assumes whoever hired him wants her to go back home.

"Did you think you could just come here and drag me back to the U.S.?"

That secretive smile of Abe's returned. "Do you think I could just drag you back?"

"Well," I scoffed, again without thinking, "you couldn't. Your guys here could. Well, maybe. I might be able to take them."

Abe laughed out loud for the first time, a rich, deep sound filled with sincere amusement. "You live up to your brash reputation. Delightful."

page 132

Abe presses for the real reason she's in Russia, but she's not talking. This isn't the last conversation the two will have, to say the least. Her connection to Zmey runs much deeper than she realizes.

Back at the memorial service, Rose is asked to tell some stories about Dimitri from his time at the Academy. Even though her heart is breaking, she does her best, relating the story of how brave and strong he was when he fought off the Strigoi in the attack that turned him. Though she doesn't admit it, it's clear to everyone that they were in love—and to her surprise, nobody has a problem with that.

Later, after too much strong vodka, Rose visits Lissa through the bond, hoping it will take her mind off the pain and grief of losing Dimitri. Lissa too was drinking heavily the night before and has a hangover to prove it, making it difficult to concentrate in class. But then there's a fire alarm—Avery pulled it so she and Lissa can ditch class and hang out. The girl's a complete rebel, and Lissa totally approves.

Rose isn't sure how she feels about that.

Anyway, the next morning she has her own hangover to deal with. Yeva wakes her, suggesting that the two take a long walk to meet a married couple named Mark and Oksana. It soon becomes clear that Mark's a dhampir and Oksana is a Moroi. Not just that, but Oksana is a spirit user and Mark is shadow-kissed. It's just like Rose and Lissa . . . well, without the "being married" part.

Oksana is talented with her magic and soon reads that Rose is out for vengeance. This discovery worries them all, especially when it also becomes clear that she helps absorb Lissa's spirit darkness. They give her a silver ring that Oksana has charmed with spirit to help her moods. This is the first time Rose has heard of silver items charmed with healing magic—but it won't be the last.

When they return to the Belikov house, Rose is disappointed to learn that Sydney has departed on Alchemist business, leaving nothing more than a note and a cell phone number. Rose is surprised to find she'll miss the tough, brainy Alchemist.

Rose settles into a routine with the Belikovs over the next few days. Being with them feels like being with the family she never had. They know she was such an important part of Dimitri's life and welcome her into their home.

Besides, she can tell through her bond with Lissa that no one really seems to miss her at St. Vlad's. As Adrian and Lissa continue practicing spirit, Christian introduces them to Jill Mastrano, the fourteen-year-old Moroi who told Rose she's interested in learning to fight using her water magic. Rose had eventually pointed her in Christian's direction, since he's always been in favor of Moroi using their power for self-defense. Jill's awestruck by the chance to spend time with these upperclassmen—especially the gorgeous Adrian, who quickly nicknames her "Jailbait."

Avery, who also has her sights set on Adrian, swings by with a big plan—they're going to Court for Easter. Christian immediately bails on this. He doesn't feel welcome there because of his family history, but he suggests Lissa take Jill so she can meet Mia, another water-magic user. Maybe the overenthusiastic young Moroi can pick up some pointers.

Through the bond, Rose can feel there's something seriously off about Lissa—a rising dark anger. She resolves to check in with her friend more often to keep an eye on things.

On a shopping trip in town, Rose runs into Mark—and can't help asking another shadow-kissed person about the ghosts she sometimes sees. Turns out that he sees them too. The shadow-kissed are able to summon ghosts, but it's dangerous and easy to lose control. Rose thinks if ghosts hate Strigoi, they might make a good weapon. Mark, however, cautions her against deliberately summoning ghosts and fighting Strigoi. Instead, she should make a safe life for herself with the Belikovs here in Baia.

The tense talk with Mark only succeeds in reinforcing her desire to find Dimitri. Rose runs into Abe again. He's losing patience with her and wants her to go back to the States. He leaves her with a warning: he can be a very good friend or a very bad enemy. His words succeed in striking fear in Rose.

That night, during a troubled sleep, Adrian pulls her into a spirit dream. It starts pleasantly enough but gets bad fast. She tells him a little about the spirit user she met and he wants to know more—

interested in anything to do with his mysterious power. But Rose pushes back. She doesn't want to reveal anything about her location, which makes him mad. The two of them can't seem to sync up. When he talks glowingly about Avery, Rose even feels a bit jealous—of how the Moroi has befriended Lissa *and* worked her way into Adrian's affections so easily. Adrian's seemingly endless patience is finally reaching a tipping point with Rose.

"Avery would never act like a little brat," he said. "She wouldn't get so offended that someone actually cares enough to check on her. She wouldn't deny me the chance to learn more about my magic because she was paranoid someone would ruin her crazy attempt to get over her boyfriend's death."

"Don't talk to me about being a brat," I shot back. "You're as selfish and self-centered as usual. It's always about you—even this dream is. You hold me against my will, whether I want it or not, because it amuses you."

"Fine," he said, voice cold. "I'll end this. And I'll end everything between us. I won't be coming back."

"Good. I hope you mean it this time." —pages 198-199

However, despite her insistence otherwise, Rose knows he was right—she *was* being a brat. She'd lashed out at him when he didn't deserve it. And now it's very possible she's ruined things with him.

For Easter, Rose goes to church with the Belikovs, which only reminds her more of Dimitri. After the service, a group of dhampirs approach her. They've heard she's unpromised and has Strigoi kills under her belt—and the *molnija* marks to prove it. They're leaving for a hunt at a nearby city tomorrow at sunrise and invite Rose to join them. But she doesn't want to leave Dimitri's family to spend time with these cocky guys, who seem like they're only interested in hunting Strigoi for the glory. Now that Rose is looking at it objectively, it seems like a suicide mission. To her, there's a big difference between dying uselessly and dying for a cause. She lets them know she's not interested in joining them.

At least, not yet.

That night, Rose goes with Viktoria to meet up with the guy she's crazy about at a club in an abandoned part of downtown. Rose quickly clues in to the fact that this is no normal nightclub—this is a blood-whore den. Dimitri's youngest sister is in love with a Moroi named Rolan, and it's clear to Rose that he wants to use her and discard her.

And gee, who else happens to be at a scummy place like this? Zmey himself. Seems fitting, actually.

But Abe has lots of info when it comes to Viktoria's situation. The Moroi guy she wants to hook up with? He's also the father of her sister Sonja's unborn child. He's bad news. And Viktoria's headed down the same road, which worries Rose. She knows Dimitri would hate knowing his sister was willingly becoming a blood whore.

Abe has ammunition now—he can use Rose's affection for Dimitri and his sister to bend her to his will. He promises to fix this situation, to scare off the Moroi jerk once and for all, *if* Rose promises to leave Baia.

She finally agrees, willing to make sacrifices to save Viktoria from making some really bad choices.

Viktoria, however, isn't too pleased Rose has chased off the man she loves.

"If you were my friend, you wouldn't be acting like this. You wouldn't try to stand in my way. You act like you loved my brother, but there's no way you could have—no way you really understand love!"

Didn't understand love? Was she crazy? If she only knew what I'd sacrificed for Dimitri, what I'd done to be where I was now . . . all for love. She was the one who couldn't understand. Love wasn't a fling in a back room at a party. It was something you lived and died for.

—*page 233*

BACK ON TARGET

The fight with Viktoria and her deal with Abe have been harsh reminders of Rose's goal in Russia. She heads back to the Belikov house, packs her things, and slips out without saying goodbye. She's never felt so alone and uncertain and wishes she had the two people she loves the most—Dimitri and Lissa—with her.

If nothing else, at least she can visit Lissa through the bond. Her friend went with Avery—and Adrian and Jill—to Court. Lissa resents having Jill tag along and wants to ditch her at the first opportunity. This selfishness doesn't feel like Lissa to Rose. Something's definitely wrong with her.

Mia meets up with them and takes Jill off her hands, but not before asking why Lissa didn't go with Rose on her quest. After all, they're best friends who support each other, right? The question troubles

Lissa, and she can't help but feel angry. After all, Rose was the one to abandon *her*, not the other way around. Lissa fights her increasingly dark mood by looking forward to partying hard with Avery.

While Rose is visiting Lissa's thoughts through the bond, she doesn't notice that Yeva has approached her. Dimitri's grandmother has grown more disappointed in Rose the longer she's stayed with the family. Gee, *thanks*. The old woman had a dream that Rose was a warrior, but she's done nothing since she arrived. Yeva urges Rose to do what she came here to do—find the monster her grandson's become and kill him.

It's the final kick in the butt Rose needs to get going. She wasn't sure what direction she'll take, but she knows now. She's going to meet the other dhampirs at sunrise for their Strigoi-hunting trip.

The group heads to Novosibirsk, the capital of Siberia, and trolls the local clubs normally frequented by Strigoi. Rose makes it clear that they don't kill any of the undead vamps until she gets a chance to question them first. Fair enough.

The first few Strigoi they take down know nothing about Dimitri. But then they find one who has seen Dimitri—*and* he speaks English.

> *"You're lying," I said. "You've never seen him."*
>
> *"I see him all the time. I've killed with him."*
>
> *My stomach twisted, and it had nothing to do with the Strigoi's proximity.* Don't think about Dimitri killing people. Don't think about Dimitri killing people. *I said the words over and over in my head, forcing myself to stay calm.*
>
> *"If it's true," I hissed back, "then I've got a message for you to*

deliver to him. Tell him Rose Hathaway is looking for him."

—page 263

She lets the Strigoi go so he can deliver the message. And then she waits.

All she can think about is what the results of this message will be. To take her mind off it, she hunts Strigoi at night with the others and mentally visits Lissa. Her best friend is still at Court and drinking hard with Avery. On the surface she seems to be having fun, but her emotions keep getting darker and darker.

At a party, Lissa drunkenly falls off a table and into the arms of Aaron, her ex-boyfriend. He's just as hot as she remembers. One thing leads to another and they kiss. But Jill witnesses the act, and she doesn't approve of Lissa "cheating" on Christian. Lissa tells her, fairly harshly, to forget about it. Things escalate to the point where Adrian needs to step in to defend Jill.

What the hell is up with Lissa? It *has* to be spirit darkness—maybe it's affecting both her and Rose, even while they're so far apart.

DARK REUNION

Rose wanders away from the rest of the dhampir group to help assist an old, homeless lady who seems to be in distress—but it turns out she's just a little out of her mind. Then she feels the nausea that indicates a Strigoi is nearby. She pulls her stake out and spins around . . .

It's Dimitri. Looks like he got her message.

Rose is stunned that the Strigoi version of Dimitri looks so much the same as he did before. All except for the eyes, and that sickening red ring around his pupils . . .

*My stake was ready. All I had to do was keep swinging to
make the kill. I had momentum on my side . . .*

*But I couldn't. I just needed a few more seconds, a few more sec-
onds to drink him in before I killed him. And that's when he spoke.*

*"Roza." His voice had that same wonderful lowness, the
same accent . . . it was all just colder. "You forgot my first lesson:
Don't hesitate."*
                                                    —*page 283*

Dimitri doesn't hesitate. He knocks Rose out cold.

She wakes to find she's trapped in a luxurious room with no way
out. *Crap.* When Dimitri visits, she fights as hard as she can, but
he immobilizes her. Just seeing him after all this time is enough
to throw off her concentration. She'd expected something different, for him not to be anything like he used to be, but that's not
the case. He's so much like the Dimitri she remembers that she's
having a really hard time separating the monster from the man.

He too looks at her as if there's something still there—some
kind of emotion tying the two together.

"Why are you here*?" His voice was low and dangerous. I'd
thought Abe was scary, but there was no competition at all.
Even Zmey would have backed off.*

"In Siberia? I came to find you."

"I came here to get away from you."

I was so shocked that I said something utterly ridiculous.

"Why? Because I might kill you?"

The look he gave me showed that he thought that was indeed a ridiculous thing to say. "No. So we wouldn't be in this situation. Now we are, and the choice is inevitable." —*page 292*

He wants to awaken her, to turn her into a Strigoi like him so they can be together forever. He wants her to choose it, but he can't wait forever. She chooses or he forces it. One way or the other, she *will* be awakened.

The chance to be with Dimitri forever is something she would have wanted once. But now—this isn't romantic. It's wrong. To say the least.

Dimitri now works for a Strigoi named Galina, who was his instructor when he was in school training to be a guardian. This is her estate. Other Strigoi work for her as well—including Nathan, the Strigoi responsible for turning Dimitri in the first place. He's definitely not a friend, though, and sees Dimitri as a direct threat to his power in the organization. But now Dimitri has a weakness—Rose. Dimitri lets Nathan know very clearly that if he touches Rose, he will die.

When Nathan leaves, Rose assures Dimitri he'll be waiting a very long time before she consents to becoming a Strigoi.

His laughter had been rare as a dhampir, and hearing it had always thrilled me. Now it no longer had that rich warmth that had wrapped all around me. It was cold and menacing.

"We'll see."

And before I could form a reply, he moved in front of me again. His hand snaked behind my neck, shoving me against him, and he tilted my face up, pressing his lips against mine. They were as cold as the rest of his skin . . . and yet there was something warm in there, too. Some voice in me screamed that this was sick and horrible . . . but at the same time, I lost track of the world around me as we kissed and could almost pretend we were back together in the cabin. —*page 301*

When Dimitri leaves her alone, tied up in the room, Rose tries everything in her power to escape. It's impossible. Waiting for Adrian to contact her through a spirit dream seems like the best solution, but then she remembers he's mad at her and won't be contacting her anymore. She's surprised by how much the thought of not seeing Adrian again in her dreams disappoints her. She knows she's treated him badly when he didn't deserve it—when he'd offered her every kindness. She abused that and feels guilty about it. And now she'll have to figure this out herself without anyone else's help.

When Dimitri visits again, he tries to convince Rose of how incredible he feels as a Strigoi—it's the greatest experience in the world to take the life of someone by drinking their blood. The world is made up of predator and prey, and he wants to be the one doing the hunting.

It sickens Rose to hear him talk about murdering people. Even still, being near him makes it hard for her to concentrate, to stay strong in the face of having him back in her life—having him want to be with her forever. It's all so confusing.

> *"The connection between us hasn't changed. You just can't see it yet."*
>
> *"Everything's changed."* With his lips so close, all I kept thinking about was that brief, passionate kiss he'd given me the last time he was here. *No, no, no.* Don't think about that.
>
> *"If I'm so different, then why don't I force you into an awakening? Why am I giving you the choice?*
>
> *A snappy retort was on my lips, but then it died. That was an excellent question. Why was he giving me the choice? Strigoi didn't give their victims choices.* —*page 314*

When Dimitri kisses her again, she doesn't want to escape. Even though the rational voice in her head screams against it, Rose kisses him back. But the bliss she feels in his kiss is nothing compared to when he bites her. That's when the Strigoi endorphins kick in, sending all her worries far, far away.

Dimitri isn't biting her to awaken her . . . that's still her choice. This? It's just for fun while she makes up her mind.

Rose loses track of the world, of her problems, of her need to escape. There's only Dimitri, who visits her daily to feed from her. She can fool herself that this is the Dimitri she remembers, the one she loves, who loves her in return. She's completely addicted to the bite now, like a drug addict.

But still, a small part of her continues to resist; she refuses to give him permission to awaken her. Time is running out, he warns.

Soon he'll have to make the decision for her.

One night, Dimitri decides to free Rose from her locked room and take her outside so he can show her the estate. On the way to the gardens, they come face-to-face with Nathan. Although he was the one who turned Dimitri, he seems to hate the pair of them. Dimitri attacks, beating the other Strigoi down to show his dominance and to protect Rose.

Outside in the garden, she realizes that she still loves Dimitri— being here with him, even though he's different than before, isn't all that bad.

I loved being close to him, loved the way he kissed me and told me he wanted me . . .

"Why?" I asked.

"Why what?" He sounded puzzled, something I hadn't heard yet in a Strigoi.

"Why do you want me?" I had no idea why I even asked that. He apparently didn't know either.

"Why wouldn't I want you?"

He spoke in such an obvious way, like it was the stupidest question in the world. It probably was, I realized, and yet . . .

I'd somehow been expecting another answer. —*page 330-331*

Being with Dimitri so much—here and in her room—has managed to push her Strigoi-induced nausea off her radar, but other Strigoi can trigger it. And one is approaching—quickly. Galina looms over them, a beautiful but scary woman. She's given Dimitri some time to sort out his issues, but she's not willing to wait any longer. He has to either awaken Rose or kill her. Time is running out.

When his boss leaves, Dimitri lets Rose know that his ultimate plan is to kill Galina and take her power and fortune . . . and having Rose at his side would make it that much better. He takes her back inside and—despite the nagging voice in her head that tells her she needs to plan her escape—Dimitri ends their "date" with a passionate kiss . . . one that quickly leads to another bite, which takes any stress or doubt away. The blissful fog rolls in and everything's okay—even when he warns that Galina's patience is running out. Soon he will have to awaken Rose, with or without her permission. He can't wait much longer.

When she falls asleep, she's surprised when Adrian pulls her into a spirit dream. She knows, somewhere, that she should be happy to see him, but even there, she's too drugged from the bite to think clearly. Adrian wants her to come back to St. Vlad's. He's worried about Lissa—she's acting reckless and doesn't seem to care about anything. But to Adrian's shock, Rose doesn't have an emotional reaction to this revelation. It's like the news about her best friend doesn't even register. That's when Adrian realizes that something's wrong, a suspicion that's confirmed when he reads her aura.

And then, worst of all, he spots the bite marks on her neck. This is enough to trigger panic that Adrian has seen something that she's deeply ashamed of, that she's lost control of her life. Rose *needs* to get out of the dream. She pulls herself out, troubled and saddened by the encounter. Then she rushes over to the bathroom mirror to inspect her throat and is shocked to see the bruises and wounds from Dimitri's regular feedings. She looks like a . . . *blood whore.*

It's a rude awakening and one that almost—*almost*—triggers a rebellion within her. But she's still too far gone in her addiction.

For now.

Nearly a day passes without another bite and she's getting twitchy. Finally, she receives a visit, but it's not from Dimitri. It's Nathan. And he wants information on Lissa. To kill the last Dragomir would be an accomplishment that would put him in good standing with Galina and would enable him to recover some of the power that he's lost to Dimitri.

It's sick, but even though she knows he wants to kill her, the lure of getting a bite—any bite—nearly has her offering up her neck to him. However, she manages to work up enough strength to fight back when he goes for her. She doesn't want to die—not like this.

Nathan easily knocks her across the room. A human servant is in there as well, and Rose, in her delusions, thinks that maybe she's the solution to her escaping. She grabs the woman and threatens to kill her if Nathan doesn't leave. If Rose were thinking straight, she'd recognize the obvious incongruity: Why would Nathan care about a meaningless human servant? The servant fights back, and Rose finds she's too weak to even fight *her* off.

Just when all seems lost, Dimitri arrives and nearly kills Nathan for what he's done. He's tempted to retrieve Rose's silver stake from the vaults so she can kill Nathan herself. It's clear that the next time the two Strigoi face each other, one won't walk away.

Rose burst into tears when Nathan and the servant leave, but she gets no sympathy from the cold Dimitri. It annoys him that she's incapable of defending herself when once she was so strong. And it's all because she refuses to be awakened.

His violent turn reminds her very strongly that he's not the tough but tender instructor she fell in love with back at St. Vlad's—he's a soulless monster.

"Time's running out. I've been lenient, Roza. Far more le-nient than I would be with anyone else."

"Why? Why have you done it?" I wanted—needed—then to hear him say it was because he loved me and that because of that love, he could never force me into anything I didn't want. I needed to hear it so that I could blot out that terrifying, furi-ous creature I'd seen a few minutes ago.

"Because I know how you think. And I know awakening you of your own free will would make you a more important ally. You're independent and strong-minded—that's what makes you valuable."

"An ally, huh?"

Not the woman he loved.   —*page 355*

It's time for Rose to get back her control—over herself, over everything. She needs to get out of there and to do that she needs to be able to think clearly.

When Dimitri tries to bite her, Rose stops him before his sharp fangs penetrate her skin. She claims that she wants to regain her energy for her awakening. But really, she's just trying to buy time to recover from the addiction. He gives her a deadline: two days before he turns her.

In other words, she has two days to figure out how to escape.

Blood Promise

ESCAPE PLAN

Breaking her addiction to Dimitri's bite is agony. To distract herself, she visits Lissa through the bond. Rose isn't the only one having a hard time.

Lissa's wild time of drinking, table-dancing, and kissing ex-boyfriends has caught up with her. Since she refused to admit any of the debauchery to Christian when they got back to school, Jill went ahead and told him for her, leaving Christian doubly pissed—not only has his girlfriend gone off the rails, but she didn't have the decency to tell him herself.

Through the bond, Rose sees that Lissa leans on Avery for moral support when she worries her boyfriend's going to break up with her. But then, suddenly, Rose is shoved right out of Lissa's head.

Okay, *that* was bizarre! While it's never happened before, something about it felt sort of . . . familiar.

Dimitri visits her again. This time, Rose avoids the bite by bombarding him with questions about becoming Strigoi—as if she's honestly interested in making the transition.

As Dimitri answers, he catches sight of the silver ring that Oksana and Mark gave to Rose. She isn't wearing it on her finger; it's on a table with some other jewelry—flashy gifts from Dimitri during her imprisonment. He picks it up to inspect it closer. She takes the opportunity to tell him about her visit with his family. As she speaks, it's as if he softens a little, becoming more like the old Dimitri. He muses that she should have stayed with his family, where she would have been safe. Then he kisses her sweetly, much differently than the previous kisses they've been sharing during her imprisonment.

135

Was it the mention of his family that triggered the softer side of the Strigoi? Or was it . . . the silver charmed with spirit?

She visits Lissa again to find that her friend's getting in trouble for trashing the library during a party. Just teens having fun, Lissa argues. No big deal. While she doesn't get suspended, she does get slapped with a bunch of counseling sessions. How *annoying*.

After a session, Lissa spots Christian and runs to him, hopeful for the chance to explain everything to him. He's wary of her— and doesn't understand why she's been acting so crazy lately, so silly and shallow. She's not the same Lissa he fell for.

> *"I can't be with you if that's your life now."*
>
> *Her eyes went wide. "Are you breaking up with me?"*
>
> *"I'm . . . I don't know. Yeah, I guess." Lissa was so consumed by the shock and horror of this that she didn't really see Christian the way I did, didn't see the agony in his eyes. It destroyed him to have to do this. He was hurting too, and all he saw was the girl he loved changing and becoming someone he couldn't be with. "Things aren't the way they used to be."*
>
> *"You can't do that," she cried. She didn't see his pain. She saw him as being cruel and unfair. "We need to talk about this— figure it out—"*
>
> *"The time for talking's past."* —page 383

It's over. When he leaves, Avery and Adrian arrive to help a heartbroken Lissa. But then . . . when Avery looks in Lissa's eyes,

Rose can feel her staring right through the bond at her. Then—
snap!—she's out of Lissa's head again.

This time she figures it out. She'd felt a familiar sensation when
Oksana read her mind. Avery Lazar is a spirit user! She's been
causing Lissa's dark moods, pushing her to do stupid things, and
using compulsion on Adrian to make him like her.

Rose's bondmate and best friend is in trouble, and Rose needs to
get out of here if she's going to help her. Time for action.

She manages to make a rough wooden stake out of a chair leg.
When the human servant arrives with a tray of food, Rose attacks
and demands the codes for the electronic door locks. Then she
knocks the girl unconscious.

Before she can escape, Dimitri arrives. It's time for her decision.
She gives him one more chance to say the right thing.

"Why do you want to awaken me so badly?"

*A slightly weary look crossed his face. "Because I want you.
I've always wanted you."*

*And that's when I knew. I finally realized the problem. He'd
given that same answer over and over, and each time, something about it bothered me. I'd never been able to pinpoint
it, though. Now I could. He wanted me. Wanted me in the
way people wanted possessions or collectibles. The Dimitri I'd
known . . . the one I'd fallen for and slept with . . . that Dimitri
would have said he wanted us to be together because he loved
me. There was no love here.* —pages 394-395

Rose kisses him goodbye. And then she plunges the makeshift stake into his heart.

Since it's only wood, it won't kill him, but it should buy her a few minutes to get past the guard. She races through the estate and forces another human servant to take her to the safe where her silver stake has been stored.

But she's not free and clear yet: Galina faces off against her. She's a much more skilled fighter than Rose, and it looks like Rose may have met her match. But then Dimitri arrives, recovered from the staking. Rose thinks he'll kill her, but instead he shocks her by protecting her from the other Strigoi. He grabs Galina and Rose stakes her—even now, they work well as a team.

Other Strigoi arrive to swarm Dimitri, and Rose finally makes the choice she's been avoiding. With one last look, she leaves him behind, leaping out of the window and running across the grounds and into the maze of hedges encircling the estate. But she's not alone for long. Against all odds, Dimitri manages to kill the other Strigoi and is hot on her heels. He calls out to Rose across the distance separating them that since she helped him kill Galina, he's in charge now. He owes her for that and won't kill her if she comes to him of her own free will.

So not going to happen. She climbs a tree and waits for him to approach, then leaps on him, fighting hard but unable to stake him again. She takes off and falls down a steep hillside into a river. There's a bridge nearby that she wants to get to, but Dimitri catches up to her again.

Feeling she has no other choice, she takes off the charmed silver ring she's wearing and summons ghosts to attack Dimitri, distracting him so she can get to the bridge. Once there, she puts the ring back on. When the ghosts fade, she's faced again with the stubborn Strigoi whom she once loved. He refuses to let her escape. She climbs onto the railing of the bridge, and Dimitri thinks she means to kill herself, something he doesn't want her to do.

"We need to be together."

"Why?" I asked softly. The word was carried away on the wind, but he heard.

"Because I want you."

I gave him a sad smile, wondering if we'd meet again in the land of the dead. "Wrong answer," I told him. —*page 425*

She lets go, but before she can fall to her death, he grabs hold of her and begins to drag her back up. It gives her the chance to finally do what she came to Russia for in the first place.

I looked him in the eye. "I will always love you."

Then I plunged the stake into his chest.

It wasn't as precise a blow as I would have liked, not with the skilled way he was dodging. I struggled to get the stake in deep enough to his heart, unsure if I could do it from this angle. Then, his struggles stopped. His eyes stared at me, stunned, and his lips parted, almost into a smile, albeit a grisly and pained one.

"That's what I was supposed to say . . ." he gasped out.

—*page 426*

Dimitri falls into the river and disappears from sight. Rose is filled with grief, and for a moment she wants to throw herself into the river after him.

But somehow she manages to pull herself together. She gets a ride to Novosibirsk and calls the only person she knows she can trust—Sydney. Sydney hooks her up with another Alchemist who takes the exhausted Rose to a safe house to rest.

When she wakes, Abe is there, as are Mark and Oksana. Oksana has been using spirit to heal Rose's wounds, and Abe has arranged a flight back to the States for her. Seeing Oksana use her spirit powers is a jarring reminder of the trouble Lissa's in.

When Rose checks on her friend, things have gone from bad to worse. She's about to fall from the ledge of a window that Avery has compelled her to stand on. But before Rose can come up with a plan, Avery senses her and shoves her out of Lissa's head.

If Rose doesn't do something fast, she knows Lissa is going to die! Fortunately, she has a crazy idea that just might work. She asks Oksana to use spirit to help link up the connection between Rose and Lissa. For the first time ever, the connection goes in both directions, and Rose is able to help Lissa fight back against the compulsion.

Avery strikes back with super-compulsion, enough to make Rose believe she's somewhere else, living a perfect fantasy life with Dimitri. *So* not fair, especially after what just happened between them. It's painful, but Rose knows Dimitri is lost to her. Lissa, however, is not. And it's *Lissa* who she needs to fight for now.

Avery's brother, Reed, and her guardian, Simon, join the fight… and they're definitely on Team Avery. It's suddenly clear to Rose what's happening—both the boys are bound to Avery. They're *both* shadow-kissed!

A combination of Lissa's physical strength and Oksana and Lissa's spirit magic, along with the timely arrival of Adrian, help Team Lissa win this fight. A last surge of spirit energy fries Avery's connection to her bondmates—and their minds as well.

Proud of her friend and of Adrian, Rose promises Lissa she'll be home soon.

A FAIRY TALE

Rose tells Oksana that the silver ring she charmed with spirit seemed to bring Dimitri back to his former self for a short time. In return, the spirit user tells Rose something incredible. There's a rumor—more like a fairy tale—that another spirit user claimed to have brought a Strigoi back to life. The man's name is Robert Doru.

Abe recognizes the name. Robert is connected to someone Rose knows very well—he's Victor Dashkov's half-brother.

The idea that something like this could be possible is stunning... and very sad. Dimitri's dead because Rose killed him. It's too late now to think about trying to save him.

Finally, she returns to Montana. In the airport, she finds Adrian waiting for her. She's exhausted and grieving but very happy to be home. Adrian fills her in—Avery planned to kill Lissa and bring her back to life, just like she did with her brother and guardian, increasing her power by having three bondmates. However, making Lissa seem like an out-of-control party girl would cover her bases if she failed to bring her back from the dead. Now Avery and her bondmates are no longer a threat—that last burst of spirit left them completely insane, and they are institutionalized.

When Rose finally sees Lissa, all is forgiven the minute the two girls embrace. They're both thrilled to see each other. Rose tells Lissa everything that's happened to her, leaving nothing out— even the heartbreaking fact that she had to kill the man she loved.

Alberta, the head guardian at St. Vlad's, wants Rose to come back so she can graduate. She's too valuable to lose permanently. Besides, a benefactor has helped pull a few strings to smooth things with the school's officials so she's welcomed back to the Academy. To Rose it's fairly obvious this "benefactor" is Abe.

Rose accepts. She's officially back at St. Vlad's.

The next day, she runs into Christian and tries to convince him to patch things up with Lissa. But he's not ready to forgive and forget— her recent actions and behavior really hurt him. While Rose would love to fix things, she agrees to give him time to figure things out.

Walking away from Christian, she's surprised by a familiar voice calling out to her. Her mother has come to the school especially to see Rose and make sure she's okay. Rose expects to be reprimanded for acting foolishly, but instead Janine comforts her, happy her daughter is okay after such a harrowing journey. She makes Rose promise to stay in school and graduate.

Janine recognizes the colorful cashmere scarf Rose is wearing— it's one Abe gave to Rose as a gift. Her mother says that it's a family heirloom that belongs to Ibrahim.

Ibrahim? It's a name Rose recognizes instantly, a Moroi her mother was romantically involved with once upon a time . . .

Oh crap.

She didn't have to tell me. It was all over her face, her expression dreamily recalling some other time and place—some time and place that had undoubtedly involved my conception. Ugh.

"Oh God," I said. "I'm Zmey's daughter. Zmey Junior.

Zmeyette, even." —page 489

It must have been Janine who sent Abe after her in Russia to convince her to come home. Or rather . . . her *father*.

She supposes there are worse fathers to have.

Abe has even looked further into the Robert Doru issue by contacting Victor Dashkov, but he refuses to say anything. It doesn't matter, anyway. Dimitri is dead.

Or is he?

An envelope is delivered to Rose that contains a silver stake—the same one she stabbed Dimitri with. There's a note attached telling Rose that she forgot an important lesson—not to turn her back until she knows her enemy is dead.

Dimitri is alive. And according to this message, they'll be going over the lesson again the next time he sees her—which will be soon.

Rose promised she'd stay in school and graduate. She will. But now she has another goal. She needs to find Victor Dashkov and learn more about how his half-brother brought a Strigoi back to life using spirit. It's a crazy quest and one she'll need Lissa's help with.

"Do you believe in fairy tales?" I asked, looking up into her eyes.

Even as I said the words, I could imagine Mark's disapproval.

"What . . . what kind of fairy tales?"

"The kind you aren't supposed to waste your life on."

—page 501

POP QUIZ:
Blood Promise

1. What intricate design does Sydney, the Alchemist, have tattooed on her face?
2. What is the name of Avery Lazar's guardian?
3. Which of Dimitri's sisters is currently pregnant?
4. What is Abe Mazur's serpentine nickname?
5. Which holiday do Lissa and her friends celebrate at the Moroi Royal Court?
6. Fill in the blanks: Abe cautions Rose that he can be a very good friend or a very _____.
7. Who does Lissa kiss at a party that will later get her into hot water with her boyfriend, Christian?
8. Finish Dimitri's quote: *"You forgot my first lesson: Don't _____."*
9. Who does Dimitri work for now that he's a Strigoi?
10. There's a rumor that a Strigoi was once brought back to life by a spirit user named Robert Doru. Who is Robert's half-brother?

They're going to break Victor Dashkov out of prison in a fleeting shot to save Dimitri. However, if Dimitri comes for her first, all this hoping for miracles will be for nothing. She'll have to fight him again, and this time she knows neither will survive.

It's a good thing Rose works well under pressure...

* For quiz answers, see p.299.

CHAPTER 5

Spirit Bound

RICHELLE ON *SPIRIT BOUND*

This was another tough book for readers, as poor Rose's torment continued. I think we get comfortable with certain well-hashed storylines and tropes in literature and just assume certain problems will resolve in an expected, happy way. It was therefore a shock to readers to see that even with one obstacle removed for Rose, the road to happiness and romance was still fraught with problems. I received a lot of frustrated e-mails from readers who couldn't understand why Dimitri behaved the way he did. I wasn't so bothered by this, just as I wasn't too upset about the endings to previous books. I think when you know how things are eventually going to end up in the series, bad things don't hit you as hard! Unfortunately, I'm the only one who has this luxury of foresight. Probably the most difficult part was writing a reaction for Dimitri that felt natural and realistic after his ordeal but that didn't slow the series down too much. It's a tough line to walk.

First line: There's a big difference between death threats and love letters—even if the person writing the death threats still claims to actually love you.

GRADUATION

Rose went to Russia to kill the man she loves. She failed. Now she's getting regular love letters from him—love letters with a deadly intent.

And we will *be meeting again. With graduation, you'll be turned out of the Academy, and once you're outside the wards, I'll find you. There is no place in this world you can hide from me. I'm watching.*

Love,

Dimitri   *page 12*

Romance from an obsessed Strigoi isn't fun. These constant and chilling reminders of the evil version of Dimitri torture Rose.

It's a miserable situation, but Rose does have a plan . . . one that still gives her hope. Her longtime enemy Victor Dashkov has a half-brother who is rumored to have brought a Strigoi back to life. To get Victor's help is going to be tricky, though. She'll need to bust him out of prison—and yes, she realizes how crazy this sounds. First on her to-do list, however, is fulfilling the promise she made to her mom by graduating from St. Vlad's. With Dimitri weighing so heavily on her mind, actually making it to graduation could be tricky.

On the day of the final guardian trials, Rose sees her father, Abe, chatting with Adrian. She finds out later he's threatening her new boyfriend with extreme bodily harm if he ever hurts Rose.

How charming.

Since coming back to St. Vlad's, Rose has held true to her deal and decided to give Adrian a chance. And . . . it's actually been great so far—Adrian is handsome, funny, and incredibly charming, and he helps add some much-needed light into her dark life. While she's extremely attracted to the sexy Moroi royal, she knows she's not ready to take their relationship to the next level and have sex. She still needs time to mend her broken heart.

Rose has already faced real threats and killed lots of Strigoi, which gives her a big advantage over the other novices. She doesn't realize it as she's going through the obstacle course in front of a large audience, but the school's rigged her test to be *way* harder than the others. Even so, she passes with flying colors, earning the highest marks in her class and impressing instructors and classmates alike. She's definitely earned her promise mark—the tattoo given to graduating guardians to show they've officially completed their training. It's a bittersweet moment. On the one hand, Rose has proven she's awesome at fighting. On the other hand, it's because she's had a lot of real-world practice—including with her Strigoi ex-boyfriend.

Abe throws her a party to celebrate. Lissa is there to support Rose, but the princess gets jealous when she sees her ex, Christian, hanging out with Jill. Christian's been teaching the younger girl defense. It's clear to Rose that Lissa and Christian still have major feelings for each other, despite all the drama Avery Lazar caused between them. But they're both too stubborn to admit their mistakes and get back together.

Even now, when she should be happy and focused on the excitement of doing so well on her tests, Dimitri remains on Rose's mind. If there's one person who might be able to get Rose the info she needs about the prison Victor's being held in, it's her pirate-mobster father. Abe tells her it's called Tarasov and it's in Alaska. The info about its location would likely be found in the guardian's headquarters at the Moroi Royal Court—but it's top secret.

Well, that works perfectly, actually. Rose happens to be headed for Court later that week. Graduates go there for orientation and to receive their assignments.

Since Jill's not a graduate, she heads home for the summer with her mom, Emily. Rose makes a point of saying goodbye to the girl she's come to consider a friend before she and the others take the flight to Court.

Driven by her need to find the answers to possibly save Dimitri, Rose visits someone she thinks could help her: Mia Rinaldi. Though Rose once considered her an enemy, Mia's since become a friend and ally. The water user confirms that the info Rose needs (records about outside security at other places—schools, royal homes . . . *prisons*) can indeed be found in the guardians' security office—although Rose doesn't reveal *why* she needs it. The two, plus Lissa, whose compulsion they need to get them in, make plans to go there mid-afternoon (which is the middle of the night in the vampire world). But before the end of the visit, Christian arrives to see Mia—and Lissa fumes with jealousy.

The girls make plans to meet later to sneak into the security office. But first, before Rose can get her hands on information to help her *ex*-boyfriend, she's got a dinner date with her *current* boyfriend. Adrian wants Rose to meet his family.

She dresses accordingly.

The small smile on his face told me he liked what he saw.

"You approve?" I asked, spinning around.

He slipped an arm around my waist. "Unfortunately, yes. I was hoping you'd show up in something a lot sluttier. Something that would scandalize my parents."

"Sometimes it's like you don't even care about me as a person," I observed as we walked inside. "It's like you're just using me for shock value."

"It's both, little dhampir. I care about you, and I'm us-ing you for shock value."   —page 68

While at the dinner party, Rose meets Adrian's mother, Lady Daniella Ivashkov. She's surprisingly warm and generous toward her son's dhampir girlfriend. His father, on the other hand ... well, Lord Nathan Ivashkov is a bit of a jerk. And not just toward Rose, toward Adrian too.

It's not the most comfortable dinner, that's for sure. And when Queen Tatiana stops by for a visit, it's even less so—though oddly, the queen seems to be treating Rose with a little more respect than she has in the past.

The queen has been having a lot of problems with disagreements in the Moroi community, which is trying her patience. Most of the issues stem from the ongoing problem of having too few guardians and too many Moroi for them to all be guarded properly. And yet, while most Moroi are worried about security, not enough are interested in learning to defend themselves. It's a hot topic that will come to a head very soon.

As Rose is about to leave, Daniella lets her know privately that she's okay with a dhampir girl dating her son. After all, she knows it won't lead to marriage. She just hopes Rose won't break Adrian's heart too badly when it inevitably ends. Rose doesn't know how to react to this. She doesn't want it to be true, but there's a small part of her that still hopes to save Dimitri and spend the rest of her life with *him*.

If only.

Making excuses (in other words, *lying*) to Adrian about where she's off to, Rose heads off to go to the security office with Mia and Lissa. Lissa's skill with compulsion gets them in, and Rose searches the files for any information she can find about Tarasov Prison. And she *does* find it. But she also finds Mikhail Tanner, one of the guardians on duty, who's wondering why she's poking around where she doesn't belong.

It's a familiar name and someone she immediately feels an important connection to. Mikhail was the dhampir in love with Sonya Karp—the Moroi teacher at St. Vlad's who went crazy from using spirit and chose to end her madness by turning Strigoi. Mikhail had searched for Sonya with the intention to kill her, much as Rose did with Dimitri, but never found her. When Rose explains her crazy theory involving Victor's brother restoring Strigoi to their former Moroi selves, Mikhail is stunned . . . and willing to give Rose the benefit of the doubt. He even volunteers to help. This is an ally who will prove very valuable in the coming weeks.

At a party where potential guardians are presented to Moroi, Rose seeks out her friend Eddie to ask him to accompany her and Lissa to Alaska. She could use all the help she can get.

> *"If you need me, I'll do it. No matter what it is."*
>
> *"You don't know what it is."*
>
> *"I trust you."*
>
> *"It's kind of illegal. Treasonous, even."*
>
> *That took him aback for a moment, but he stayed resolute.*
>
> *"Whatever you need. I don't care. I've got your back."* —*page 104*

His loyalty is amazing—despite Rose's warnings—and the plan is set. Rose, Lissa, and Eddie meet later, and Mikhail smuggles them out of Court in the trunk of a car. Together they head to the airport.

PRISON BREAK

When they arrive in Alaska, Rose and Eddie go to the prison to scope out the tight security. The only way in seems to be through the front gates.

Lissa's been charming silver jewelry with spirit to help them today. When she'd returned to the school from Russia, Rose gave Lissa the silver ring Oksana had charmed with spirit, and just holding it helped give Lissa an idea how she could work the same kind of magic with other jewelry. When they each wear a piece, it gives them a magical disguise, enough to sneak them into the prison, and Rose and Lissa take on the form of human feeders delivered by Eddie for the Moroi prisoners.

It's been a difficult journey so far, but one that pays off when Victor is brought to the feeding room. Though he's quite weakened, both from being a prisoner and from his disease, he recognizes Rose right through the magical disguise . . . and he's intrigued by what this means.

"Oh my. This might be the best meal I've ever had." His voice was barely audible, covered by the conversation of the others.

"Put your teeth anywhere near me and it'll be your last meal," I murmured, voice just as quiet. "But if you want any chance of getting out of here and seeing the world again, you'll do exactly what I say."

He gave me a questioning look. I took a deep breath, dreading
what I had to say next.

"Attack me."   —*pages 126—127*

An opportunist like Victor recognizes a chance when he sees
it. He lunges at Rose, creating a distraction for Rose to attack the
oncoming guards. It's a struggle to get Victor out of the prison
without anyone getting killed, but they do it.

Just being around the man who'd had her tortured freaks Lissa
out, but she tries to be strong for Rose. On their way out of the
prison, they pass a wing for the criminally insane, and Lissa senses
other spirit users there. It's another chilling reminder that the use
of her rare ability usually leads to darkness and insanity.

They flee the prison, pursued by guardians, but manage to lose
them on winding roads. Now it's time to tackle phase two of Rose's
"Save Dimitri" plan. She tells Victor they need to get to Robert
Doru, Victor's brother. And if Victor wants to stay out of prison,
he's going to help them.

Next stop: Las Vegas.

WHAT HAPPENS IN VEGAS

Once they arrive, they get a room at the Luxor, and Victor calls
his brother. It takes a lot of convincing to have Robert agree to
meet them for dinner.

When there's a knock at the door, everyone braces themselves.
They've been discovered. Luckily for them, it's somebody out to
have a little fun in the City of Sin. Adrian followed Rose's
credit card trail and has decided to crash her "girls' weekend."

An exclusive peek into the *Vampire Academy* graphic novel. Rose, Lissa, Dimitri, and all the characters you know and love from the VA world are even more daring and impressive than you imagined!

Rose

"Technically I was half-Moroi, but my looks
were human. . . . I knew I was pretty, but
to Moroi boys, my body was more than just
pretty: it was sexy in a risqué way."

Lissn

"Those fangs contrasted oddly with the
rest of her features. With her pretty face
and pale blonde hair, she looked more
like an angel than a vampire."

Dimitri

"He was older than us, maybe mid-twenties, and as tall as I'd figured, probably six-six or six-seven. And under different circumstances—say, when he wasn't holding up our desperate escape— I would have thought he was hot."

"Mason Ashford snapped out of his haze, giving me a lopsided smile. With red hair that stuck up everywhere and a smattering of freckles, he was nice-looking, though not exactly hot. He was also one of the funniest guys I knew."

Rose & Lissa

"Her fear poured into me through our psychic bond, but there was something else too: her complete faith that I would take care of everything, that we would be safe."

Rose & Dimitri

"The sound of his voice thrilled me, and I couldn't answer. I couldn't stop staring at him. The force that had pulled me up here pulled me to him. I wanted him to touch me so badly, so badly I could barely stand it. He was so amazing. So unbelievably gorgeous."

Lissa & Christian

"Lissa met Christian's eyes and smiled, surprised she'd never noticed how icy blue they were before."

SYMBOLS

Tattoos, signs, and marks rule the VA world. Whether you're a Spirit User or have three molnija marks, the symbol says a lot about who you are.

GUARDIAN MARKS:

Guardian marks are powerful in Vampire Academy. Find your mark below!

MOLNIJA   PROMISE   ZVEZDA

MOLNIJA MARK:

Are you instinctive and quick on your feet? Would you do anything to protect those you love? Russian for lightning, guardians receive the molnija mark on their necks to indicate how many Strigoi they have killed. See page 282 for more!

PROMISE MARK:

Are you selfless and determined to do your best for others? Do you stop at nothing to prove your loyalty? Guardians put their own needs aside in a promise to protect, defend, and uphold. The promise mark proves their elite level of training and commitment.

ZVEZDA MARK:

Are you the best of the best? Consistently excelling at everything you do? From the Russian word for star, the zvezda mark, or "the battle mark," is awarded only to the top guardians—those with too many Strigoi victories to count.

MOROI ELEMENTAL SIGNS:

Using their powers only defensively, Moroi make their magic from the elements earth, water, air, and fire. Spirit users draw their powers from their own mind and body. Which element are you connected with? See page 274 for more!

AIR

EARTH

WATER

FIRE

SPIRIT

ALCHEMIST TATTOOS:

THROUGH THE YEARS

Since Rose and Lissa first rocked the vampire world, the VA covers have gone through a number of changes. But one thing remains the same: the iconic, foreboding gates of Saint Vladimir's Academy.

BOOKS 1-3 ORIGINAL COVERS

BOOKS 1-6 NEW COVERS

GRAPHIC NOVEL COVER   **MASS MARKET EDITION COVER**

THE ADVENTURE
CONTINUES IN *Bloodlines*

BY THE AUTHOR OF THE INTERNATIONAL #1 BESTSELLING VAMPIRE ACADEMY SERIES
RICHELLE MEAD

Bloodlines

"Re-ink Sydney," said Stanton decisively. "No point in inking Zoe until we know what we're doing with her."

My eyes flickered to my sister's noticeably bare—and pale—cheeks. Yes. As long as there was no lily there, she was free. Once the tattoo was emblazoned on your skin, there was no going back. You belonged to the Alchemists.

—*Bloodlines*, page 8

"Sydney is the one narrating *Bloodlines*. She's the polar opposite of Rose. Rose has more of that impulsive, jump-into-it nature. And Sydney, if anything, over-thinks. Ironically, Rose's continual issue was: *How do I get that control? How do I stop doing things that maybe I shouldn't?* And Sydney, one of her struggles through the series is kind of the opposite: *How do I stop being so timid? How do I stand up for myself and jump out when I need to?* So, it's definitely going to give us a new perspective. . . ."

—RICHELLE MEAD

BEHIND THE SCENES:
Book trailers from the world of Richelle Mead

Vampire Academy

Is the mastermind behind the VA world right around your corner? Richelle has traveled to meet fans and talk about her book everywhere from New York to Australia. Here are some snapshots from her travels.

RICHELLE'S TOP 8 FAVORITE LINKS *and* FAN SITES:

www.richellemead.com/books/vampireacademy.htm

us.penguingroup.com/static/packages/us/
yreaders/vampireacademy/merch.html

vampireacademybooks.ning.com

www.shadowkissed.net

www.shadowkissed.com

vampireacademy.heavenforum.org

www.facebook.com/BloodlinesBooks

www.facebook.com/pages/
Richelle-Mead/103765809662856

Only, he's a bit surprised by what he finds.

"You guys didn't really think you could go off on a party
weekend without me, did you? Especially here of all places—"
He froze, and it was one of those rare moments when Adri-
an Ivashkov was caught totally and completely off guard.
"Did you know," he said slowly, "that Victor Dashkov is sit-
ting on your bed?"
—page 153

The normally easygoing Adrian knows a bad situation when he
sees it—and Rose can't help but feel guilty. It doesn't take him long
to find out the motivation behind the whole trip. This is all to help
Rose save Dimitri. Adrian is furious. He feels like Rose has been
shamelessly using him for his affection and money. It's enough to
trigger his crazy side. He needs a drink to get control of himself,
something he promised Rose he'd give up when they started dating.

Rose feels terrible about all of this, but she's determined not to let
it change their plans. Although Adrian doesn't exactly come around,
when it comes time to meet Robert, he reluctantly decides to join
them, intrigued by the thought of meeting another spirit user.

Just like Lissa, Robert once had a shadow-kissed bondmate, but
he died, leaving Robert to face his spirit darkness alone. It's dete-
riorated his mental health—to put it mildly. It's obvious now why
Victor didn't go directly to his spirit-using brother to help cure his
disease. Robert's way too fragile.

Fragile, yes. But the rumor he brought a Strigoi back to life?
Absolutely true.

"That which is dead doesn't always stay dead…" Robert's words weren't directed at Adrian. They were spoken to me. I shivered.

"How? How did you do it?"

"With a stake. She was killed with a stake, and in doing so, was brought back to life."

"Okay," I said. "That is a lie. I've killed plenty of Strigoi with stakes, and believe me, they stay dead."

"Not just any stake." Robert's fingers danced along the edge of his glass. "A special stake."

"A stake charmed with spirit," said Lissa suddenly.

—pages 165–166

But it's not that easy. For a Strigoi to be brought back, the stake must be wielded by a spirit user like Lissa or Adrian, not a trained guardian like Rose. Lissa speaks up to say she will do it, but Rose shuts her down. After all, protecting Lissa is her first priority. Using enough spirit to cure Dimitri could be enough to finally push Lissa over the edge when it comes to her own sanity. Rose refuses to lose her too.

Robert does agree to talk more about this—in private. But on their way back to the hotel room, they run into a snag. A big one.

Dimitri's tracked down Rose, just as he promised he would. And this time, he's not interested in being lenient—he's in it for the kill, and he's brought two of his Strigoi cronies to help him.

"I told you I'd find you."

"Yeah," I said, trying to ignore the grunts of Eddie and the other

Strigoi. Eddie could take him. I knew he could. "I got the memos."

A ghost of a smile curled up Dimitri's lips, showing the fangs

that somehow triggered a mix of both longing and loathing in me.

page 175

Eddie and Rose fight the Strigoi, allowing the Moroi to escape into the daylight. Rose and Eddie make a great team, successfully slaying two of the Strigoi until there's only one left standing: Dimitri. Rose feels like she and Eddie *could* kill him together. And Eddie gets the chance, his stake aimed directly for Dimitri's chest.

But this *isn't* the time—not when Rose is so close to finding the answer to cure him. Despite all the evil he's done, Dimitri *can't* die. Not now. She interferes with Eddie's aim and they barely manage to escape.

Eddie turns on Rose, furious about what just happened. He doesn't understand—at least not until she tells him her true motivation for this quest: she loves Dimitri. Eddie can't believe that he's risked everything so Rose could try to *save* a Strigoi. Rose is ripped apart by guilt over her actions that have led them here. She knows letting Dimitri live means more people will have to die. But it's done.

When they find Lissa and Adrian, Rose realizes she's lost something else—Victor and Robert have escaped.

Not a good day, that's for damn sure.

Adrian takes them to a Moroi hotel and casino called the Witching Hour so they can establish an alibi and have a safe place to hang out till they wait to catch a flight back to Court.

While at the Witching Hour, Rose learns that Eric Dragomir liked coming there and spending time with the sexy showgirls. Rose bristles at the surprising and racy rumors about Lissa's father—rumors that will come to mean a great deal more in the weeks to follow.

BACK AT COURT

Of course, when they arrive back at Court, no one knows Rose's real reasons behind the trip. If they did, her punishment would be *way* more severe. As it is, it's believed she took Lissa on an irresponsibly wild weekend in Vegas, putting the Dragomir princess in danger, especially now that the news of Victor's prison break is known by all.

Eddie is also punished alongside Rose. They're both given grunt work to do around Court, and Rose is threatened by the head guardian, Hans, with something even worse for the future: a desk job.

Through the bond, Rose sees Christian confront Lissa about their little trip. He knows enough to see it wasn't just a fun and frivolous vacation. Lissa confides what they learned about bringing Strigoi back to life and how, even though Rose is against it, she wants to help. Christian wants to come along on her upcoming trip to tour Lehigh University. While there, he's promised to teach her how to stake a Strigoi.

Since Rose is barred from socializing as part of her punishment, Adrian visits her in a spirit dream. She knows he's not happy with her, even though he's acting cool about everything. His support is heartening, and she knows that she cares deeply about him, despite her many Dimitri issues.

I suddenly felt unworthy. He was so easy to underestimate.
The only thing I could do was lean my head against his chest
and let him wrap his arms around me.

"I'm sorry."

"Be sorry you lied," he said, pressing a kiss to my forehead.
"Don't be sorry you loved him. That's part of you, part you have
to let go, yeah, but still something that's made you who you are."

—page 225

LISSA THE VAMPIRE SLAYER

Lissa and Christian head with an entourage—minus Rose, because she's still being punished—for the university tour. At the hotel, Christian and Lissa practice fighting. It's an encounter that triggers both their tempers... *and* their passions. A punch *almost* leads to a super-hot kiss until Lissa's current guardian Serena comes in to figure out what's causing all the commotion. When she sees they're trying to learn to fight, she volunteers to help out.

Great, someone else who doesn't seem to see how dangerous this is. Rose isn't happy her friend seems so intent on this, but there's not much she can do about it at the moment, especially since she's only witnessing this on a psychic level.

Rose is summoned before the queen and the Moroi Royal Council for questioning. She assumes it's about the "fun trip" to Vegas, but it's actually about her past actions—such as going to Russia to extract personal revenge after the attack at the Academy and killing many Strigoi even before that. The queen wants to establish if Rose is in favor of direct strikes against Strigoi. Rose most certainly is, as her actions prove without much doubt. Later, she will learn that this testimony would be instrumental in the queen's upcoming controversial decisions—ones that will affect the future of all dhampirs—and not in a good way.

At the moment, though, Rose has to go back to her lousy desk job.

It's Lissa's birthday, so while sorting paper, Rose visits through the bond to learn her friend loved the tour of the university and is looking forward to attending in the fall. Back at the hotel, Lissa and Christian begin their tutelage. Grant, the other guardian who's been assigned to the Dragomir princess, also pitches in to help Serena show the two Moroi how to fight. Topics discussed include such important skills as how to properly use a stake. It's hard work—especially for two who aren't trained to be Strigoi hunters. But Christian persists.

> *"I just need more practice."*
>
> *"You don't need to do anything," she shot back, fighting to keep her voice quiet through her anger. "This isn't your fight. It's mine."*
>
> *"Hey," he snapped, eyes glittering like pale blue diamonds, "you're crazy if you think I'm going to just let you go and risk—"*

—page 257

To Rose, it's obvious Christian doesn't want the girl he loves to be in danger. It's a romantic moment, but Lissa forces herself to pull away from it.

Later, Rose checks in to find the entire entourage leaving a restaurant where they celebrated Lissa's birthday. It's been lots of fun for all. But the fun's about to end.

DIMITRI'S PLAN

Rose watches in horror as suddenly, Lissa and the group are surrounded by Strigoi. They attack without mercy, killing Moroi and guardians alike—including Grant. Serena is seriously injured. With no guardians to protect them, Lissa and Christian find themselves face-to-face with the one Strigoi who Rose least wants to see: Dimitri himself. Rose can only watch on in horror as her friends look like they're about to be murdered—and it's all her fault. Dimitri's only alive because she chose not to kill him. And there's nothing she can do . . .

Christian summons his fire magic as a last-ditch attempt to protect Lissa, but Dimitri advises him to put it out—or Lissa dies.

> *"Actually," said Dimitri, voice pleasant amid the grim scene, "I'd rather you two stay alive. At least for a little while longer."*
>
> *I felt Lissa's face move to a frown. I wouldn't have been surprised if Christian's did too, judging from the confusion in his voice. He couldn't even manage a snarky comment. He could only ask the obvious: "Why?"*
>
> *Dimitri's eyes gleamed. "Because I need you to be bait for Rose."* —page 262

Even though it's an obvious trap, Rose needs to save her friends. She races to get Hans and the rest of the guardians. Teams quickly form for the rescue mission. Rose is going, as are fire-using Moroi, like Christian's aunt Tasha, who has always been in favor of Moroi fighting back against Strigoi.

Enough's enough. Rose let Dimitri live last time. This time? It's different. He can mess with her, but he can't put her friends in danger. Even though there might be a way to restore a Strigoi, she knows it's too late for Dimitri. He's stepped over the line and has to die. Adrian agrees.

"Good," said Adrian, relief flooding his features. "I'm glad."

For some reason, that irritated me. "God," I snapped. "Are you that eager to get rid of any competition?"

Adrian's face stayed serious. "No. I just know that as long as he's still alive—or, well, kind of alive—then you're in danger. And I can't stand that. I can't stand knowing that your life is in the balance. And it is, Rose. You'll never be safe until he's gone. I want you safe. I need you to be safe. I can't . . . I can't have anything happen to you."

—page 268

Rose's anger toward Adrian fades, and she hugs him goodbye, allowing herself a brief and fleeting moment of comfort. She knows her heart will be crushed tonight—to her it's inevitable that she's going to lose somebody she loves tonight, either Dimitri or Lissa. Adrian begs her to be careful—he can't bear the thought of losing her.

Rose kisses him—and in the midst of all of this death, the kiss feels more powerful and alive than any they have ever shared before. She wants to return to Adrian's arms when all of this is over.

Rose's bond to Lissa guides the convoy to the Strigoi's location, an abandoned warehouse where Lissa and Christian are tied up. Lissa is terrified as she faces this evil version of Dimitri. He grips her throat so he can speak to Rose directly through the bond. He knows she won't abandon her friends and that she's coming after him. He knows what he's doing.

It's Rose's worst nightmare come to life.

At the warehouse, the guardians and fire-magic-using Moroi fight through the waves of Strigoi protection. Rose is on the team headed for the room with Lissa and Christian. It's what she was born to do—fight and kill Strigoi. Eventually, Rose maneuvers into the small room where her friends are tied up—and she's finally face-to-face with Dimitri himself.

> *"You're beautiful in battle," said Dimitri. His cold voice carried to me clearly, even above the roar of combat. "Like an avenging angel come to deliver the justice of heaven."*
>
> *"Funny," I said, shifting my hold on the stake. "That is kind of why I'm here."*
>
> *"Angels fall, Rose."* —page 280

It's time for this to end—all the heartbreak and all the hope that have led Rose to this moment. Dimitri must die for her friends to be saved. And she needs to be the one to kill him.

Dimitri doesn't see things her way. He reminds her that this is all her fault. If she'd agreed to become Strigoi in Russia, they could be together in their own vampiric happily ever after.

Rose isn't stupid. If that had happened, she'd be killing innocents now just like he does.

Christian burns through Lissa's ropes and the two join the fight. To Rose's shock, Lissa suddenly has a silver stake in her hand!

Dimitri is still not convinced Rose is ready to kill him. Oh, but she is. As horrible as it is, Dimitri's given her no other choice.

And she tries to do just that—but Lissa shoves her out of the way! Before Rose can figure out what is going on, a wall of fire encircles Dimitri. It traps him in place while—with great effort—Lissa manages to sink her stake into his heart. Rose screams. *She* was the one who was supposed to kill Dimitri!

But she's about to learn that this particular stake isn't meant to kill.

It's charmed with spirit, just as Robert instructed. White light bursts out, and Rose can feel the healing magic come through the bond, more intense than anything she's ever felt before. The bond temporarily disappears—shorted out by the sheer amount of spirit that's just been used. And then . . . the results speak for themselves.

> *I'd expected him to be burned to a crisp—some sort of black-ened, skeletal nightmare. Yet when he shifted his head, giv-ing me my first full view of his face, I saw that he was com-pletely unharmed. No burns marked his skin—skin that was as warm and tanned as it had been the first day I'd met him. I caught only a glimpse of his eyes before he buried his face against Lissa's knee. I saw endless depths of brown, the depths I'd fallen into so many times. No red rings.*
>
> *Dimitri . . . was not a Strigoi.*
>
> *And he was weeping.* —*pages 289-290*

A MODERN MIRACLE

That a Strigoi could be restored has shaken everyone who witnessed it. Despite Rose and Lissa's protests, Dimitri's taken away by guardians. Rose, meanwhile, is hauled in a different direction. She's freaking out—no one will give her any damn information about what's going on—or let her see Dimitri.

The trip back to Court is a blur, and it's followed by a frustrating amount of secrecy. Dimitri's been locked up somewhere, and nobody will tell her where. Lissa's been taken to the medical center for treatment—Hans tells Rose she isn't welcome there. It's chaos and she'll just be in the way. Adrian's busy using spirit to help heal those who were injured in the fight, and everyone is buzzing with the rumor about Lissa working a miracle by restoring a Strigoi back to his former dhampir self.

When Rose finally gets to Lissa, her friend is making her second visit to see Dimitri. Rose wants to go too, but Lissa gives her some shocking news: Dimitri doesn't want to see her.

What? He doesn't want to see her? After everything she's done, everything she's sacrificed to help him? Rose is deeply hurt—he is supposed to be *her* Dimitri. The man she went to Russia to find. The one who she made a deal with the devil to save. Lissa begs her to understand, to give Dimitri the time he needs to heal.

Not like she has any choice. Rose watches through the bond as her friend goes to Dimitri's holding cell. As a former Strigoi, he's being kept under constant guard. Rose can't get over the way Dimitri looks at Lissa—it's with awe and wonder that she was able to bring him back from the nightmare of being an evil Strigoi.

"I swear, whatever you need, anything—if it's in my power—I'll do it. I'll serve and protect you for the rest of my life. I'll do whatever you ask. You have my loyalty forever."

Again, Lissa started to say she didn't want that, but then a canny thought came to mind. "Will you see Rose?"

He grimaced. "Anything but that."

"Dimitri—"

"Please. I'll do anything else for you, but if I see her . . . it'll hurt too much." —page 316

This sure isn't the fairy-tale ending Rose always hoped for. Dimitri isn't running into her arms. He's running *away* from her.

While she finally lets herself cry in the privacy of her room, Adrian stops by to invite her to a party. But not any party. It's a Death Watch, an official Moroi ceremony to honor those who died in the attack. It's by invitation only for the most elite Moroi bloodlines—but he has some passwords he's stolen to sneak his friends into the masked event.

The ceremony begins, and both Moroi and dhampirs who were lost in the battle are honored. Rose is surprised to see that the dhampir guardians are treated with such respect. Even if they weren't actually invited to the party . . .

Christian and Mia are there as well, also courtesy of Adrian. And again, Lissa is jealous. To Rose, it's obvious the two aren't dating, but Lissa thinks the worst. Any romantic drama is put on hold, though, when someone outs Rose as a party crasher. To make matters worse, she's the only dhampir in attendance, and this is considered a major breach of tradition. Adrian's mother chastises him for letting this happen; however, the queen actually seems somewhat pleased that Rose was able to witness the respect paid to her race. Sadly, now even more guardians have been lost, leaving holes in the ranks.

Rose leaves the party—she can take a hint—and runs into

Mikhail. And does he have a surprise for her: he says he can get her in to see Dimitri. *Right now.*

Well, okay then. Eager and apprehensive, she's led to Dimitri's holding cell. She finds him standing with his back to her. This is exactly what he *didn't* want to happen.

He probably knew the sound of my heartbeat and breathing. As it was, I think I stopped breathing while I waited for his response. When it came, it was a little disappointing.

"No."

"No what?" I asked. "As in, no, it's not me?"

He exhaled in frustration, a sound almost—but not quite— like the one he used to make when I did something particularly ridiculous in our trainings. "No, as in I don't want to see you."

—page 353

How can Dimitri just turn her away? What about the life that they almost had together, that they could have again? And what about everything she did for him? Rose's anger starts to burn through the hurt when she tells him he should be grateful. He tells her he *is* grateful—to Lissa, his savior.

She demands that he turn around and face her. Finally, he does. When their eyes meet, all the memories of falling in love with him in the first place come flooding back. And it's not just how she feels—she knows he feels it too. He might not want her there now, but he still feels something for her. Something big.

The way Dimitri was looking at me . . . it confirmed every-thing I'd suspected. The feelings he'd had for me before he'd been turned—the feelings that had become twisted while a Stri-goi—were all still there. They had to be. Maybe Lissa was his savior. Maybe the rest of the Court thought she was a goddess. I knew, right then, that no matter how bedraggled I looked or how blank he tried to keep his face, I was a goddess to him.

—*page 356*

Dimitri finally breaks down and tells her he's racked with guilt over his actions as a Strigoi—including what he did to Rose, keeping her imprisoned in Russia and feeding off her like a blood whore. Even his thoughts of killing her and using her friends as bait against her haunt him. He can't forgive himself for any of it.

Rose assures him she forgives him for everything. She loves him and knows he still loves her.

Dimitri's the one to bring up the subject of her new boyfriend—Adrian. But he's not jealous; he's glad. Besides, he assures her he *doesn't* love her anymore. He can't love *anyone*.

Her continued protests start to break him, and he shouts for the guards to get her out of there. When she finally leaves, her heart feels like it's shattered into a million pieces.

THE QUEEN'S DECREE

Meanwhile, the Council has been debating something for days—the same thing that they had Rose testify about—and they've finally reached a verdict. Queen Tatiana has been the deciding vote in a decree to lower the age of official guardians. Now, instead of eighteen, guardians will graduate at sixteen and immediately be assigned to Moroi. It's a controversial decision—to say the very least.

Rose is furious when she realizes it was her testimony that was held up as a shining example of what underage Strigoi killers can do. It's clear to her now—Tatiana hadn't begun to accept her. Instead, she'd shamelessly used her as a way to pass her new ruling.

Tasha is equally appalled by this decision. She's been pushing for Moroi to learn how to fight to avoid just such a decision. The last thing she wanted was to put sixteen-year-olds in the line of fire.

The ruling brings up an important debate. Lissa is the last in her royal line. Even though she's now eighteen, she had no vote on Council because of something called a *quorum*. In order to be eligible to vote, a family must have more than one member. If Lissa had a vote, this ruling would have gone a very different way.

Rose makes her opinion known to all about this ridiculous decision. She should be an exception. Not all teens are well trained enough to deal with what she's had to face. She just had a great instructor—one the Court insists on keeping locked up even though he's not a danger anymore.

To stop her outburst, Tatiana orders her removed from the Council room. But a pissed-off Rose has a few last words for the queen.

"You could change the quorum law if you wanted, you sanctimonious bitch!" I yelled back. "You're twisting the law because you're selfish and afraid! You're making the worst mistake of your life. You'll regret it! Wait and see—you'll wish you'd never done it!"

—page 377

They're harsh words, spoken in a public forum, and Rose will come to regret them in the days that follow. But for now, they're heartfelt and full of passion. Even the guardians who give her the boot think what she said was pretty fantastic.

Through the bond, Rose can see that Tasha is still arguing with everyone on the Council who'll listen. To her, it's been proven that a spirit user can restore a Strigoi. Why would they need to find new ways to kill them if they can save them?

To Rose, though, the amount of spirit needed to restore Strigoi makes it impossible for it to become the ultimate solution. The more spirit used, the quicker the spirit user will succumb to insanity. She'd seen it herself—Lissa had used a staggering amount of power to restore Dimitri. It had even temporarily hurt the bond. Even if she might be naively compassionate enough to do it again, Rose knows that road is a dangerous one for her friend or any other spirit user. It's not worth it.

Rose has heard enough. She cuts off the connection to Lissa, planning to talk more to her friend later. She'd been so absorbed by the bond, she didn't even realize that someone she knows is standing right in front of her—Ambrose, the queen's masseur and secret lover. Since Rose is waiting around to talk to Lissa later, he suggests that she see his aunt Rhonda for another tarot card reading.

Actually, she could use a little insight on her future at the moment—so she agrees. Just like last time, though, the cards aren't all that helpful.

I scanned the cards. Heartache. An enemy. Accusations. Entrapment. Travel. "Some of it tells me things I already know. The rest leaves me with more questions."

She smiled knowingly. "That's how it usually is." —page 390

Great. Real helpful there. But there's one card—the Page of Cups—that confuses Rhonda. It's possible that it points to the reason for the journey Rose will go on—a search for an unknown girl or a boy. Unfortunately, she can't be of much more help.

As they leave, Rose vents to Ambrose the anger she feels toward Tatiana about the quorum and the age law, but Ambrose defends the queen. It wasn't her sole decision—the Council voted. Even so, he believes the queen will eventually change the decree.

Sure. Rose will believe that when she sees it.

Lissa calls to her through the bond. There's something Rose should see—and it involves Dimitri.

Say no more. Rose finds Lissa and Dimitri outside in the sunshine sitting opposite three Moroi—and Hans. They're being interrogated in front of a scattering of guardians and a crowd of curious Moroi onlookers. The officials want to determine once and for all if Dimitri is still Strigoi. Well, being out in the sunshine should clue everyone in. But no, they're still asking questions. Lots of them.

When Lissa testifies on Dimitri's behalf, he watches her with with wonder . . . and worship. Again, Rose is jealous of the connection the two seem to have formed without her.

His feelings weren't romantic, but it didn't matter. What mattered was that he had rejected me but regarded her as the greatest thing in the world. He'd told me never to talk to him again and sworn he'd do anything for her. Again I felt that petulant sense of being wronged. I refused to believe that he couldn't love me anymore. It wasn't possible, not after all he and I had been through together. Not after everything we'd felt for each other. —*pages 397-398*

By the end of the session, the official determination is that Dimitri is no longer Strigoi and that Lissa, somehow, has worked a miracle to restore him. He won't be held in the locked cell anymore but will still be kept under watch by guards for now.

Lissa warns Rose to back off and not to provoke Dimitri. He needs to stay in control—something he definitely *doesn't* do whenever Rose is around—to ensure that he's not seen as a threat. If Rose keeps pushing, it will ruin everything they've worked toward.

It totally sucks. But even Rose can see it's the truth.

Rose becomes aware of someone lurking nearby. She confronts the stranger, and he identifies himself as a messenger from her father. He gives Rose a laptop and a satellite modem for a meeting she's to have momentarily. She quickly returns to her room to set up the equipment. But instead of her father, she's surprised to come face-to-face with Sydney, the Alchemist she met in Russia.

Sydney questions Rose about a recent break-in she thinks Rose might have been involved with (thankfully, it's not at Tarasov!). The Alchemists had some files stolen—files about Eric Dragomir, Lissa's father. He'd made some large deposits to an anonymous woman's bank account in Las Vegas.

Rose didn't steal the files, but now she's wondering who did and what this all means.

She goes to sleep, forgetting all about a promise she'd made to meet Adrian for a cocktail party. *Oops.* Adrian's waiting in Rose's lobby the next morning, and he's not too cheerful at being stood up. It's obvious to him she's been so distracted visiting Dimitri that he's the last thing on her mind.

Rose tries to assure him that it's not true—she values their relationship. *Really* she does. He gives her another chance but warns that she needs to really mean it this time. He isn't interested in playing games with her.

She takes the opportunity to pick his brain about Eric Dragomir and what trouble he might have gotten into in Las Vegas. Adrian figures gambling debts, but the family's rich, so that doesn't make much sense. Why would anyone want to steal info like that anyway?

Rose heads to church. Not so much to worship, but because she has a hunch who might be there. And she's right. Dimitri's there, with guards in tow. She sits next to him, which he doesn't appreciate very much. Too damn bad.

She tries to convince him again that his Strigoi deeds are in his past. Besides, what he did as a Strigoi was completely out of his control. She presses for some sign that he still cares about her, but Dimitri begins to lose his patience, and his desperation and frustration bleed through. Her being there with him is too hard. He wants them to stay away from each other. It's better that way.

But Rose is nothing if not stubborn. After everything they've been through together, it *can't* end like this. She still feels the connection between them.

Without even realizing it, I reached toward him, needing that touch. He sprang up like I was a snake, and all of his

171

guardians shot forward, braced for what he might do.

But he did nothing. Nothing except stare at me with a look that made my blood run cold. Like I was something strange and bad. "Rose. Please stop. Please stay away." He was working hard to stay calm.

I shot up, now as angry and frustrated at him. I had a feeling if I stayed, we'd both snap. In an undertone, I murmured, "This isn't over. I won't give up on you."

"I've given up on you," he said back, voice also soft. "Love fades. Mine has." —page 430

The words are like a stake to Rose's heart. But she finally accepts that he doesn't want her around. She runs out of the church and lets out her grief and pain in the privacy of her room.

Lissa calls to her through the bond, but she just wants to be alone. She avoids everyone and wanders the Court grounds. When she returns to her room, Adrian stops by to see her. He has some info on Lissa's father courtesy of his mother. Daniella thinks the anonymous woman might have been a mistress he was supporting. It's unbelievable and shocking, but it doesn't sound like anything that could put Lissa in danger, which is a definite relief.

The rejection by Dimitri has made her realize how much she's been taking Adrian's affections for granted. He's a great guy and endlessly supportive of her. She apologizes for how much she's been taking him for granted lately. He needs to know that she's willing to give him a real shot—that what she'd had with Dimitri is truly over.

"I realize now that it's over with him. I'm not saying that's easy to get past. It'll take a while, and I'd be lying to both of us if I said it wouldn't."

"That makes sense," Adrian said.

"It does?"

He glanced at me, a flicker of amusement in his eyes. "Yes, little dhampir. Sometimes you make sense. Go on."

"I . . . well, like I said . . . I've got to heal from him. But I do care about you . . . I think I even love you a little." That got a small smile. "I want to try again. I really do." —page 436

Dimitri's in her past, but Adrian could be her future. At the moment, she doesn't want to feel *anything* for Dimitri—it only causes her pain. She wants to block out those feelings completely. He's rejected her and she wants to feel wanted again. Adrian makes her feel wanted . . . and loved. What more could she ask for?

A passionate moment between them leads them to do something Rose never thought she'd do again. She bares her neck to Adrian, and he hesitates only briefly before sinking his fangs in. The endorphins kick in and all is blissful and perfect. Nothing else seems to matter—for a little while, anyway.

ACCUSATIONS

Getting breakfast at the café the next morning seems like an innocent enough way to start the day. Of course, Dimitri's there with his ever-present guards. Rose tries to avoid him but gets to talking to one of the guardians about the age law, which gets Dimitri's attention and stirs his passions. In the moment, he spots the bite marks on her neck and knows where they come from. He's dry about this observation—almost triumphant, as if he's known she'd get over him all along; it was only a matter of time. This is the proof. Despite her claims to still love him, Rose has moved on with her Moroi boyfriend in a very physical way. She's about to argue when guardians suddenly storm the café.

Rose fears they're there for Dimitri. They're not. They're there for her. Dimitri immediately springs into action when they grab her. He can't help but fight them off—protecting Rose is like second nature to him. But no, he *can't* be violent—Rose realizes what will happen if the guardians perceive him to be a threat. They'll think there's still some Strigoi left in him! Rose does the only thing she can think of—she gives herself up so Dimitri doesn't get in any more trouble.

Too bad Rose didn't realize how much trouble *she's* in. She's under arrest for high treason—

—for the murder of Queen Tatiana!

There will be a hearing first to determine if there's enough evidence for the trial. Alibis are questioned—and Adrian steps forward to say he and Rose were together last night. *All* night.

Christian tries to comfort Lissa, who is now frantic and worried. This leads to the first kiss they've shared since their breakup. As far as any jealousies she's had . . .

> *"There is only one person I have ever wanted," he said. The steadiness of his gaze, of those crystal blue eyes, left no question as to who that person was. "No one else has ever come close. In*

spite of everything, even with Avery—"

"Christian, I'm so sorry for that—"

"You don't have to—"

"I do—"

"Damn it," he said. "Will you let me finish a sent—"

"No," Lissa interrupted. And she leaned over and kissed him,
a hard and powerful kiss that burned through her body, one
that told her there was no one else in the world for her either.

—*pages 468-469*

Rose always meant to help bring Lissa and Christian back together. Who knew it would be her murder accusation that would do the trick?

In the courtroom, Rose is introduced to her Moroi lawyer. But there's suddenly a commotion as someone else strolls in. It's Abe and he wants to represent his daughter. Except . . . he's not *exactly* a lawyer. Still, he asks Rose to trust him. She's understandably worried about how this will all turn out.

"They're going to send me to trial and convict me!"

Every trace of humor or cheer vanished from his face. His ex-
pression grew hard, deadly serious. A chill ran down my spine.

"That," he said in a low, flat voice, "is something I swear to
you is never, ever going to happen." —*page 478*

Zmey doesn't make promises he can't fulfill. Rose takes him on as her official representation. The investigation has led to some pretty

POP QUIZ:
Spirit Bound

1. Where does Rose sneak into a security office in order to get info on Tarasov Prison?
2. What is the name of the guardian who was in love with former St. Vlad's teacher and current Strigoi Sonya Karp?
3. In order to sneak into the prison, Lissa and Rose wear charmed silver jewelry that makes them appear to the guards as what?
4. Complete Robert Doru's quote: *"That which is dead doesn't _____ stay dead ..."*
5. To restore a Strigoi back to his or her Moroi self, they must be stabbed through the heart with a silver stake charmed with which element?
6. What is the name of the Moroi casino in Las Vegas?
7. When Dimitri is restored and willing to do anything to prove his loyalty and gratitude to Lissa, what is the one thing he refuses to do?
8. What is the name of the secret, masked ceremony that Moroi royals hold to honor the dead?
9. Queen Tatiana's controversial royal decree is that guardians will now graduate from their training at what age, ready to be assigned to protect Moroi?
10. Who shows up just in time to act as legal representation for Rose after she's accused of murder?

* For quiz answers, see p.299.

damning evidence, though. Rose's silver stake, with her fingerprints, was the murder weapon. Adrian's alibi is confirmed by a witness and has him at her room *after* the murder occurred.

There's more than enough evidence to warrant a full trial.

It's obvious that she's been framed. Somebody wants her to take the blame for this horrible crime. But who?

As she's leaving the courtroom, stunned by what's happened, Ambrose manages to slip her a note. It's from Queen Tatiana herself, written before her death. She wasn't in favor of the age decree, but it was better than what some Moroi wanted—to force *all* dhampirs into becoming guardians.

But that's not all the note says.... It also reveals that

there's another Dragomir—Eric Dragomir's illegitimate child. Lissa's half-sibling! If Rose can find this child—and the queen trusts only her to take on this important task—then Lissa will have an official vote on the Council. It would make the difference for Lissa, for everyone.

It's an amazing amount of information to take in.

But at the moment, Rose is a bit busy dealing with the thought of being sent to prison for the rest of her life. Abe assures her that she won't go to trial . . . *or* anywhere else.

"Even you have your limits, old man."

His smile returned. "You'd be surprised. Besides, they don't even send royal traitors to prison, Rose. Everyone knows that."

I scoffed. "Are you insane? Of course they do. What else do you think they do with traitors? Set them free and tell them not to do it again?"

"No," said Abe, just before he turned away. "They execute traitors."

—page 489

CHAPTER 6

Last Sacrifice

RICHELLE ON *LAST SACRIFICE*

What was most surprising about *Last Sacrifice* was what a high-powered action novel it became! The love story, friendships, and emotional content have always made up the heart of this series. While they were still present in this book, they were also sharing the spotlight with C4 explosions and car chases, which was certainly a long ways from how the series had started!

It's amazing how difficult it can be to wrap up all the subplots and threads in a series, particularly when you've fallen into a pattern of just ending books on cliffhangers. There are so many nuances to address, and as I tried to cover all of them, the book just kept getting longer and longer. Equally difficult was that I also wanted to seed some plotlines for *Bloodlines*, which meant purposely leaving a few threads open. My hope was that this would excite readers for the spin-off series, but it backfired on me a little! Those who didn't realize there was more to come thought I'd been sloppy and forgotten to wrap certain things up, not realizing those threads had been left by design.

Overall, I'm happy with the way this book and the series turned out. Ask any writer, and he or she will always wish there was more time to go back and keep fixing or adding things. I'm no different and probably could've kept perfecting this for years! At some point, though, you have to step back and say, "It's time we wrap this up."

First line: I don't like cages.

ROSE BEHIND BARS

Framed for the murder of Queen Tatiana, Rose is awaiting trial, under constant guard, behind cold steel bars in a holding cell at the Moroi Royal Court—frustrated that she's helpless to do anything at the moment but wait. And if she's found guilty of this crime, she'll immediately be sentenced to death.

Her father, Abe—who's also working as her lawyer—visits to tell her that her trial might be moved up to two weeks from now. To Rose, that's great news. It means she'll be free earlier than expected once they prove her innocence.

To Abe, it's a bad thing. He anticipates it will be exactly the same as her hearing—same evidence and a guilty verdict. After which, she'll be executed. Immediately.

Abe assures her before leaving her cell that he believes in her innocence—his daughter might be capable of murder, but not this one—and he's working on a way to fix this. Just as he promised her in the courtroom, she *won't* stand trial. But even she knows that her dangerous and influential father has limits to what he can fix—especially in the amount of time they have.

But her impending fate is not all that's on Rose's mind . . . The visit from Abe did nothing to distract her from the other important matter at hand: the possible existence of another Dragomir. Rose rereads the note the queen wrote to her before she died. In it, she disclosed her belief that Lissa's father's had an illegitimate child. If this is true and the child can be found, the Dragomir family would gain quorum, and Lissa would be given an official voice on the Moroi Royal Council. This would be *big*. One vote could change everything—including whether or not Rose is found guilty.

Rose reaches out to her friend through their bond, but it feels as if Lissa is trying to hide something from Rose—something huge. But what?

It doesn't take long before she finds out.

During Queen Tatiana's funeral procession, statues rigged with explosives detonate to distract guardians while Eddie and Mikhail help free Rose from her cell. They're helped by another conspirator, one who's a big surprise to Rose given their many issues and difficulties: Dimitri. Adrian is also doing his part to help by using compulsion on any guards who try to stand in their way as they get Rose away from the Royal Court.

With the help of her friends, Abe has masterminded this prison break. If Rose isn't at Court, she won't stand trial. And if she doesn't stand trial, she can't be found guilty. It's not a perfect solution, but drastic times call for drastic measures. Rose is told she must go with Dimitri and stay safely hidden away while her friends work on finding evidence to prove her innocence.

Adrian warns Rose of one problem—by escaping, she'll be confirming her guilt in the eyes of the guardians. And if she's caught, they'll have the authority to kill her on sight. If she stays, there is a slim chance she will be found innocent during her trial. Either option is a gamble.

To Rose, it isn't a difficult decision. She'd rather risk living as a fugitive, and if death came for her, she'd rather face it fighting.

They fight their way past guardians to get to their getaway car— a nondescript Honda—where Abe meets up with them.

There isn't much time for goodbyes, and Rose quickly hugs Eddie and Mikhail—and then shares a brief moment with her current boyfriend before she flees the scene with her ex-boyfriend.

Adrian was the hardest to leave behind. I could tell it was difficult for him too, no matter how relaxed his grin seemed. He couldn't be happy about me going off with Dimitri. Our hug lasted a little bit longer than the others, and he gave me a soft, brief kiss on the lips. I almost felt like crying after how brave he'd been tonight. I wished he could go with me but knew he'd be safer here.

"Adrian, thank you for—"

He held up his hand. "It's not goodbye, little dhampir. I'll see you in your dreams." —pages 63-64

Finally, Rose says goodbye to her father, who has planned all of this, right down to one more explosion—one that will blast a hole in the Court's walls so they can get out. Dimitri races the car through the opening, leaving the Moroi Royal Court behind them.

The longer she sits there—in the passenger seat next to him— the more the truth of what's happened sinks in. And the more she realizes that she is really and truly alone with Dimitri for the first time since he'd become a dhampir again.

He'd risked so much for her by doing this. He was now a fugitive too. She lets him know that he's free to take off at any time. But he refuses to even consider it. He warns that if she tries to get away from him, he'll just find her.

She wants to know why . . . she wonders to herself if he might

181

still feel a lingering attraction to her despite his harsh words from before—*"love fades, mine has."*

Dimitri makes sure she knows exactly why he's doing this.

> *"Lissa asked me to protect you."*
>
> *"Hey, I don't need anyone to—"*
>
> *"And," he continued, "I meant what I said to her. I swore I'd serve her and help her for the rest of my life, anything she asks. If she wants me to be your bodyguard, then that's what I'll be." He gave me a dangerous look. "There's no way you're getting rid of me anytime soon."*
>
> —*page 67*

If the guardians find her—they'll find Dimitri too. He's destroying his life by helping her—by agreeing to do this. Staying with her is definitely the wrong decision, and she needs to convince him of that. But there's no time to argue. It's not long before pursuing guardians start to tail them. Dimitri swerves off the highway and into a mall parking lot, where he decides they need to split up temporarily to lose those following them. They're to meet up at the nearby movie theater in half an hour.

Rose does as he says and tries to blend in with other teens at the mall while she waits out the half hour. As she exits the mall and heads for the theater, she's ambushed by a guardian. She knows he has the authority to kill her on sight, so she dodges his blows and manages to take him to the ground, where she knocks him unconscious.

Breathlessly, she reaches the theater—but there's no sign of Dimitri. Finally an unfamiliar car pulls up beside her and Dimitri calls out to her. He stole this car and ditched the other one. When

Rose gets in, he hits the gas, and they get back to the main road, leaving the guardians far behind them.

A few hours later, Dimitri pulls off the road into a McDonald's, where they meet up with another surprising ally—Sydney. She now works out of New Orleans. Abe had been responsible for getting her out of Russia, which is where the girls first met during Rose's quest to find and kill the Strigoi version of Dimitri. This "favor" has left Sydney in open-ended debt to him, and he kept getting favors from her—this is just the most recent. Helping a wanted fugitive and a former Strigoi isn't exactly part of an Alchemist's regular work, and Sydney's not thrilled with being a part of this drama. But here she is. And she also has a new car for them to continue on in, leaving the stolen one behind.

Back at Court, order has been restored, but the guardians are grilling Rose's friends about what happened and who's involved. However, everyone involved with her breakout has alibis. Lissa suspects that Rose is watching and doesn't want her to worry. She sends a message through the bond that they will clear Rose's name. It's crazy, really. Rose has always been the one to protect Lissa, and now it seems to be the other way around.

At an ordinary motel in an uninteresting town, Sydney checks them in. Rose and Dimitri have to share a room, since it's all the better to defend themselves if there's any trouble. However, if they do get caught, Sydney doesn't want to be anywhere near them, so she gets a separate room. Abe has strictly instructed Sydney that the three are to get comfortable at the motel and stay out of trouble while her friends try to gather evidence to help Rose's case back at Court, but Rose is frantic. She hates the idea of sitting around and doing nothing. Who knows how long it will take to clear her name? When she and Dimitri are alone in their room, she heads for the motel room door, but Dimitri blocks her way. So now what is she supposed to do?

Clearly, there's only one answer. Fight. Dimitri, however, throws her on the bed and pins her down. This is totally infuriating. But it's also kind of intoxicating to have his body so close to hers. Fighting isn't working so well, so she tries a different tactic.

> *My body might be constrained, but my head and neck had just enough freedom to shift up—and kiss him.*
>
> *My lips met his, and I learned a few things. One was that it was possible to catch him totally by surprise. His body froze and locked up, shocked at the sudden turn of events. I also realized that he was just as good a kisser as I recalled. The last time we'd kissed had been when he was Strigoi. There had been an eerie sexiness to that, but it didn't compare to the heat and energy of being alive.* —*page 96*

Dimitri kisses her back—passionately. She wonders, not for the first time, if it's possible he might still love her. However, this isn't the time to think about romance; it's time to think about escape. She manages to catch him by surprise—again—with a very non-sexy punch to his face and flees the motel, headed into the woods.

While she tries to get her bearings and put space between herself and Dimitri, she slips into Lissa's head to find her friend being questioned by guardians. The subject turns to Dimitri and why he'd help an accused murderer escape if he's no longer an evil Strigoi.

It's time for Lissa to reveal a big secret—Rose and Dimitri were romantically involved. This admission establishes a very strong motive. But it also proves that Dimitri and Rose would have been together at St. Vlad's when she was still underage.

Not good . . .

After they're released from questioning, Lissa and the others are met by Abe. They brainstorm other suspects in the queen's murder, knowing it would had to have been someone who had access to her private chambers. Ambrose, the queen's secret dhampir lover, is discussed as a possibility. Abe remembers seeing him speak briefly with Rose in the courtroom. They all agree that he is definitely a suspect.

Back in the woods, Dimitri catches up with Rose. He grabs hold of her and attempts to take her back to the motel, but she puts up a major fight.

> *"Rose," he said wearily. "You can't win."*
>
> *"How's your face feeling?" I asked. I couldn't see any marks in the poor lighting, but I knew the punch I'd given him would leave a mark tomorrow. It was a shame to damage his face like that, but he'd heal, and maybe it would teach him a lesson about messing with Rose Hathaway.*
>
> *Or not. He began dragging me again. "I'm seconds away from just tossing you over my shoulder," he warned.*
>
> *"I'd like to see you try."* —page 118

Perhaps fighting with Dimitri isn't the best use of her time. She realizes there's something else she can do to help Lissa while she's away from Court. She's going to find the lost Dragomir!

Sure, this will go against the orders Dimitri and Sydney were given by Lissa and Abe, respectively—to keep Rose safe and out of trouble—but they all agree that it's a worthy pursuit. To find a sibling of Lissa's would mean she can get a vote on the royal council, and that vote could mean the difference between life and death for Rose. The only problem is that they don't have any real leads. Sydney knows a place they can stay while they figure it out. On the drive there, Rose visits Lissa through the bond.

She finds her friend at Adrian's parents' home, recovering with Adrian and Christian from the questioning session. Lissa isn't confident she convinced the officials that she had nothing to do with Rose's escape, but the guardians don't have any proof.

They're interrupted by a knock on the door. An unfamiliar young Moroi guy is looking for Adrian's mother. Adrian recognizes him—this is Joe, the janitor, who gave Adrian his alibi the night of the murder so he wouldn't be implicated along with Rose.

Joe wants Adrian to relate a message to his mother—that he's leaving Court, but "everything's set." He's about to go, but a suspicious Lissa uses compulsion to get him to go into further detail about what he meant. It turns out Joe was given money by Adrian's mother, Daniella, to put a specific time on when he saw Adrian—even though Joe didn't remember precisely when it was. For a price, he'd fudged the details for Daniella in order to protect her son. Joe says he was also paid off by another Moroi to give false testimony about Rose's whereabouts—and that was testimony that made Rose the prime suspect.

Rose's friends are desperate to find out who it was that bribed him. But unfortunately, the janitor is no more help to them. All he knows is that there was something strange about the Moroi's hand . . .

THE KEEPERS

Rose, Dimitri, and Sydney near their destination, deeper and deeper into darkness, surrounded by mountains and forest. They leave the main road and drive down a tiny gravel one toward what looks like a campground. There are other old-looking vehicles here, and all around them is dark forest.

Finally, they get out of the car since they have to continue on foot.

They're suddenly surrounded by vampires—they're Moroi, but still, they're dangerous, and Rose and Dimitri both have their stakes in hand in an instant, just in case they're attacked. They aren't. This is a commune of Keepers—Moroi who keep to the old ways and will marry humans or dhampirs without concern for social protocol. They consider modern Moroi to be "Tainted."

The leader of the Keepers, Raymond, generously allows the trio to stay with his family. Raymond has four children, including a cute dhampir son Joshua and an extremely angry and unwelcoming dhampir daughter, Angeline.

That night, Rose is pulled into a spirit dream by someone who's never previously summoned her: Robert Doru. His brother, Victor Dashkov, is in the dream as well, and Rose's first response is to attack—Victor clearly has something devious up his sleeve. But her fighting abilities prove to be of little worth in the dream—since Robert is the one controlling it, she can't get to either of them.

"Are you done with your tantrum?" asked Victor. "Behaving like a civilized person will make our talk so much more pleasant."

"I have no interest in talking to you," I snapped. "The only

thing I'm going to do is hunt you down in the real world and drag you back to the authorities."

"Charming," said Victor. "We can share a cell." —*page 156*

Victor has great interest in the queen's murder. He's deceitful but smart, and Rose decides to tell him about the missing Dragomir. He offers to help in the search, but she still doesn't have any leads. She needs time.

Victor offers a suggestion that would provide Rose with some additional time—have Lissa run as a candidate for queen. Sure, she'd never be elected since her family doesn't have quorum. But still, she *can* run. And her doing so would certainly incite some major debate at Court, which in turn would cause a sizable delay . . .

The dream ends, but Rose is pulled into another—this time with a much better-looking guy: Adrian. He compliments her on the dress she's wearing—and Rose realizes she's unconsciously chosen the dress she wore the night she and Dimitri almost had sex thanks to Victor's lust charm. Of course, Adrian doesn't realize that. All he sees is a sexy black dress on a beautiful girl. But is her subconscious trying to tell her that spending so much time with her ex is affecting her more than she'd like to admit?

Despite this distraction, before the dream ends, Rose is able to tell Adrian about the potential plan to nominate Lissa for queen.

The next day, Rose, Sydney, and Dimitri go to a nearby town so Sydney can get internet access to start their search to find the missing Dragomir. While Sydney looks up information online, Rose and Dimitri go for a walk around town to kill some time. They end up at the local library, where they flip through travel books and imagine where they'd like to travel to one day. Being with Dimitri like this feels . . . good. Very good.

> *If anyone had told me forty-eight hours ago that I'd be lying in a library with Dimitri, reading a travel book, I would have said they were crazy. Almost as crazy was the realization that I was doing something perfectly ordinary and casual with him. Since the moment we'd met, our lives had been about secrecy and danger. And really, those were still the dominant themes in our lives. But in those quiet couple of hours, time seemed to stand still. We were at peace. We were friends.* —*pages 185-186*

They head back to the café to see if Sydney's found anything useful. She has. She was able to track down Eric Dragomir's bank records and transactions, hoping they might lead to his mistress. Instead, they led to the mistress's next of kin—and it's a shockingly familiar name: Sonya Karp. This is the same teacher from St. Vlad's who specialized in spirit and chose to turn Strigoi as the only way to escape her madness. But how are they supposed to track down a Strigoi?

THE SEARCH FOR SONYA

Grimly, Dimitri makes a call during which he speaks Russian. Rose recognizes the change in his tone, and it scares her deeply.

> *A strange sensation spread over me as he spoke. I was confused, lost because of the language . . . but there was more than that. I*

felt chilled. My pulse raced with fear. That voice . . . I knew that voice. It was his voice and yet not his voice. It was the voice of my nightmares, a voice of coldness and cruelty.

Dimitri was playing Strigoi. ———*page 192*

Sydney translates Dimitri's demands for Rose—he wants to know where to find Sonya Karp, and he wants to know NOW. He threatens the Strigoi on the other end with extreme violence if he fails to provide answers. It's an effective call, but pretending to be Strigoi shakes Dimitri—and Rose—to their cores.

When they get back to the commune, Joshua wants to show Rose his future living quarters—a nearby cave. Dimitri looks like he doesn't approve of this outing and warns Rose not to lead the young dhampir on. Well, that makes zero sense. Is he jealous she's thinking about spending time with another cute guy? He doesn't have control over her. It's *his* choice to keep Rose at arm's length. She proves her independence by agreeing to go for a tour of the cave. There, Joshua surprises her by proposing marriage.

Um . . . unexpected. Very unexpected. Rose lets him down as easy as possible. He takes the rejection well—especially when Rose makes it clear that she's already dating somebody else. When Rose sorts out her issues, Joshua hopes she might come back for him. He then gives her a finely carved wooden bracelet as a gift. Since she turned down his marriage proposal, she doesn't want to insult him, so she accepts the gift—although she hopes this isn't encouraging his interest.

They head back to the big campfire, where Rose is promptly attacked by Angeline. She wants Rose to prove she's really a badass guardian by fighting her. The girl is scrappy but untrained, and Rose is able to restrain her. Angeline is finally impressed by Rose—and it's okay with her that Rose marries her brother. When the young girl had spotted the bracelet Rose wore, she'd assumed the two were engaged. It's a Keeper custom that the prospective bride and groom must battle it out with the other's nearest relative of the same sex.

Dimitri wryly reminds Rose that he told her not to encourage Joshua's interest.

His humor fades when he decides it's time to leave the commune to make another call to his Strigoi contact—the cell phone they have can only get a signal ten minutes away from the Keeper village. Since Rose wants to check in with Lissa, she asks that Sydney go with him for support as he is forced to relive his Strigoi days.

When they leave, Rose sees through the bond that Lissa, Adrian, and Christian are now questioning Ambrose about the murder. The dhampir resents that they think he might have had something to do with it. He cared deeply about Tatiana.

Ambrose thinks the murderer was politically motivated. The queen wasn't happy about making the guardian age decree, but her only other option was to force all dhampirs into service as guardians. Her ultimate decision was the lesser of two evils. Tatiana had also been secretly working to have a group of Moroi trained in defense. The group's instructor was Lissa's previous guardian Grant. Unfortunately, he was killed the night of Lissa's birthday in the Strigoi attack led by Dimitri.

Ambrose lets them know that the queen was also romantically involved with Blake Lazar, a royal party boy who makes Adrian look like an upstanding member of society. Perhaps the real murderer wasn't politically motivated. It could be that another woman, jealous of the queen's romantic interludes, decided to take her life. Ambrose promises to check the queen's bedroom for any further evidence.

Back at the Keepers' commune, Dimitri and Sydney return from their phone call. Dimitri has a solid lead on a Strigoi who could tell them where to find Sonya. They need to leave immediately for the six-hour trip to Lexington. Angeline begs them to take her with them. Her pleas show that not all Keepers are thrilled about being stuck where they are. Rose feels bad about leaving her behind, but she can't risk the girl's safety.

On the drive to Lexington, Rose views the nomination ceremony through Lissa's eyes. The Royal Ballroom is packed with royals and commoners alike. A member of each royal family is nominated.

When it's believed all nominations have been made, Tasha steps forward to nominate Lissa—much to the princess's surprise. It's seconded by Christian and confirmed by Adrian. Some Moroi are unhappy about this, but others are now watching Lissa with interest—this princess from a dying line who can allegedly work miracles.

Lissa retains her composure until she gets back to her room with Christian and Adrian, where she promptly freaks out. She doesn't want to be queen! They assure her it's only to buy time for Rose so they can find the real murderer.

DIMITRI'S BREAKDOWN

The Strigoi they're after, Donovan, works in a tattoo shop. Since he would sense a dhampir, the plan is to send in a very reluctant Sydney so that she can lure him out into Rose and Dimitri's trap.

Despite Sydney's fears, it works! Donovan and his two henchmen enter the alley, where Rose and Dimitri attack. Rose takes out one of the henchmen, and Dimitri pummels the other. Being faced with Strigoi reminds him of the horrors he was responsible for when he too was a monster. He begins to lose control of himself.

Dimitri's face. It was . . . terrifying. Ferocious. He'd had a similar look when he'd defended me at my arrest—that badass warrior god expression that said he could take on hell itself. The way he looked now . . . well, it took that fierceness to a whole new level. This was personal, I realized. Fighting these Strigoi wasn't just about finding Sonya and helping Lissa. This was about redemption, an attempt to destroy his past by destroying the evil directly in his path. —page 249

He stakes the Strigoi henchman—hard—but he's so fixated that he's almost blindsided by Donovan. He and Rose restrain the Strigoi and demand answers. Donovan finally reveals what he knows, giving them a town and description of Sonya's house.

As soon as they have the information they came for, Dimitri stakes him. And not just once. He thrusts his stake into Donovan's chest over and over again. The carnage gets out of hand, and Rose has to beg Dimitri to stop before he loses himself completely.

"It's over. You've done enough."

"It's never enough, Roza," he whispered. The grief in his voice killed me. "It'll never be enough."

"It is for now," I said. I pulled him to me. Unresisting, he let

go of his stake and buried his face against my shoulder. I dropped my stake as well and embraced him, drawing him closer. He wrapped his arms around me in return, seeking the contact of another living being, the contact I'd long known he needed.

"You're the only one." He clung more tightly to me. "The only one who understands. The only one who saw how I was."

—*page 253*

The pain he feels is palpable. It breaks Rose's heart. She tries to comfort him, tries to remind him that he said he wants to appreciate life now that he's a dhampir again. But at the moment, he can't find anything beautiful . . . there's only death. She forces him to focus on one thing that's beautiful; one thing will be enough to make him realize he is no longer Strigoi.

Finally, he finds something. Her hair—Rose's hair is beautiful to him. Since Strigoi don't see beauty in the world, only death, this is definitely progress.

Later, in a spirit dream, Rose is visited again by the brothers Dashkov. Against her better judgment, she shares their quest to find Sonya Karp, a major lead in locating the missing Dragomir. Victor and his brother promise to join them tomorrow to assist her in her efforts. Then the dream ends.

Awesome.

One spirit dream follows another as Adrian checks in with his dhampir girlfriend, who he believes is still safely tucked away at the original motel—and Rose isn't filling him in on their current plan since she doesn't want to worry anyone. Adrian shares his concerns with Rose about his own mental stability. Unlike Lissa, who has Rose to take away some of her spirit darkness when it gets to be too much to handle, Adrian doesn't have anyone to whom he's bonded. He's afraid he's going insane—the alcohol only masks his deterioration. Adrian tells Rose that she's his strength. She's about to tell him that she'd rather he find that strength inside himself when she's abruptly woken from the dream by the blare of the alarm clock, leaving her frustrated—both because she misses Adrian and also because she hadn't been able to tell him all she wanted to. She can only hope that he'll be able to manage on his own.

GETTING ANSWERS THE HARD WAY

On the way to Sonya's house, Rose shares a little info with the others.

"So," I began casually, "Victor Dashkov might be joining us soon."

It was to Sydney's credit that she didn't drive off the road.

"What? That guy who escaped?"

I could see in Dimitri's eyes that he was just as shocked, but he kept cool and under control, like always. "Why," he began slowly, "is Victor Dashkov joining us?"

"Well, it's kind of a funny story . . ."   —*page 267*

Rose fills Dimitri and Sydney in on Robert Doru's background and also the spirit dreams she's been having with the Dashkov brothers. While she glosses over Victor's "mysterious" escape from prison a few weeks ago, something tells her that Dimitri is putting the pieces together for himself about what really happened—and just what extremes Rose took to find a way to restore him from his Strigoi self.

When they arrive at Sonya's house, Rose and Dimitri scout the area, until finally they break in. Rose bangs her head hard while fighting Sonya, but at last they're able to chain her to a chair. Even restrained, Sonya refuses to tell them anything about her connection to the missing Dragomir. No surprise there—she's a Strigoi.

Dimitri's concerned about Rose's head injury and instructs her to rest, which she does begrudgingly.

While resting, Rose mentally visits Lissa and finds that she's now taking part in the first of three monarch tests. The test takes place in the wilderness and is designed to assess the candidates' physical endurance. The royals are given cell phones, maps, and compasses to guide them. If, however, they decide to use their phones to call for help, they'll have failed the test and be out of the running for the throne.

The map contains a riddle Lissa must follow to find her way to the finish as well as the locations of helpful items. It's a miserable, cold, and rain-drenched day, but Rose is impressed by how well Lissa can take care of herself. The princess is far from helpless.

When Rose is drawn back to Sonya's house, the Strigoi still isn't saying a word—and is extremely dangerous, even restrained.

When Sonya makes her move to break free, it takes both Dimitri and Rose to hold her down. Shockingly, the Dashkov brothers arrive with their own solution to make her talk—they're going to stake her! Robert plunges a silver stake into the Strigoi's heart— one that's been charmed with spirit. A brilliant, blinding white light throws everyone back as spirit returns Sonya to her former self, just as it did Dimitri only recently.

The former Strigoi is in shock—being restored to a Moroi is

something she never thought possible. And she's not the only one who finds it miraculous. Sydney is staring, wide-eyed.

> *The Alchemist met my eyes wonderingly.*
>
> *"I heard . . . but I didn't believe."*
>
> *"Sometimes," I told her, "I still don't. It goes against every rule of the universe."*
>
> *To my surprise, she touched the small gold cross around her neck. "Some rules are bigger than the universe."* —*page 302*

A now-protective Dimitri takes Sonya into another room where she can recover. Witnessing the spirit conversion for himself has made him understand that a gift like this—life emerging from death—is something that shouldn't be wasted.

Through the bond, Rose sees that someone else is coming to a similarly inspired realization back at Court. Lissa has returned victorious from the test to be greeted by a mob of admirers who are treating the nominees like celebrities and whispering about the "return of the dragon," the symbol of Lissa's family. Even though this started as an act to buy more time to solve the queen's murder, Lissa resolves to treat the election process with respect. Anything else would be an insult to her society.

Adrian brings Christian and Lissa to a local bar to meet Blake Lazar, the queen's other lover. It doesn't take them very long to determine that this guy is a total jerk. The initial pleasantries turn into a heated discussion about the queen's murder and Ambrose's other lovers, who could be suspects. They press for names and are stunned by what they learn. Among Ambrose's lovers is Daniella Ivashkov, Adrian's mother.

Adrian's appalled by this possibility and storms out. To Lissa and Christian, however, it puts Daniella on the short list of potential murder suspects.

THE MISSING DRAGOMIR

While Dimitri gets some rest, the others go and sit in Sonya's garden. Dimitri didn't want Sonya grilled in her delicate state, but Rose knows they don't have time to waste. She questions Sonya about her relative—the mother of Lissa's brother or sister—but she's resistant. Robert tries to compel her to talk, but this just pisses her off, and the spirit users attack each other. Rose calls Dimitri to help, and he's angry they refuse to let Sonya recuperate.

Sydney is the one who finds a solution. Sonya doesn't want to go back on her promise not to *tell* who her relative is—but she can *show* them where to find her, can't she? It's shaky logic at best, but it works. Sonya reluctantly agrees to lead the way.

Which means only one thing—another road trip! The six of them, the Dashkov brothers included, bundle into Sydney's SUV and off they go.

On the way, Rose is able to watch through the bond as Lissa takes part in the second monarch test. She's taken to a room where a very old Moroi woman—who Lissa will later learn is Ekaterina Zeklos, the queen prior to Tatiana—waits for her with a silver goblet filled with water. The goblet is charmed with magic from the four elements—and likely with spirit too, Lissa decides, when she finds herself in a spirit dream after drinking from it.

She quickly comes to the horrible realization that this is a test that will force her to face her darkest fears, starting with learning that Rose is dead. While Lissa is filled with grief over losing her dearest friend, dream-Christian announces that he too is leaving her. Lissa knows it's only a dream—a nightmare—but she's desperate for it to end. She can't take the thought of being alone.

Would she give up over a dream? A dream about being alone? It seemed like such a minor thing, but that cold truth hit her again: I've never been alone. *She didn't know if she could carry on by herself, but then, she realized that if this wasn't a dream—and dear God, did it feel real—there was no magic "stop" in real life. If she couldn't deal with loneliness in a dream, she never would be able to while waking.* —page 355

Pulling out of the dream would mean failing the test. She forces herself to hang on, and the dream shifts to one in which she's a Council member unable to properly represent the Dragomir family name due to her lack of confidence in this intimidating setting. She gropes for words when faced with the strong speakers and personalities from other royal representatives. They mock and jeer at her, calling for a removal of this "tongue-tied child" from Council. It isn't until the Dragomir family seal is pulled off the wall that she finds her courage—and her voice. She snatches the seal back. It's *hers*. Just like the seat on Council is *hers*. And no one has the right to take that away from her!

The Council room and members disappear and silence falls. Next she finds herself in the St. Vladimir medical examining room. Her spirit darkness has taken over, causing her to become a danger to herself and to others. They're threatening to lock her up in the criminally insane wing of the Tarasov Prison. Rose bravely volunteers to take all of Lissa's darkness and be driven mad in her place. But no—Lissa can't let her make such a sacrifice. She will accept this fate and be sent away in order to protect her best friend.

And that's when the dream ends, and with it, the test. Lissa has faced her fears and passed the test. She exits the room to the enthusiastic crowd shouting for the "dragon."

Happy her friend is doing so well, Rose drifts off to sleep and finds herself in a spirit dream of her own with Adrian. They're in a location picked by Rose's subconscious—Sonya's beautiful garden. When Rose accidentally lets it slip where they are, Adrian finally clues in that his girlfriend is not safely tucked away in the original motel, she's been on a mission to find a dangerous Strigoi with Victor Dashkov as one of her allies. Adrian's furious—staying at the motel was the only way to ensure Rose's safety. When she's anywhere else, she's putting her life at great risk. She assures Adrian that her quest is worth it, but she can't fill him in on the details . . . he just has to trust her. As the dream fades, she begs him not to say anything to the others. It'll just worry them.

In the morning, they finally arrive at the house Sonya has directed them to. The face that greets them is a familiar one. Rose is completely shocked to realize that the missing Dragomir is someone they've known all along—it's Jill Mastrano!

Jill's mother, Emily, is scared when she sees her cousin Sonya. After all, Sonya's supposed to be a *Strigoi*. It takes a bit of explaining before they're allowed in the house, especially since Rose is a wanted fugitive.

The gravity of the situation is not lost on Rose.

I'd rushed into this, ready to find Lissa's sibling—her sister, we now knew—with little thought of the implications. I should have known this would be a secret from everyone— including the child in question. I hadn't considered what a shock this would be to her. And this wasn't just some random stranger. This was Jill. Jill. My friend. The girl who was like a little sister to all of us, the one we looked out for. What was I about to do to her? —pages 378-379

The truth is hard to tell and even harder to take for Emily, who's tried to shield her daughter from anything royal for her entire life. But Jill, while young and fearful, understands what's at stake and wants to help. Finally, after much debate, Emily relents. Jill can go to Court. For now, the others are allowed to spend the night in the Mastrano home.

Meanwhile, Lissa's been sent word that Ambrose wants to talk. He's gone through Tatiana's belongings and stolen some documents from her safe, including a letter from someone chastising her for both the age law and for the secret group of royal Moroi she had arranged to practice defense. Tatiana definitely had enemies. The writer of this letter could be the murderer.

On their way back from this meeting, a man heads directly for Lissa—with a knife in his hand! Christian jerks her back as Eddie leaps to her defense and forces the guy to the ground. Even restrained, he's able to aim his blade for Eddie's neck. Eddie deflects the blow, but there's no doubt that this man is out to kill. Before the man can get a death blow in, Eddie takes his shot and stakes him.

Other guardians arrive and take one look at the scene—there's a dead Moroi and someone holding a bloody weapon. They throw Eddie against the wall and pry his weapon away. Lissa's shouts that he saved her life fall on deaf ears. Eddie has killed a Moroi. Guardians are supposed to *protect* them. *Killing* one is unimaginable.

A frantic Rose is brought back to her reality, desperate to help her friends at Court. Dimitri assures her all will be okay—Lissa is protected even without Rose by her side. The Dragomir they need to worry about is Jill. And Dimitri praises Rose for the single-minded determination she's shown thus far—it's only because of it that they were able to find Jill.

Rose wonders if Adrian, who was so angry with her in their last dream, will feel the same. The mention of her current boyfriend definitely spoils the mood.

> *"Do you love him?"*
>
> *There were only a few people in the world who could ask me such insanely personal questions without getting punched. Dimitri was one of them. With us, there were no walls, but our complicated relationship made this topic surreal. How could I describe loving someone else to a man I'd once loved?* A man you still love, *a voice whispered inside my head. Maybe. Probably. Again, I reminded myself that it was natural to carry lingering feelings for Dimitri. They would fade. They had to fade, just like his had. He was the past. Adrian was my future.*
>
> *"Yeah," I said, taking longer than I probably should have. "I . . . I do love him."*

page 403

Even though Rose has admitted she loves Adrian, it's impossible to ignore the connection between her and Dimitri. Being this close to him makes her dizzy. The attraction to each other hasn't vanished—if anything, this trip has only made it stronger.

"What?" I asked uneasily. "Why are you looking at me like that?"

He shook his head, the smile rueful now. "Because sometimes, a person can get so caught up in the details that they miss the whole. It's not just the dress or the hair. It's you. You're beautiful. So beautiful, it hurts me."   —*page 404*

Rose is reminded of how it was between them before Dimitri was turned Strigoi and everything went horribly wrong. Back when they were in the cabin in the woods . . . He'd looked at her the same way then, only with less sadness than there is now. He still thinks she's beautiful—the confirmation helps free all the feelings for him she'd locked away—and feels that sense of oneness they'd shared. It's as if they're bound . . . but not in the way Lissa and Rose were, by a bond forced on them.

The moment—and it was most *definitely* a moment—is broken by Sydney's appearance. The Alchemist would much rather hang out with the evil creatures upstairs that she knows than the ones downstairs that she doesn't.

But then, suddenly, guardians are raiding the house! Rose and Dimitri must escape or else they'll be killed, and in doing so they must leave everyone else behind. Rose only has enough time to shout at Sydney that she has to get Jill to Court before she and Dimitri jump out of the window to the ground below. Racing to get away from the gun-wielding guardians hot on their heels, Rose and Dimitri steal a car and finally manage to give their pursuers the slip. All their plans have fallen apart, but at least they're still alive.

Dimitri picks up some supplies, and he and Rose head to a campground to pitch a tent for the night. They each take turns keeping watch while the other sleeps. Rose sleeps first and is pulled into a spirit dream. And this is a first—it's with Sonya. She has some bad news to break to Rose. Everything that Rose worked for may have been for nothing—Victor and Robert took Jill from the house during the chaos earlier. Victor's always wanted power and control—well, now he's got a major bargaining chip in the form of a certain missing Dragomir. Sonya promises that she'll help Rose get Jill back. She is a spirit user, after all. She'll visit Jill in a dream and then from there determine her location.

Before the dream ends, Sonya comments on Rose and Dimitri's auras—since her powers are the same as Adrian's, she can also see them. She was surprised to hear Rose had another boyfriend, one who *wasn't* Dimitri. Sonya doesn't believe in soul mates, but she believes in souls being in sync—which is exactly what Rose and Dimitri's auras show.

She also warns of the darkness she sees in Rose's aura—Rose carries that dangerous darkness with her. One spark could be enough to make it explode.

Rose recounts the dream to Dimitri—minus the romantic soul-sync stuff. She's deeply disturbed that Victor has innocent Jill in his nasty clutches.

While Dimitri sleeps, Rose visits Lissa. She finds her with Eddie, as Hans questions them about the Moroi staking. Everyone sticks to the truth—Eddie protected her from an attack. There was something weird about the Moroi's hand—Lissa wonders if it's the same Moroi who paid off Joe the janitor to give false testimony about Rose.

Hans tells Lissa the latest—her pal Rose has kidnapped Jill Mastrano. This is a complete shock for Lissa. Last she heard, Rose was safely tucked away at the original motel. And what would Rose want with Jill? It doesn't make any sense.

Three Alchemists are brought into the room, including Sydney, who'd been taken into custody by the guardians who raided the Mastrano house. She denies she played any part in Rose's escape from Court. Still, the guardians aren't exactly convinced. The Alchemists will be kept under guardian surveillance at a hotel close to Court. As they're leaving, an Alchemist named Ian spots the picture of the bad-handed Moroi and seems to recognize who it is. Rose mentally logs this for later reference.

Eddie's detained, but Lissa needs to get to her last monarch test. This one is also presided over by Ekaterina. It's a question that Lissa will be given time to consider: *"What must a queen possess in order to truly rule her people?"*

Rose snaps back to the reality of the tent when she senses movement. It's Dimitri, who, in his sleep, has rolled up against her. The contact brings forth a flood of emotions she can't control. The smart thing to do would be to push him away. She doesn't. Instead, she pulls him closer.

His eyes opened, instantly alert. I expected him to jump

205

away from me, but instead, he only assessed the situation—
and didn't move. I left my hand where it was on the side of his
face, still stroking his hair. Our gazes locked, so much passing
between us. In those moments, I wasn't in a tent with him, on
the run from those who regarded us as villains. There was no
murderer to catch, no Strigoi trauma to overcome. There was
just him and me and the feelings that had burned between us
for so long. —page 446

They come close to kissing, but at the last second Dimitri pulls away from her, seemingly frustrated.

Sonya arrives. She knows where Jill is. They head as a group to the motel where Victor and Robert have her. As the three of them close in, Rose tries to talk about what happened in the tent. They almost kissed! How could he stop something like that? But he knows it would be wrong—he refuses to try to take Rose away from Adrian, a man she's admitted to loving. He's very focused on doing the right thing after being Strigoi. Stealing Rose from another man would be wrong.

Their conversation is cut short when the brothers exit the motel with Jill in tow. Rose doesn't wait for an invitation—she takes Victor down to the pavement hard.

> *"Well done," he gasped out.*
> *"I've been wanting to do that for a very long time," I growled.*
> *Victor smiled through the pain and the blood. "Of course you*
> *have. I used to think Belikov was the savage one, but it's re-*

206

Last Sacrifice

ally you, isn't it? You're the animal with no control, no higher reasoning except to fight and kill."   —page 454

Victor summons his earth magic to create a mini-earthquake centered around Rose. But it's not his magic that throws her off balance the most—it's his threats toward Jill and Lissa and his claims that he can control them both now.

At the thought of the Dragomirs being in danger, Rose loses it. That darkness Sonya saw in her aura overwhelms her and suddenly, Victor becomes the epitome of every evil in the world. She lashes out at him with violence and strength, slamming him into a concrete wall like the uncontrollable animal he just accused her of being.

The strength of the blow is enough to kill Victor Dashkov.

Robert is grief stricken, and Dimitri has to restrain him before he can try to work his spirit magic to bring his brother back to life. Meanwhile, Sonya directs Rose back to the car. She's a murderer now—stunned, distraught, and talking crazy. The darkness that has always been at the edges, waiting to destroy her, has taken over.

Sonya takes Jill's silver bracelet and charms it with healing magic to help Rose think a bit clearer. After disposing of Victor's body, they head toward a hotel, where they can gather themselves and prepare for the next day. It should be a momentous one: they plan to head to Court with Jill.

Trying to escape herself, Rose visits Lissa through the bond. Adrian has located Serena, Lissa's previous guardian. They want to question her about the secret Moroi training sessions—the ones mentioned in the threatening letter to the queen. She agrees to provide a list of names as soon as she can.

At the hotel, Sonya and Jill take a separate room so that Dimitri

207

can talk to Rose alone. It's a good thing too—Rose is destroyed over what she's done. Victor was a villain, a bad guy, but he wasn't really a threat to her. She murdered him without even a second thought. And her spirit darkness is no excuse.

Rose and Dimitri are the same now. He can't forgive himself for what he did when he was Strigoi—even though he couldn't control any of it—just like Rose couldn't control her darkness that led her to kill Victor. Rose knows they're the same. Sonya even confirmed it when she commented on their matching auras.

But it's more than that . . .

"She was right about something else too," Dimitri said after a long pause. My back was to him, but there was a strange quality to his voice that made me turn around.

"What's that?" I asked.

"That I do still love you."

With that one sentence, everything in the universe changed.

Time slowed to one heartbeat. The world became his eyes, his voice. This wasn't happening. It wasn't real. None of it could be real. It felt like a spirit dream. I resisted the urge to close my eyes and see if I'd wake up moments later. No. No matter how unbelievable it all seemed, this was no dream. This was real. This was life. This was flesh and blood.

"Since . . . since when?" I finally managed to speak.

"Since . . . forever."

—page 480

Dimitri's feelings have been repressed since he was restored—but in the alley, after Donovan, he could see Rose's goodness, her hope, her faith, and her beauty—inside and out. She's the most amazing woman he's ever met.

But Dimitri believes they can't be together. He knows she's moved on with Adrian. That she *loves* Adrian.

Yeah, he's right. She *does* love Adrian—she loves hanging around with him and having fun with him. Adrian's wonderful on so many levels. But Dimitri . . . well, he's the only one in the world who really *gets* her. And she's never, ever stopped loving him.

> *"I don't belong to anyone. I make my own choices."*
>
> *"And you're with Adrian," said Dimitri.*
>
> *"But I was meant for you."*
>
> *And that did it. Any pretense of control or reason either of us possessed melted away. The walls crumbled, and everything we'd been holding back from each other came rushing out. I reached up, pulling us together for a kiss—a kiss he didn't let go this time. A kiss I didn't end by punching him.* —*page 484*

It's enough to finally stop his protests. They can't deny their feelings for each other, feelings that overwhelm them as they give into their mutual passion. They were meant to be together.

But before they can truly be together, there are a couple of very important things standing in their way.

Adrian. Rose realizes what she's done. She's cheated on him. He deserves better than that because she does truly love him. He's amazing, but . . . he's not Dimitri. She needs to give Adrian the respect he deserves and let him go once and for all. The last thing she'd ever want to do is flaunt her feelings for Dimitri in front of him.

And also, before she and Dimitri can even think about having a real relationship, she has a single request: he needs to truly forgive himself. If he can't be happy with himself, he can't be happy with her.

When Rose falls asleep in Dimitri's arms, she's faced with something she didn't think she'd have to deal with yet—Adrian. Talk about unfortunate timing. She knows she can't break up with him in a dream, even when he comments that her aura is shinier than he's ever seen it before. He doesn't realize it's because of what's happened between her and Dimitri—and she can't exactly tell him. Um, *awkward*.

Rose tries to be all business. She asks Adrian to have Mikhail meet her at a restaurant near the Alchemists' hotel. She needs to get in to see Ian, to find out the identity of the Moroi he recognized in the photograph.

When the dream ends, she checks in with Lissa, who's on her way to complete the last of the monarch tests by answering the question. And she's deeply scared that she will answer incorrectly. On the way, Serena stops her to give her the list of Moroi defense trainees. A familiar name is among them—Daniella Ivashkov.

Lissa goes to face the former queen for her test and is tongue-tied when she's asked the question again: *"What must a queen possess in order to truly rule her people?"*

The answer finally comes to her. *"A queen must possess nothing to rule because she has to give everything she has to her people. Even her life."*

It's the right answer! Even so, Lissa confides that she can't become queen due to the rules of quorum. She's hoping that Ariana Szelsky will be elected. She's the only one from the remaining nominees who Lissa believes would make a great ruler.

Ekaterina breaks the bad news to Lissa: Ariana failed this test. She's out of the running.

ENDGAME

Rose, Dimitri, Sonya, and Jill must gather their things from the hotel and hurry to the restaurant to meet Mikhail. Rose finally has a prime suspect for the murder—and a quick visit to Lissa confirms that her friend is also putting the pieces together . . .

It's Daniella Ivashkov.

Adrian's mother had both the method and the means to kill the queen. She did it—Rose is *certain* of it—even though it breaks her heart to think what this will mean for Adrian when he learns his mother is a murderer.

Both Rose and Lissa believe that Daniella did it. Now they just have to prove it.

At the moment, Lissa needs to focus on giving her pre-election speech, which is taking place in the huge Royal Ballroom—there are so many people in the audience that it looks like a rock concert. Lissa will be speaking along with the remaining two other nominees—only three left from the original pool of twelve. When Lissa speaks about Moroi and dhampirs being one people and how they must work together for a strong future, she receives loud cheers.

But then the enthusiastic crowd receives some bitter news. Despite Lissa's popularity, she has no family and is therefore not allowed to win this election. The crowd goes crazy, and it's clear there will be no vote today. Order must first be restored.

Lissa is not eligible to be queen—but Rose and the others already knew this. This was supposed to simply be a diversion to buy them more time to find evidence to clear Rose's name.

And yet it's become so much more than that.

Rose listened in on Lissa's incredible speech with pride—and with every word her friend spoke, the truth became clearer and clearer to her. This was meant to be.

She would be queen.

I decided then and there that I would make it happen. We wouldn't bring Jill simply to give Lissa her Council vote. Jill would give Lissa the status that would allow Moroi to vote for her. And Lissa would win. —page 513

Rose, Dimitri, Sonya, and Jill arrive at the restaurant where Mikhail . . . and Adrian . . . are waiting for them. When Mikhail and Sonya see each other, she immediately runs into his arms. After three years being apart, they're still in love. Mikhail is desperately grateful to Rose and the others for making this reunion possible.

Before Rose leaves with Mikhail to sneak into the hotel where the Alchemists are being held so she can get more evidence to prove Daniella is the murderer, Dimitri tells her to be careful and kisses her forehead . . .

But once again, Adrian's timing is impeccable.

"Little dhampir, are you—"

Adrian came strolling around the car, just in time to see that small kiss. I dropped my hand from Dimitri's. None of us said anything, but in that moment, Adrian's eyes . . . well, I saw his whole world come crashing apart. I felt sicker than if a fleet of Strigoi were around. I felt worse than a Strigoi. Honor, I thought. For real: the guardians should have taught it. Because I hadn't learned it.

page 519

Talking to Adrian about this is her responsibility—but it's one that will have to wait until later. Her heart twisting from what just happened, Rose goes with Mikhail to the hotel and dons a magical disguise, courtesy of Sonya, to help her get past the guards to go see Sydney. Once they drop their disguises and the young Alchemist sees who has just barged into her room, she's hopeful that they're there to free her.

No, sorry. They're actually there to talk to Ian—he knows something important. And they need Sydney's help to get to him.

The other Alchemist clearly won't help a couple of dhampirs, but Rose thinks he'll help Sydney—it's clear to Rose that Ian has a crush on Sydney. If she asks him to talk, he'll talk.

Rose is right. When Sydney flirts—just a little bit—Ian caves. He confirms that he recognized the Moroi with the bad hand he'd seen in the photo during their earlier interrogation at Court. The Moroi was a hired bodyguard for a non-royal Moroi. The Moroi woman he describes, though, is definitely not Daniella—but it *is* someone else Rose knows *very* well.

Shocked by what she's learned, Rose returns with Mikhail to Dimitri, Jill, and Sonya—Adrian's still there too, but he's now keeping his distance from Rose—and compares notes on the real killer. The threatening letter likely *was* from Daniella. But she wasn't the one who killed the queen.

With Dimitri and Rose in magical disguises, they slip past Court security and into the ballroom, where chaos still reigns. Rose finds her father and asks him to take charge of this situation—especially when he realizes that it's his rebellious daughter who's broken back into Court. Abe grabs the microphone to get the crowd's attention so Rose can speak.

She wastes no time in introducing Jill—Eric Dragomir's illegitimate daughter.

It's a major surprise for the crowd, and there is a flurry of shouted commentary. One person's voice carries through the room to confirm that it's all true. It's Daniella Ivashkov. She knew all along. Eric had personally asked her to help keep this secret—and to help with certain tasks to facilitate this.

Pieces click in Rose's head—Daniella was the one responsible for having the files stolen from the Alchemists to cover up the existence of another Dragomir. But it's over now and Daniella knows it—the truth is out there, and one simple DNA test will prove that Jill is Eric's daughter.

Daniella turns on Rose, demanding to know who she is.

Rose faces the crowd before her—those all too willing to accuse her of a crime she didn't commit and toss her away. She wants to face them and let them all know that she's innocent.

She drops her disguise.

The crowd reacts with cries and screams, and guardians move in to capture her and Dimitri. Rose still has the microphone, and she announces to all who the real murderer is—and it's not her.

It's Tasha Ozera.

Christian's aunt springs to defend herself, shocked and hurt that Rose would make such an accusation. But the facts speak for themselves: Tasha hated the queen for the guardian age law and her refusal to let Moroi learn how to fight back against Strigoi. That the queen didn't *actually* feel this way would have been too little, too late. Tasha's hired Moroi bodyguard had a bad hand—it would have been impossible for him to stake the queen. Tasha did it herself.

Tasha's also been working hard to change the quorum so Lissa could become queen—having the new queen's confidence would have helped Tasha pass the laws she wanted. As far as her bodyguard attacking Lissa, Dimitri thinks that was supposed to have been a fake attack to throw off suspicion. Tasha seems crushed by Dimitri's accusations. She's still in love with him, which only adds to her motive. Having the murder pinned on Rose would mean she'd have another chance with him after Rose's execution.

When guardians move in to take Tasha into custody, she grabs Mia Rinaldi and holds a gun to her head, planning to use the girl as a hostage. But Mia's come a long way in her abilities to defend herself—and uses her powers to fight back.

Lissa fears that one of them is going to die and leaps forward in an attempt to compel Tasha to drop her weapon, but Tasha turns the gun on Lissa and fires.

Rose jumps in front of her friend, shielding Lissa with her own body, and is shot in the chest. Pain rips through her.

She escaped death once before. She doesn't think she'll escape this time—death has finally come to claim her . . .

Just before the light completely vanished, I saw Dimitri's

face join Lissa's. I wanted to smile. I decided then that if the
two people I loved most were safe, I could leave this world. The
dead could finally have me. And I'd fulfilled my purpose, right?
To protect? I'd done it. I'd saved Lissa, just like I'd sworn I'd
always do. I was dying in battle. —page 551

But Rose isn't meant to die today. She wakes up three days later
in a huge, luxurious bedroom with a canopied bed. And Dimitri
is by her side.

Since Court went into lockdown and Adrian and Lissa were
taken away and couldn't heal her, she healed *herself*—because she's
a fighter and because she has a very strong will to live.

Dimitri fills her in on what she's missed. Tasha was caught, and
Rose and Dimitri are clear of all charges. Rose is more than free—
she's a hero! And almost losing her made Dimitri realize that he
truly loves her and that she forgives him for being Strigoi—all this
time, he hasn't been certain. But now he is.

We kissed, lightly at first, and the sweetness of the moment
overpowered any pain I felt. The intensity had just barely
picked up when he pulled away.

"Hey, what gives?" I asked.

"You're still recovering," he chastised. "You might think
you're back to normal, but you aren't."

"This is normal for me. And you know, I thought with all
this freedom and self-discovery and expression of our love stuff

that we could finally stop with the whole Zen master wisdom and practical advice crap."

This got me an outright grin. "Roza, that's not going to happen. Take it or leave it."

I pressed a kiss to his lips. "If it means getting you, I'll take it."

pages 557–558

There's more good news. They've both received guardian status again . . . and Rose has officially been named Lissa's guardian! However, it brings up old worries. From the beginning, they didn't think they could be together because protecting Lissa got in the way. Dimitri had once told her that if he let himself love Rose, then he wouldn't throw himself in front of Lissa to protect her—he'd throw himself in front of *her*.

When Rose had been shot, she knew she wasn't the only one to move into the line of fire . . .

"You followed when I jumped in front of Lissa, didn't you? Who were you going for? Me or her?"

He studied me for several long seconds. He could have lied. He could have given the easy answer by saying he'd intended to push both of us out of the way—if that was even possible, which I didn't recall. But Dimitri didn't lie. "I don't know, Roza. I don't know."

I sighed. "This isn't going to be easy."

"It never is," he said, pulling me into his arms. I leaned

217

against his chest and closed my eyes. No, it wouldn't be easy, but it would be worth it. As long as we were together, it would be worth it. —page 560

When Lissa visits, Rose makes a stunning realization. She can feel her own happiness surging through her at the sight of her best friend . . . but she had absolutely no idea how Lissa felt.

The bond is gone.

It isn't just muted; there is literally nothing there. Rose is alone in her mind for the first time in years. How is this possible?

Lissa isn't certain, but she thinks she knows. The bond was created when Lissa brought Rose back from the dead with spirit—and it was spirit that kept them tied together all this time. But when Rose used her own strength—rather than spirit—to pull herself back from death, she freed herself from Lissa.

It's so surreal to Rose. Something like this is going to take *a lot* of time to process.

As she recovers from this news, she notices the lush room she's in. Lissa tells her it's palace housing.

Palace?

Lissa shares her other major news with Rose: she was elected queen. It's not something she ever wanted, but she's going to give it her all. She'll find a way to deal with the spirit darkness without burdening Rose with it. They still have a bond—one of love and loyalty. They'll still get through everything that awaits them together.

But it can't be all good news. Rose needs to deal with someone else who has hard questions for her—Adrian. When he comes to see her in private, he's clearly not happy and smells of cigarettes and alcohol. This *so* isn't going to go well.

Rose tries to apologize—she honestly did *want* things to work between her and Adrian. But Dimitri is the one she's meant to be with.

Adrian's pain over her betrayal is palpable. He isn't willing to let her off the hook. He reminds her of the path of destruction she's left behind—he's only one of her victims. That he thinks of himself as a victim and is unwilling to take control of his life is only another reason Rose knows they can't be together. He can't give up his destructive habits for someone else. It needs to be for himself.

When he leaves, Rose wonders sadly if she'll ever see him again.

THE FUTURE AWAITS

On the day of the coronation, a few familiar people are in attendance whom Rose makes a point of speaking to.

> *"Well, well, well," I said. "If it isn't the people responsible for unleashing Rose Hathaway on the world. You've got a lot to answer for."...*
>
> *"Don't blame us," said my mother. "We didn't blow up half of Court, steal a dozen cars, call out a murderer in the middle of a crowd, or get our teenage friend crowned queen."*
>
> *"Actually," said Abe, "I did blow up half of Court."*
>
> —*pages 586–587*

They're proud of their daughter, despite (or in Abe's case, be-

POP QUIZ:
Last Sacrifice

1. Why does Dimitri say he agreed to help Rose escape from Court and protect her while her friends stay behind to try to prove her innocence?
2. At which fast-food restaurant do Rose and Dimitri meet up with Sydney?
3. Who paid off Joe the janitor to help give Adrian his alibi the night of the queen's murder?
4. What do "Keepers" call Moroi who've abandoned the old ways in favor of the modern world?
5. What is the name of the Keeper who asks Rose to marry him?
6. Who are the three Moroi who nominate Lissa as a candidate for queen?
7. How many "monarch tests" are there to help weed out the competition?
8. What relation are Emily Mastrano and Sonya Karp?
9. Complete Dimitri's quote about Rose: "You're beautiful. So beautiful, it ___ me."
10. Who does Tasha grab as a hostage when she's accused of the queen's murder?

* For quiz answers, see p.299.

cause of) her extreme means of getting what she wants. However, Dimitri gets a very chilly reception from the two. Abe's got a few pressing questions for the man seven years older than his still-teenage daughter. But Dimitri's willing to take some heat in order to be with Rose. She's worth it.

They watch as Lissa is crowned Queen Vasilisa Sabina Rhea Dragomir, first of her name, and it's a glorious moment. While they no longer share the psychic bond, Rose tells Dimitri she knows exactly what Lissa would say to her right now.

"I think she'd ask, 'What have we gotten ourselves into?'"

"What's the answer?" His warmth was all around me, as was his love, and again, I felt that completeness. I had that missing piece of my world back. The soul that complemented

mine. My match. My equal. Not only that, I had my life back—my own life. I would protect Lissa, I would serve, but I was finally my own person.

"I don't know," I said, leaning against his chest. "But I think it's going to be good." —*page* 594

PART TWO:
THE WORLD OF VAMPIRE ACADEMY

Q&A WITH RICHELLE MEAD

WHO WAS YOUR FAVORITE CHARACTER TO WRITE AND WHY?

I loved writing Rose in this series. Of course, when you're writing in first person POV, it's easy to fall in love with your narrator. You almost have to, since you're in that person's head so much! But Rose is wonderfully complex, and that's a joy for any writer. She has a wry, witty outlook on the world that makes a nice contrast for the darkness that so often pops up in the series. She's not afraid to point out the ludicrous, and I had a lot of fun putting in her asides and observations. At the same time, behind this humor, Rose has a depth and vulnerability that I think really speak to a lot of people. She's larger than life in many ways, but at her heart, she shares the same kind of love and yearning we all do. Those qualities are what readers really love about her and are the reason I enjoyed writing her so much.

I'm amazed how, in all of my series, there are always a few side charac-ters that readers absolutely adore—to the extent that I start seeing fan clubs and T-shirts made up in honor of those characters! For the VA se-ries, Abe definitely wins the prize in this category. I get a lot of comments from readers who are excited to hear about his next wardrobe choice, be it scarves or fedoras. The more out-landish, the better! He's a great char-acter because most of his lines are completely absurd, but at the same time, you never doubt for an instant that he's pretty fierce when push comes to shove. One of my most memorable moments as a writer was being contacted by a reader from Saudi Arabia who was happy to see someone of Middle Eastern descent on the side of the good guys. This comment meant so much to me, es-pecially because despite all his lay-ers of intrigue and questionable mo-tives, we never doubt that Abe has a heart of gold.

CHAPTER 7

Characters

MAIN CHARACTERS

ROSEMARIE "ROSE" HATHAWAY

DHAMPIR | Novice guardian | AGE: 17 | HEIGHT: 5'7"
HAIR: Very dark brown | EYES: Brown
FAMILY: Janine Hathaway, mother; Ibrahim "Abe" Mazur, father
NICKNAMES: Roza, little dhampir, ghost girl

She had no idea what it was like to be filled with a love so strong that it made your chest ache—a love you could only feel and not express. Keeping love buried was a lot like keeping anger pent up, I'd learned. It just ate you up inside until you wanted to scream or kick something. —*Shadow Kiss, page 5*

With the beauty of a semi-exotic desert princess and the butt-kicking ability of a fierce warrior, half-human/half-vampire Rose Hathaway has been raised to believe that "they come first." They being the Moroi that dhampirs protect from evil Strigoi.

The one Moroi who Rose has always put first is her best

225

friend, Lissa, with whom she shares a one-sided bond. The bond was formed when Lissa used spirit to bring Rose back to life after she died in the same car accident that killed Lissa's parents and brother.

This act made Rose "shadow-kissed," allowing her to sense Lissa's thoughts and emotions and to see events through her eyes. Being shadow-kissed also gives Rose the ability to summon ghosts and sense the presence of Strigoi. In addition, it enables Rose to take some of Lissa's spirit darkness into herself—something that has serious consequences.

Two years after running away from St. Vladimir's in an attempt to keep Lissa safe, the girls are found and returned to the school. Even after missing two years of training, Rose is a natural when it comes to being a guardian, something that is clearly seen by Dimitri Belikov, a guardian and instructor at the school who is part of the initial Lissa-Rose rescue operation. He agrees to tutor Rose after she and Lissa are brought back to the Academy.

The sarcastic, quick-witted, and extremely stubborn Rose falls hard for Dimitri. Even though Dimitri's her older mentor and a relationship between the two is prohibited, they're drawn to each other, and it's not long before they begin a roller coaster of a forbidden romance. When a future with Dimitri seems impossible, Rose is also briefly romantically involved with Mason, a friend who is murdered by Strigoi, and later Adrian, a Moroi royal.

Rose has a strained relationship with her mother, Janine, a famed guardian who Rose feels abandoned her in favor of pursuing her own career goals. Over time, Rose and Janine slowly become closer and more understanding of each other. At eighteen, Rose finally meets her father, Abe Mazur, a Turkish Moroi who, despite not being royal, is powerful, influential, extremely dangerous, and fiercely protective of his equally dangerous daughter.

When Dimitri is turned into a Strigoi, Rose travels to Russia to find and kill him, just as she had promised. Ultimately, however, she fails, having missed his heart at the time of staking him. This turns out to be a good thing when she discovers that it's possible to restore Strigoi to their former life. Rose breaks laws and hearts in her single-minded quest to bring Dimitri back to her. She finally succeeds in restoring him to a dhampir with Lissa's spirit-infused help.

Rose puts "they come first" to the ultimate test when she saves Lissa's life as Tasha Ozera, just accused of the murder of Queen Tatiana, turns her gun on the Dragomir princess. Rose throws herself in front of her friend and ends up getting shot instead. Because she uses her own healing abilities this time, rather than the magic of her friend, Rose permanently loses her psychic bond with Lissa—bittersweet since the girls are happy with their newfound privacy from each other but sad to lose the closeness of their unusual and often helpful connection.

While her questionable and risky—but well-intentioned—decisions have left a great deal of damage in her wake, Rose gets what she most wanted in the end—the chance to be Lissa's official guardian and the love and devotion of Dimitri.

VASILISA "LISSA" SABINA RHEA DRAGOMIR

MOROI ROYAL I ELEMENT: Spirit I AGE: 17
HAIR: Pale blond I EYES: Jade green
FAMILY: Rhea Daniels, mother; Eric Dragomir, father; Andre,
brother; Frederick, grandfather (all deceased); Jill, half-sister

Those fangs contrasted oddly with the rest of her features. With her pretty face and pale blond hair, she looked more like an angel than a vampire. —*Vampire Academy, page 3*

A Moroi royal, Lissa is the last of the Dragomir line. A car accident tragically took the lives of her parents and brother, and she relies on her best friend, novice guardian Rose, to keep her safe in a dangerous world. Lissa comes to realize that she wields "spirit," a mysterious fifth element that allows her to heal injuries and use very strong compulsion.

When Lissa uses too much spirit, she's taken over by darkness, which manifests itself in anger and insanity. Fortunately, Rose is there to help her through this by taking away some of that darkness through their bond. Christian, a school outcast whom Lissa finds herself romantically drawn to, also lends his support. Adrian, another spirit user, helps Lissa get a handle on her ability and keep it from overwhelming her.

Lissa is naturally kind and generous and has a warm heart. If Rose is the risk taker, Lissa tries to stay cautious—to a point. She discovers that she holds the key to restoring a Strigoi to life—all it takes is a spirit-charmed silver stake wielded by a spirit user. She learns how to fight and use a stake, so she can help restore Dimitri to his former self, something viewed by others as a saint-like miracle.

When trying to buy time to find Queen Tatiana's real killer, Lissa surprisingly finds herself a candidate to become the next queen. As the last Dragomir, she doesn't fulfill the requirements of having a family and being eligible for votes, but when her half-sister, Jill, is discovered, Lissa is officially in the running and ultimately elected as the new Moroi queen.

DIMITRI BELIKOV

DHAMPIR | Guardian | AGE: 24 | HEIGHT: 6'7"
HAIR: Brown, shoulder length | EYES: Dark brown
NICKNAMES: Dimka, Comrade
FAMILY: Olena, mother; Karolina, Sonja and Viktoria, sisters; Paul, nephew; Zoya, niece; Yeva, grandmother

And then, suddenly, he was there, charging down the hallway like Death in a cowboy duster. — *Vampire Academy, page 322*

Well known among guardians and novices alike as a badass "god," tall, dark, and gorgeous Russian-born Dimitri prefers to keep to himself, read western novels, and listen to bad eighties music. Some might call him "antisocial," but it's more that he's fiercely private, highly dedicated to his job, and doesn't easily trust others. Raised in a dhampir commune in Baia, Siberia, Dimitri beat up his abusive Moroi father at age thirteen in order to protect his mother.

He graduated top of his class and became a guardian for his friend, a Moroi lord, who was killed when Dimitri wasn't on watch. Dimitri was then sent to St. Vladimir's and became part of the team to find runaways Rose and Lissa and bring them back to the school. He sees potential in Rose and starts to give her extra training sessions to help her catch up on what she's missed. She's seven years younger than he is and still underage, so he fights hard against the attraction he feels for her—but it's a losing battle.

Shortly after Rose and Dimitri finally admit and consummate their love, there's a Strigoi attack, and Dimitri is bitten and turned into an evil Strigoi. Dimitri heads to Russia to put some distance between him and Rose, but when she tracks him down, he kidnaps and imprisons her. She's there to fulfill a promise they made to kill each other if they were turned Strigoi, but since being "awakened," Dimitri has had a change of heart. Now he wants to turn Rose into a Strigoi too, so they can be together forever. She manages to escape after unsuccessfully staking him, but, now obsessed with Rose, Dimitri begins to stalk her.

Dimitri is restored to his former dhampir self when Lissa stakes him with a spirit-charmed silver stake, but he is racked by guilt over what he did as a Strigoi. It's only thanks to Rose's stubbornness and love that he pulls through and is able to look toward a bright future together with his Roza.

CHRISTIAN OZERA

MOROI ROYAL I ELEMENT: Fire I Age: 17
HAIR: Black and messy I EYES: Ice blue
FAMILY: Lucas, father; Moira, mother (both deceased); Tasha, aunt

"Don't worry," he said. *"I won't bite. Well, at least not in the way you're afraid of."* He chuckled at his own joke.

—*Vampire Academy, page 58*

Christian is forced to live in the shadow cast by his parents' decision to become Strigoi, something that makes him a major social

Q&A WITH RICHELLE MEAD

HOW DID YOU FEEL ABOUT THE PASSIONATE RESPONSE OF FANS TO THE LOVE TRIANGLE? WHAT DO YOU THINK DIFFERENTIATES TEAM DIMITRI FROM TEAM ADRIAN?

It was a surprise to me how early and how passionately readers began to divide themselves up between Dimitri and Adrian! Even before Adrian was a serious contender for Rose's heart in the series, he already had a faithful following. It's really hard to say for sure what makes readers pick one guy over the other. Dimitri (aside from when he's passing time as an evil vampire) shines as the choice for those who love strong, dependable men. You know he's always going to be around for Rose, and he dominates any situation he walks into. Even when he's a Strigoi, he's still a badass! On the other hand, I think the Adrian fans love his flippant, easy-going nature. Adrian knows how to turn on the romance and charm, and we occasionally get glimpses that maybe—just maybe—he's not the slacker party boy he so often portrays. Every once in a while, I'll see someone come to a signing with a "Team Mason" shirt. They're so sweet, but I always feel a little sad because that's one romantic choice I can say with certainty is out of the running!

outcast at St. Vladimir's. Most people are wary he'll make the same choice one day. And while they're actually quite wrong about him, he's not exactly going to be all warm and fuzzy if they're not willing to do the same. Now he likes to wear all black and views the world around him with a wry and snarky outlook.

When Lissa finds Christian's private hideaway in the chapel attic, he tentatively agrees to share it, sparking an attraction between the two that quickly turns to love.

Christian believes Moroi should learn to use their powers defensively against Strigoi. He stands by these words when he uses his fire magic to help his friends escape from the Strigoi in Spokane and later fights side by side with Rose during the attack at the school.

While strong defensively, he constantly questions Lissa's commitment to him and his worthiness as the princess's boyfriend. He is quick to jealousy and self-doubt but is a true hero at heart.

ADRIAN IVASHKOV

MOROI ROYAL I ELEMENT: Spirit I AGE: 21 I HAIR: Sable brown, stylishly messy I EYES: Dark emerald green
VICES: Smoking and drinking
FAMILY: Nathan, father; Daniella, mother; Tatiana, great-aunt

"Dreams, dreams. I walk them; I live them. I delude myself with them. It's a wonder I can spot reality anymore." The weird sound of his voice made me nervous. I could recognize one of his slightly crazy, spirit-induced lapses. Then he turned from me with a sigh. "I need a drink." —*Spirit Bound, page 157*

Adrian has a reputation. He's rich, charming, and good-looking—with a bad-boy streak. It's a lethal combination. That he has a good heart underneath it all is definitely his saving grace.

He drinks and smokes a lot and is usually in some state of inebriation. This self-medication is his primary method of dealing with the dangerous side effects of spirit, the element he wields. Adrian and Lissa work together to learn the secrets of the powerful magic they share. But because of his use of spirit, Adrian has moments of madness, sometimes babbling incoherently before he gets himself together. On the surface, he's fine and breezy. Inside, he's desperately afraid he's going insane.

While he has no problem with girls wanting him, he decides that *he* wants Rose—and not just for a fling, for real. He pursues her, even in her dreams, and finally convinces her to give him a chance, though not until after Dimitri turns Strigoi. But Rose and Adrian's romance is to be short-lived. Try as she might, Rose can never fully return his affections—her heart belongs to Dimitri. And Adrian's left angry and hurt when she cheats on him with Dimitri after her true love is restored to life as a dhampir.

Still, despite her betrayal, Rose assures Adrian that he has the potential to be a true hero someday. He's not quite as convinced.

MASON ASHFORD

DHAMPIR | Novice guardian | AGE: 17 | HAIR: Red | EYES: Blue

To my annoyance, he laughed. "How do you not know where the heart is? Especially considering how many of them you've broken." — *Frostbite, page 46*

Rose's good friend Mason harbors a not-so-secret crush on the beautiful dhampir. While she thinks he's cute and one of the funniest guys she knows, she doesn't exactly reciprocate his romantic interest. However, she decides to give him a chance during the school's trip to the ski lodge. He'd definitely be good boyfriend material, and she's still stinging from the thought that Dimitri might be leaving the school (and her) to be with Tasha.

It becomes clear fairly soon that since her heart is elsewhere, it would be better if they were just friends. But before Rose can break things off with him, she realizes that the reckless, risk-seeking Mason has taken off to hunt Strigoi with Eddie and Mia.

Rose goes after them, concerned for her friends, but shortly after she finds them, the group is kidnapped by Strigoi. She and Mason work together to escape, but when Mason returns to save her from the clutches of a Strigoi, it grabs him and breaks his neck, killing him instantly.

Mason's sad and restless spirit returns to St. Vladimir's, sending the already grief-stricken Rose into a panic. At first, Rose can't figure out why Mason is back or if he's even really there at all. Part of her suspects that maybe she's just seeing things . . . It could be that her guilt over Mason's death is causing her to have visions or that Lissa's spirit darkness is beginning to overwhelm her. Eventually, Rose realizes that Mason is truly visiting her. On several occasions, he even tries to get a message across, but it's difficult for him. When he finally is able to say a few words (*"They're . . . coming . . ."*), they're enough to warn Rose that the wards around the school have been tampered with, allowing Strigoi to pass over them and attack.

Just before Mason's finally able to move on from this world and find peace, he confirms to Rose that Dimitri has been turned into a Strigoi.

EDISON "EDDIE" CASTILE

DHAMPIR | Novice guardian | AGE: 17
HAIR: Sandy blond, messy | EYES: Hazel

"This is . . . well, it's something that could ruin everything for you. Get you in big trouble. I can't do that to you."

That half smile vanished. "It doesn't matter," he said fiercely.

"If you need me, I'll do it. No matter what it is."

—*Spirit Bound, page 104*

Best friends with Mason, Eddie is a friendly and funny dhampir who is training to become a guardian at St. Vlad's. But things begin to change for him when he goes with Mia and Mason to hunt Strigoi in Spokane. After they're kidnapped, he's repeatedly fed on by a Strigoi. He becomes dazed and weakened from the endorphins and loss of blood. When Mason is killed, Eddie feels a great deal of blame for not being able to save his friend. He never fully recovers from this tragedy.

Eddie is also one of the kidnapped victims taken during the Strigoi attack on the school but is later rescued from the caves. His harsh experiences make him a very serious and determined guardian and a loyal friend who will help Rose without question. When asked, he goes with her and Lissa to break Victor Dashkov out of prison in Alaska. He then continues with them on their quest to Vegas to find Robert Doru, only later becoming angry when he realizes the reason behind it all is to try to save Dimitri. To Eddie, Strigoi are supposed to be killed, not saved.

Regardless, Eddie's first impulse is to protect his friends, so when an attempt is made on Lissa's life at Court, Eddie ends up staking the person responsible. But because the individual in question is a Moroi, not a Strigoi, he finds himself in very hot water.

JANINE HATHAWAY

DHAMPIR I Guardian I AGE: 37 I I HEIGHT: 5' I
HAIR: Cropped, curly auburn I EYES: Brown I FAMILY: Rose,
daughter

"So, what?" I asked. "This is your way of making up for maternal negligence?"

"This is my way of making you get rid of that chip on your shoulder. You've had nothing but attitude for me since I arrived. You want to fight?" Her fist shot out and connected with my arm. "Then we'll fight." — *Frostbite, pages 79–80*

A guardian with a stellar reputation, the Scottish-born Janine is dwarfed by most dhampirs but holds her own in a fight and has the *molnija* marks to prove it. While she has excelled at being a guardian, she hasn't always been the best mother. And Rose feels a great deal of resentment toward the woman she feels abandoned her to the Academy's care and only gave birth to her in the first place in order to help replenish the well of potential guardians.

While she might not be winning any "Mother of the Year" competitions, Janine feels great affection for her daughter, and their relationship begins to improve after Rose returns to St. Vladimir's. There is strong evidence that Janine didn't just have a child to further the dhampir race but that she was actually in love with Abe at the time of Rose's conception. For Christmas, Janine gives Rose a gift that was once given to her by Abe—a *nazar*, an eye-like pendant meant to protect anyone who wears it.

IBRAHIM "ABE" MAZUR

MOROI | NICKNAME: Zmey (the serpent) | AGE: 40ish
HAIR: Black; goatee | FAMILY: Rose, daughter

"Ah, my daughter," he said. "Eighteen, and already you've been accused of murder, aided felons, and acquired a death count higher than most guardians will ever see." He paused. "I couldn't be prouder." — *Last Sacrifice, page 64*

Powerful and wealthy but non-royal, Turkish-born Abe meets Rose during her trip to Siberia to find and kill Dimitri. Although Rose doesn't immediately recognize Abe as her father, he tries to convince her to return to the States, where she will be safe. His nickname is *Zmey*, the serpent, and despite the flamboyant way he dresses, with colorful scarves and gold earrings, he seems like the kind of guy who breaks kneecaps of the people who cross him.

Even though Abe succeeds in scaring Rose, everything he does—even the extreme stuff like issuing veiled threats and later blackmailing Rose by agreeing to help Dimitri's troubled sister only if Rose agrees to leave Russia—is in her best interest. It isn't until Rose's return to the Academy that she comes to the stunning realization that Abe is her father.

When Rose is accused of Queen Tatiana's murder, Abe acts as her lawyer—despite not actually *being* a lawyer—and he promises her that she'll never stand trial for this crime. And he's right about that. He masterminds Rose's breakout—explosions and all.

JILLIAN "JILL" MASTRANO DRAGOMIR

MOROI | ELEMENT: Water | AGE: 14
HAIR: Long, light brown curls | EYES: Jade green
NICKNAME: Jailbait FAMILY: Emily Mastrano, mother; Eric
Dragomir, father; Lissa Dragomir, half-sister

"I knew it! I can't even imagine that—I'd be freaking out all

the time around him. I'd never get anything done, but you're so

cool about it all, kind of like, 'Yeah, I'm with this totally hot guy,

but whatever, it doesn't matter.'" —Jill, impressed by Rose's

teacher–student relationship with Dimitri

—*Shadow Kiss, page 126*

Jill is an awkward Moroi teen in ninth grade at St. Vlad's when she first meets the infamous Rose. At Rose's suggestion, she starts learning defensive magic with Christian and gets to occasionally hang out with his super-cool friends, including Adrian, on whom she quickly develops a big crush. Lissa reluctantly brings Jill along to Court so she can meet Mia, a fellow water user.

When Rose's search for Eric Dragomir's illegitimate child leads her directly to Jill, she suddenly becomes much more than a tall, skinny teenager—she becomes incredibly important to the future of the Moroi race. It takes some convincing for Jill to accompany the others to Court to help gain Lissa the family standing she needs for a vote on Council, but she ultimately agrees to go because she knows it's the right thing to do. Jill joining Rose and her friends proves to be more important than anyone could have guessed—it also gives Lissa the opportunity to be voted in as the new queen.

Jill's safety is now a priority. If anything happens to Lissa's half-sister, the young queen's position is at grave risk by those who might wish to see her removed from the throne.

Talk about being critical to the future of the Moroi race.

SYDNEY SAGE

HUMAN ALCHEMIST I AGE: 18 I HAIR: Dark blond
EYES: Brown I DEFINING FEATURE: Gold tattoo of flowers
and leaves on her lower left cheek

P.P.S. Just because I like you, it doesn't mean I still don't think you're an evil creature of the night. You are.

—From Sydney's goodbye letter to Rose

— Blood Promise, page 168

Sydney, an Alchemist who speaks five languages, works hard to keep the existence of Moroi and dhampirs hidden from the rest of the world. The tattoo on her cheek—made from gold ink, Moroi blood, and elemental magic—has given her good health and a long life, but it also prevents her from revealing the secrets of her job to those who are not part of the vampire world.

While interning in Russia, Sydney meets Rose and assists her in finding the village of Baia. While Sydney is strictly religious and believes vampires—*including* dhampirs—are evil creatures of the night, she forms a strong friendship with Rose.

After making a mysterious deal with Abe, Sydney gets transferred to New Orleans but is required to help hide Rose when she's accused of murder. She accompanies Rose and Dimitri on the search for the missing Dragomir—Jill. Little does Sydney know, Jill will play a key role in her future . . .

NATASHA "TASHA" OZERA

MOROI ROYAL I ELEMENT: Fire I AGE: Early 30s
HAIR: Jet black I EYES: Pale blue
DEFINING FEATURE: Scarring on one side of her face
FAMILY: Christian Ozera, nephew

"We run and hide behind the dhampirs and let the Strigoi go unchecked. It's our fault. We are the reason those Drozdovs died. You want an army? Well, here we are. Dhampirs aren't the only ones who can learn to fight." — *Frostbite, page 169*

Tasha protected her nephew Christian from his Strigoi parents so that he could live a full life as a Moroi. But she was scarred in the process—emotionally and physically—which drove her to become a fighter. She now teaches martial arts, which is a very unusual occupation for normally peaceful, passive Moroi.

Tasha is romantically interested in Dimitri and wants him to become both her official guardian and the father of her children— a rare choice for a Moroi woman, who typically will only want to have purebred Moroi children. But he turns her down because he's in love with someone else.

Tasha works very hard to try to make the queen and other Moroi see that fighting defensively against Strigoi is the best solution for the continued survival of the Moroi race, but she's met with great opposition, especially when she suggests that Moroi learn to harness their elemental magic. She comes out strongly against the queen's age decree and argues for change at all levels.

Tasha is ultimately revealed to be Queen Tatiana's murderer and to have framed Rose as the prime suspect. Tasha isn't evil per se; she committed these heinous crimes out of anger over the queen's politics and figured that with Rose out of the way, she'd be able to win Dimitri back. All she ends up winning is an arrest for high treason.

VICTOR DASHKOV

MOROI ROYAL | ELEMENT: Earth | AGE: Early 40s
HAIR: Thin and graying before being healed, thick and black afterward | EYES: Jade green

"The greatest and most powerful revolutions often start very

quietly, hidden in the shadows." He eyed me. "Remember that."

—Vampire Academy, page 318

Victor Dashkov was next in line to the throne before he became ill with Sandovsky's syndrome. Now, instead of being in the running for king, he's headed toward death, thanks to the debilitating disease.

But Victor isn't one to simply succumb to the hand fate dealt him. He kidnaps Lissa—a girl who has been like family to him—and has her tortured until she finally agrees to use spirit to heal him. Victor knows that Rose will be on high alert the second she senses that Lissa's in trouble, so he devises yet another twisted plan. He gives Rose a lust charm that heightens the desire between her and Dimitri, thereby distracting them from everything but their intense passion. Fortunately, Victor's attempts prove to be in vain—Rose and the other guardians rescue Lissa just in time. Later, Victor uses this episode to taunt Rose and Dimitri about their forbidden romance.

When Victor's captured and imprisoned, he convinces his daughter Natalie to turn Strigoi to help in his rescue. Much later, it becomes evident he did this believing that she could be restored to her previous Moroi self—but it was a risky gamble that didn't pay off when the dangerous Natalie is killed.

A few months after being found guilty and sentenced to life in Tarasov Prison, Rose and Lissa break him out of jail. They're desperate to learn the secrets of restoring a Strigoi to life, and they've been told that Victor's half-brother, Robert Doru, has prior experience in this area. Victor takes them to his brother, who does indeed tell the girls his secrets.

But Victor's turnaround isn't exactly long-lasting. He's protective of his brother Robert, who's half-mad and very weakened from his own use of spirit, and escapes with him at the first opportunity.

After appearing to Rose in several spirit dreams, Victor and his brother join her search to find the missing Dragomir. But again, Victor double-crosses them. He kidnaps Jill, wanting to use Lissa's half-sister to gain power over Lissa. Unfortunately for him, he doesn't make it too far this time. In a moment of spirit-darkness rage, Rose kills Victor to protect the Dragomirs.

OTHER CHARACTERS

NATALIE DASHKOV (MOROI)

Unpopular Natalie becomes Lissa's roommate when the girls return to school for the first time. Natalie shies away from the social scene at St. Vladimir's and is seemingly naive and innocent. But she also has some tricks up her sleeve . . . Just like her father, Victor Dashkov, Natalie specializes in earth magic. She helps her father plant dead animals to test Lissa's use of spirit. Ultimately, Natalie chooses to become an evil Strigoi to help rescue her father. Natalie doesn't last long as a Strigoi, however—she's quickly staked by Dimitri.

MIA RINALDI (MOROI)

A former sexual conquest of Lissa's deceased brother, Andre, the very young-looking, blond Mia hates Lissa on sight and sets out to destroy her and Rose at school. She's now dating Aaron, Lissa's ex, and will stop at nothing to get revenge—going so far as to sleep with both Jesse and Ralf to get them to help ruin Rose's reputation. Lissa fights back, using compulsion and charm to get back in the popular royal clique's good graces. She encourages them to shun the non-royal Mia and even goes so far as to steal Aaron back, leaving Mia socially destroyed and with a broken nose (courtesy of Rose).

After Strigoi kill her mother, Mia comes to build a grudging friendship with both Lissa and Rose. She's part of the kidnapping by Strigoi in Spokane because the grief-driven Mia accompanies Mason and Eddie to hunt the Strigoi responsible for her mother's death. Ultimately, Mia saves Rose's life using her water magic. After they escape and return to St. Vlad's, she leaves school for good to live with her father at Court. There, she secretly trains in self-defense with some guardian friends she's made.

AARON DROZDOV (MOROI)

Aaron is Lissa's popular and gorgeous but fairly boring ex-boyfriend. He gets another chance to date the princess during her attempt to get back into the royal students' clique and destroy Mia's social standing. But Lissa ends up dumping Aaron—again—for the guy she really likes, Christian. Later, a meaningless, drunken kiss between Lissa and Aaron at Court will cause big problems between her and Christian—now that they're dating.

JESSE ZEKLOS (MOROI)

A really hot Moroi royal, with bronze-colored hair and dark blue eyes, Jesse gets in trouble with Dimitri when the guardian catches him fooling around with Rose. Later, he becomes part of Mia's plan to destroy Rose's reputation by spreading the rumor that she's a blood whore. Jesse proves that he's truly an elitist jerk when he helps form the *Mânǎ*, a group of Moroi students who want to use compulsion to get whatever they want. When this leads to Lissa's forcible initiation—more like torture—Lissa uses super-compulsion to torture him back, after which he is almost beaten to death by a magically enraged Rose. Lissa manages to heal his injuries—whether he deserves it or not.

RALF SARCOZY (MOROI)

Jesse's best friend and part of Mia's original plan to destroy Rose's reputation, fire-user Ralf is only royal on his mother's Conta side. He's a bully, evidenced by his participation in the *Mânǎ*.

CAMILLE CONTA (MOROI)

Prim, beautiful, and perfectly groomed, Camille is the self-appointed leader of the Academy's royal Moroi cliques and was close friends with Lissa before she and Rose ran away.

ABBY BADICA (MOROI)

Abby is a St. Vlad's student with a lot of bad luck. Not only is she abused in the *Mână* initiation tests—her bruises become one of Rose's first clues that something nasty is going on at St. Vlad's—but she's also unfortunate enough to be kidnapped by Strigoi during their attack on the school. Luckily, she's successfully rescued from the caves.

ST. VLADIMIR (MOROI)

St. Vladimir, the fourteenth-century patron saint of the Academy, used his spirit magic for good, healing the sick and helping crops to grow. Although he suffered greatly from depression and madness caused by his use of spirit, with help from his bondmate, Anna, he lived to a very old age and died of natural causes.

ANNA (DHAMPIR)

After St. Vladimir brought her back to life as a child, Anna became his shadow-kissed guardian and was always with him to defend him from Strigoi. She also helped take Vladimir's darkness and madness away, absorbing it into herself, which led her to commit suicide shortly after his death.

ALBERTA PETROV (DHAMPIR)

In her fifties but wiry and tough, Alberta is the captain of St. Vladimir's guardians and wears a pixie cut to show off her promise and *molnija* marks.

SONYA KARP (MOROI)

A pretty Moroi teacher in her early thirties, students called her "Crazy Karp" when her use of spirit triggered deep instability. To escape her madness, she made a desperate choice—to become a Strigoi. She was then hunted by her lover, Mikhail Tanner, who never found her. When Rose and Dimitri locate her on their quest to find the lost Dragomir, she is restored to her former Moroi self by Robert Doru's spirit magic and gratefully reunited with Mikhail.

MIKHAIL TANNER (DHAMPIR)

A dedicated and serious guardian, Mikhail left everything behind for a year to hunt down his former lover, Sonya, who had become Strigoi. Returning to the Moroi world, he faced his punishment for defying orders by being given a glorified desk job at the Moroi Royal Court. When he learns of the possibility of restoring a Strigoi to life, Mikhail goes out of his way to help Rose find the answers she seeks and is ultimately reunited with his true love.

FATHER ANDREW (MOROI)

The priest at the Academy's Russian Orthodox chapel, Father Andrew is a wealth of information to Rose when it comes to finding out more about the mysterious St. Vladimir.

HEADMISTRESS ELLEN KIROVA (MOROI)

Tall and slim Kirova—who reminds Rose of a vulture—runs the school with a strict but fair hand. Rose spends a lot of time in the headmistress's office.

QUEEN TATIANA MARINA IVASHKOV (MOROI)

Moroi queen and great-aunt to Adrian, Tatiana holds very strongly to tradition. While it appears that she made some very harsh decisions, including lowering the graduation age from eighteen to sixteen, she did the best she could to keep the situation from worsening. While putting on a regal and prickly front, she was more open-minded about change than she let on—when it came to the survival of her race. She even chose to have a group of elite Moroi royals secretly trained in defense. Queen Tatiana is murdered by Tasha Ozera, who strongly opposed her political views, but before the queen's death she composed a letter to Rose—the only one she trusted with the information that Eric Dragomir had an illegitimate child who, if found, would give Lissa quorum and allow her to have a council vote.

246

DANIELLA IVASHKOV (MOROI)

With a strong sense of Moroi etiquette, Adrian's mother likes to stick strictly to the social norms lest her family be judged harshly by others. She gives permission for Rose and Adrian to date, if only because she knows it won't lead to a long-term relationship. She pays off a janitor to give false testimony about her son's whereabouts at the time of the queen's murder so he won't be implicated alongside Rose. Unbeknownst to everyone, Daniella is part of the queen's secret Moroi defense training sessions and is also having an illicit affair with the queen's lover, Ambrose. It's because of these actions that she becomes one of the prime suspects in the murder of Queen Tatiana.

NATHAN IVASHKOV (MOROI)

With a deeply judgmental and snobbish air about him, Lord Ivashkov isn't exactly the friendliest guy around. He disapproves of his son Adrian's seemingly lazy and disinterested behavior and refuses to welcome his son's lowly dhampir girlfriend, Rose, into his life. He would likely be even less welcoming to his wife's blood-whore boyfriend if he actually knew about his existence.

AMBROSE (DHAMPIR)

An extremely attractive dhampir in his early twenties, Ambrose works as a masseur at the Royal Court and is Queen Tatiana's secret lover and blood whore. While he has other lovers on the side, including Daniella Ivashkov, he cares deeply for Tatiana and, after her death, helps deliver a message from the queen to Rose.

RHONDA (MOROI)

Ambrose's forty-something Roma aunt (Dimitri calls her a *vrăjitoare*, Romanian for something similar to "witch"), Rhonda works at Court telling fortunes to those who want a glimpse at their futures. Her insightful predictions come true more often than not, and because of this, Lissa guesses she might be a spirit user. Turns out she isn't. Rhonda actually specializes in air magic.

AVERY LAZAR (MOROI)

The very beautiful Avery graduated from her high school last year but is forced to join her father at St. Vladimir's to help assist him in his duties as headmaster. She's soon befriended by Lissa and is the catalyst for a lot of bad behavior on the latter's part, including Lissa's becoming a shallow party girl, which ends up causing Lissa's breakup with Christian.

Avery is actually a spirit user who is manipulating everyone as part of her quest for power. She'll stop at nothing to get what she wants and even stoops to using compulsion on Adrian so he'll become romantically interested in her. Her ultimate goal is to kill Lissa and bring her back to life, therefore binding them together and strengthening her power.

Avery is already bound to both Reed, her brother, and Simon, her guardian. During a surge of spirit magic, all three bondmates' minds are fried. All are currently in mental institutions.

— THE BELIKOV FAMILY (DHAMPIR) —

OLENA

Living in a dhampir commune in a Siberian town called Baia, Dimitri's mother has had medical training and has a reputation among her peers for healing.

KAROLINA

Dimitri's eldest sister, Karolina, has a baby girl named Zoya and a ten-year-old son named Paul.

SONJA

Dimitri's sister Sonja is currently pregnant with the child of a scummy Moroi named Rolan who, unbeknownst to everyone, is currently romancing Viktoria.

VIKTORIA

Dimitri's youngest sister, Viktoria, is madly in love with Rolan but too naive to see that he is using her as a blood whore just as he used her sister Sonja. To help protect her, Rose makes a deal with Abe to scare the Moroi off but is given no thanks by an angry and heartbroken Viktoria.

YEVA

Yeva is Dimitri's grandmother and a former guardian who chose to quit to raise her family and read tarot cards to make a living. While very old and thin, standing barely five feet tall, she's sharp and alert. Yeva had a prophetic dream of Rose's visit prior to her arrival and urges her to continue her hunt for the Strigoi version of Dimitri. Despite speaking Russian most of the time, Yeva prefers to hide the fact that she is also fluent in English.

OKSANA (MOROI)

A spirit user Rose meets in Baia, Oksana helps Rose learn more about the element, teaching her that silver can be charmed with healing magic and helping her to connect psychically with Lissa and thereby defeat Avery. She is also the one to first mention the "fairy tale" of a Moroi rumored to have brought a Strigoi back to life.

MARK (DHAMPIR)

Oksana's much older husband (it's very unusual to find a married Moroi-dhampir couple) and shadow-kissed bondmate, Mark has found a way to heal from the darkness he takes from his wife, keeping both of them sane and happily married.

GALINA (STRIGOI)

Dimitri's former school instructor, Galina has been a Strigoi for several years and has quickly risen in power. She presides over her vast estate near Novosibirsk, the capital of Siberia. She is staked by Rose, which inadvertently helps Dimitri take her power—his master plan all along.

NATHAN (STRIGOI)

One of Galina's henchman, blond Nathan was responsible for turning Dimitri into a Strigoi. He also had a great interest in being the one to find and kill Lissa, the last Dragomir. He is ultimately killed by Dimitri after Galina's death.

EMILY MASTRANO (MOROI)

Emily is a beautiful, black-haired, blue-eyed ballerina and also the former secret lover of Eric Dragomir—who met her when she was a Vegas showgirl. Before his death, Eric created a bank account for Emily to help her raise their illegitimate daughter, Jill.

ROBERT DORU (MOROI)

Victor Dashkov's half-brother, Robert, is a spirit user driven mad by his magic after his bondmate died. He's rumored to have restored a Strigoi to life, and while it sounds like a fairy tale, Rose moves heaven and earth to find out that it's all true. Robert also uses a silver stake charmed with spirit to restore Sonya Karp to her former Moroi self.

HANS CROFT (DHAMPIR)

Head of guardians at the Moroi Royal Court, Hans is in charge of Rose's punishment after her seemingly irresponsible "girls weekend" to Vegas with Lissa. He's very stern but also really good at his job. He soon recognizes Rose's skill and talent as a guardian and eventually comes to respect her as being more than just a troublemaker.

SERENA (DHAMPIR)

Serena is the queen's selection as Lissa's guardian when Rose is deemed unworthy. The pretty blond dhampir is similar in age to the princess and open-minded about teaching Moroi self-defense. Both she and Grant help Lissa learn to use a silver stake. While badly injured in the Strigoi attack on Lissa's birthday, Serena is still able to make a distress call to the other guardians. After her recovery, she is assigned to work security at the front gates of Court during the elections.

GRANT (DHAMPIR)

Lissa's temporary guardian, Grant helps Serena teach Lissa and Christian some defense moves. He was also secretly training a group of elite Moroi in how to fight as part of the queen's experiment. Grant is killed in the Strigoi attack on Lissa's birthday.

— THE KEEPERS —

RAYMOND DAWES (MOROI)

Leader of the Keepers, a group of Moroi who have shunned the modern ways and live in small backward communes, bearded Raymond is married to Sarah, a human, and has a Moroi mistress named Paulette. They all live happily together.

JOSHUA DAWES (DHAMPIR)

Raymond's eighteen-year-old son Joshua is a good-looking dhampir with sandy blond hair and blue eyes. After taking a liking to Rose during her visit to his village, he takes her for a tour of his bachelor cave and promptly proposes marriage. She declines the offer.

ANGELINE DAWES (DHAMPIR)

Joshua's fifteen-year-old sister, Angeline, is angry at everyone and seems to have a big chip on her shoulder. After Joshua's marriage proposal, Angeline challenges Rose in hand-to-hand combat to make sure she's worthy of her brother—a Keeper tradition. The potential is there for her to be a good fighter, but she's untrained, so Rose wins easily. When Angeline begs Rose to take her along when they leave the village, it's clear that not everyone is happy with the rustic Keeper lifestyle.

CHAPTER 8

Love & Friendship

ROSE & DIMITRI

PRIVATE LESSONS

When Rose first meets Dimitri, he's the one in charge of dragging her and Lissa back to St. Vladimir's. But he sees her potential as a guardian and steps in to give her extra training to help her catch up. Good thing, too—the alternative would have been her expulsion. It's not long before Rose starts to realize that Dimitri isn't just a good-looking jerk with a Russian accent, he's somebody who supports her, protects her, and is helping her to become who she was meant to be.

> *Feeling his eyes on me like that made something flutter inside of*
> *me—which was stupid, of course. I had no reason to get all goofy,*
> *just because the man was too good-looking for his own good.*
>
> —*Vampire Academy, page 64*

Despite knowing that he's seven years older and her teacher, she ends up falling for him. The feeling is mutual, but Dimitri takes the age gap—and the potential ramifications of a relationship with an underage student—a bit more seriously. Still, it's impossible to ignore the attraction between the two, especially when they're zapped with a lust charm, courtesy of Victor Dashkov. It almost—*almost*—results in the bespelled Rose losing her virginity to Dimitri before they are able to fight back against the charm's very strong magic.

Q&A WITH RICHELLE MEAD

WHAT WAS THE EXACT MOMENT THAT DIMITRI FELL IN LOVE WITH ROSE?

I'm not sure that we can pinpoint the exact moment that Dimitri fell for Rose. It was definitely a gradual thing that crept up on him (and her!). I can say for sure, though, that he was awestruck by her at their very first meeting. Rose throwing herself between Lissa and the guardians, even when she was hopelessly outnumbered, is definitely one of the most powerful scenes in the series. It establishes Rose's nature right away—both her bravery and intense devotion to those she loves. Dimitri possesses those exact same traits, and I think seeing that in her was definitely a moment when the world stood still for him.

It's magic that never would have worked if there weren't already feelings on both sides of this forbidden relationship, though. Feelings they need to fight. They're both set to become Lissa's guardians, so how can they protect the princess—their first priority as guardians—if they're too busy protecting each other?

"Rose, I'm seven years older than you. In ten years, that won't mean so much, but for now, it's huge. I'm an adult. You're a child."

Love & Friendship

Ouch. I flinched. Easier if he'd just punched me.

"You didn't seem to think I was a child when you were all over me." —*Vampire Academy, page 313*

They try to ignore their feelings, but feelings this strong only continue to grow. When Dimitri's given the opportunity to become Tasha Ozera's guardian and maybe even the father of her children, Rose is torn apart with jealousy. She tries her best to find love with her friend Mason. But it doesn't work. What she has with Dimitri is real. And when he declines Tasha's offer, it just shows that their feelings for each other are impossible to ignore.

Finally, Dimitri's resistance wears away as he realizes just how deeply he cares about Rose during her traumatic fight against Lissa's spirit darkness. He comforts her, tells her he loves her, and they finally make love in the privacy of an abandoned cabin in the woods surrounding St. Vlad's. He promises that they'll find a way to be together, no matter what, and for a little while—a *very* little while—everything is wonderful and golden between them.

But then Dimitri is attacked and bitten by a Strigoi, and Rose fears that the man she loves has been killed—but it's even worse than that. He's been turned into a Strigoi.

ADDICTED TO LOVE

Holding true to a promise they once made to each other, Rose travels to Russia to hunt down and kill Dimitri, knowing the man she loved is gone forever, replaced by an evil monster. But when Rose finally finds him, she's stunned by how similar this Dimitri is to the one she fell in love with—apart from the fangs, red eyes, and cruel demeanor.

Dimitri kidnaps Rose and holds her prisoner at a Strigoi-controlled estate. He's cold and evil and readily admits to enjoying the act of murder, but there's something inside him that prevents him from killing Rose. Instead, he wants to awaken her as a Strigoi so they can be together forever. It's chilling . . . but kind of romantic, too. While Rose is tempted by the idea of being with Dimitri, she's held back by her strong sense of good and evil. She knows being a Strigoi is wrong and Dimitri isn't thinking right. But his kiss feels similar to his kisses before—and when he bites her, she quickly becomes addicted to the pleasure his Strigoi endorphins bring her.

Q&A WITH RICHELLE MEAD

WAS WRITING THE EVIL STRIGOI VERSION OF DIMITRI FUN FOR YOU AS AN AUTHOR—OR DIFFICULT?

Writing Dimitri as an evil Strigoi was challenging on a lot of levels. First, I simply had to overcome my own difficulties with allowing a character I knew and loved to do bad things! When you write someone long enough, you really get comfortable with that character's personality. So, it was definitely weird having to portray him in a totally different—and at times, awful—way. From a craft point of view, this was also a difficult writing task because I needed to make Dimitri terrifying and consumed by his monstrous side—while still giving readers a reason to be hopeful for him. If you make a character too evil and too unlikeable, readers will lose faith and stop caring. I needed readers to still love him—but also be a little afraid of him! It was a very tricky balance to manage.

She begins to live in a daze, content with her visits from this dark version of Dimitri. He continues to give her the time she needs to make up her mind about becoming Strigoi—with the caveat that he will decide for her . . . soon.

Rose questions his true motives for making her a Strigoi— wanting him to say it's because he loves her—but he never says the words she wants to hear, words that might possibly have tempted her to make a different decision.

A glimpse in the mirror after a brief and troubled spirit dream with Adrian makes Rose realize that with the bruises over her neck and the fresher wounds where Dimitri has bitten her, she looks like a blood whore. This realization begins to help her slowly pull out of her addiction until she's finally able to escape, pursued by an obsessed Dimitri at every turn. He refuses to let her run away from him.

Knowing she has no other choice for survival, Rose stakes Dimitri. His body falls into a river and is washed away. She's grief-stricken that it's come to this and thinks he's dead—that she's killed the man she loves—but Dimitri isn't quite that easy to kill. She missed his heart—she always did have trouble figuring out where it is.

On her return to St. Vlad's, she begins to receive love letters from him that promise they'll be seeing each other again—and next time, she will die.

> *One of the few downsides to being awakened is that we no longer require sleep; therefore we also no longer dream. It's a shame, because if I could dream, I know I'd dream about you.*
>
> —*Spirit Bound, page 11*

FINDING BEAUTY

In Russia, Rose heard a rumor about a man who restored a Strigoi to life. It seems impossible—but that's never stopped Rose before. Driven by the possibility that there's a way to save Dimitri, she breaks Victor Dashkov out of prison so he'll lead her to his brother, a spirit user who was responsible for the miracle she heard about.

Q&A WITH RICHELLE MEAD

DO YOU FEEL THAT ROSE WAS TOTALLY JUSTIFIED IN WHAT SHE DID TO SAVE DIMITRI—BREAKING BOTH LAWS AND HEARTS? IS ALL FAIR IN LOVE AND WAR?

Rose's decision to save Dimitri in *Spirit Bound*—and the choices she made to pull it off—was definitely a key moment in the series for her identity and growth as a person. Throughout the entire series, Rose has been shaped by two powerful forces. One is her loyalty to the guardians and the rules they've established for her world. The other is her devotion to those she loves and willingness to do anything for them. These two forces clashed frequently in the series, but she was always able to balance them just in time—until *Spirit Bound*. Dimitri's salvation forced Rose to finally choose where she truly stood, and despite her faith in the guardians, it was her love for others that won out. Once that decision was made, everything else that followed was justified as far as Rose was concerned. She certainly regretted the laws and hearts that were broken along the way, but standing by and abandoning Dimitri was not an option at this point.

But Lissa is the one who must ultimately wield the spirit-charmed stake and restore Dimitri to his former dhampir self—although he's guilt-ridden and nearly destroyed by the knowledge of what he's done as a Strigoi. The thought of seeing Rose, facing what he did to her in Russia, is too much for him to bear, and he avoids her at all costs.

But Rose is stubborn and won't give up on him. Even though she's now dating Adrian, she refuses to let Dimitri go—but his repeated rejection wears at her confidence that he still loves her.

When Rose is accused of murdering Queen Tatiana, Dimitri can't turn his back on Rose any longer. While he continues to fight his true feelings, his duty calls him to step up and help the woman who has been there for him at every turn. He assists in Rose's escape from Court and tries to keep her safe, but her plans veer elsewhere—toward the search for the missing Dragomir. Dimitri goes along for the ride—what other choice does he have when dealing with Rose logic?—and the more time they spend together, the more he sees it's impossible to ignore how much he loves her.

But Dimitri's guilt over being Strigoi continues to torture him. One night he loses control of himself, and his bloodlust takes over as he slaughters a Strigoi. It's only Rose who's able to pull him back. She makes him try to see beauty in the world again—and he does. He sees it in her.

> *"Your hair," repeated Dimitri. His eyes were wide, almost awestruck. "Your hair is beautiful."*
>
> *I didn't think so, not in its current state. Of course, considering we were in a dark alley filled with bodies, the choices were kind of limited. "You see? You're not one of them. Strigoi don't*

see beauty. Only death. You've found something beautiful. One thing that's beautiful." — *Last Sacrifice, pages 255–256*

When they give in to their passion for each other and make love again, Rose knows the only thing stopping them from being together is Dimitri's guilt. If he can't love himself, it's impossible for him to truly love Rose. She insists that before she can be with him for real, he has to forgive himself once and for all.

But then Rose gets shot in the chest while trying to save Lissa's life—and Dimitri automatically chooses to protect Rose over Lissa. In that moment, it's finally clear to them both that they're meant to be together now and always.

ROSE & ADRIAN

THE WARRIOR AND THE BAD BOY

It only takes one look at the bruised and sweaty—but *gorgeous*—Rose Hathaway for Adrian Ivashkov to be smitten by the girl he nicknames "little dhampir." In the beginning, Rose believes he's only pursuing her for the same reason other Moroi guys pursue dhampir girls—for sex. But despite his royal, rich-kid trappings, Adrian's deeper than that.

And Adrian has a special ability to help him spend more time with Rose. Because he's a spirit user, he can dream-walk through Rose's dreams. He's also able to see auras and smartly pinpoints that Rose's dark moods are directly related to her taking Lissa's spirit darkness away and absorbing it into herself.

He is continually intrigued and amused by Rose's brash, tough-chick exterior and falls hard for her, willing to do pretty much anything she asks of him, even funding her trip to Russia to try to

Q&A WITH RICHELLE MEAD

HOW DID ADRIAN FIRST DISCOVER HIS SPIRIT MAGIC?

When we first meet Adrian, he doesn't even really know what his magic is called or that it might be bigger than he realizes. Adrian's had a mixed history of both belonging and being an outsider. He can easily fit into any social situation and always stands out as the life of a party. People love him, and he's always invited to the hottest, most popular events. At the same time, there's a part of Adrian that always feels a little different, and that's why we often see him put on this lazy, wacky persona that Rose finds so infuriating. That's Adrian's way of coping. So, when he initially thought he had no element and then later realized he had bizarre and unknown powers, he pretty much accepted that as par for his life. It was just one more way in which he didn't quite fit in with everyone else. It wasn't until he met Lissa (and other spirit users) that he began to realize he wasn't weird. He was special. That's gone a long way to change his attitudes about himself and the world (though not done much to change his crazy partying nature...yet).

kill Dimitri after he's turned into a Strigoi. He does it because he knows it will help Rose heal and finally let go of Dimitri . . . and maybe give him a chance.

When she returns, haunted by what she did in Russia, she does give Adrian that chance. They date . . . and it's kind of awesome. They have a lot of fun together. He is even willing to go so far as giving up cigarettes and drinking to please Rose, vices that normally are his crutch to deal with the side effects of his spirit magic.

Even though Rose has agreed to date Adrian, she hasn't given up on finding a way to help Dimitri—especially once she learns of a potential way to restore a Strigoi to life. She feels bad about lying to Adrian, but she can't tell him when she takes off on a quest to find the answers she needs. Adrian follows her credit card trail—it's the credit card he provided her with for her trip to Russia—and surprises Rose by showing up in Las Vegas, thinking she's there for a fun weekend with Lissa. And Adrian's all for fun Vegas weekends!

He's hurt and angry to learn her real reasons—and that she lied to him—but he still gathers himself together enough to help when she continues to assure him that her feelings for him are true. After Dimitri's restored and rejects Rose to her face, she almost sleeps with Adrian just to feel like somebody still wants her. *Almost.* Instead, she lets him bite her, a mutually satisfying alternative—but ultimately empty since Rose's heart is still with another.

> *I shifted closer to Adrian on the bed and pressed my head against his chest. "We can make this work, I know we can. If I screw up again, you can leave."*
>
> *"If only it were that easy," he laughed. "You forget: I have an addictive personality. I'm addicted to you. Somehow I think you could do all sorts of bad things to me, and I'd still come back to you."*
>
> —*Spirit Bound, page 437*

Adrian helps Rose escape from Court after she's accused of murder and visits regularly in her dreams to make sure she's okay. While he's uneasy about her spending so much time with Dimitri, she continues to assure Adrian that she's with him now.

Q&A WITH RICHELLE MEAD

WHAT WAS IT THAT ATTRACTED ADRIAN TO ROSE? IS HE NATURALLY INCLINED TO FALL FOR GIRLS WHO ARE LIKELY TO BREAK HIS HEART?

Rose made things difficult for Adrian from the very beginning, and honestly, I kind of think that's what attracted him! Adrian has a lot of problems with a lot of things in his life, but charming people (especially women) isn't one of them. He's always been able to get former girlfriends, his mother, and even prickly Queen Tatiana to do whatever he wants. So, it was kind of a shock for him when Rose wasn't instantly taken in by his usual tricks. The part of Adrian that just likes to be contrary and difficult couldn't resist the challenge. It's almost impossible for him to believe that a girl wouldn't instantly fall for him. At the same time, he secretly likes that. Girls who give in too easily bore him, and he had been waiting for someone to stand up to him. Rose's strength spoke to him and ignited a hidden piece of his personality that actually longs to be stronger too.

So, when Adrian learns that Rose has cheated on him with Dimitri, the man she loves more than him, Adrian can't help but be heartbroken ... and really pissed off that she's abused his feelings for her. He's not willing to just forgive her for betraying him. It's clear to Rose that Adrian is strong, he's wonderful, but he's not meant for her—and that he's leaning on his addictions when he should be leaning on the strength he hasn't yet found within himself.

"You're better than this . . . better than whatever it is you're going to do now."

Adrian rested his hand on the doorknob and gave me a rueful look. "Rose, I'm an addict with no work ethic who's likely going to go insane. I'm not like you. I'm not a superhero."

"Not yet," I said. — *Last Sacrifice, page 581*

Rose is convinced that despite his current heartache, Adrian's a hero in the making. He just has to realize it for himself someday soon . . .

ROSE & LISSA

Lissa and I had been best friends ever since kindergarten, when our teacher had paired us together for writing lessons. Forcing five-year-olds to spell Vasilisa Dragomir and Rosemarie Hathaway *was beyond cruel, and we'd—or rather, I'd—responded appropriately. I'd chucked my book at our teacher and called her a fascist bastard. I hadn't known what those words meant, but I'd known how to hit a moving target.*

Lissa and I had been inseparable ever since.

— *Vampire Academy, page 8*

BEST FRIENDS FOREVER

Rose and Lissa were best friends for years, even before the event that would bond their lives even closer together. After a horrible car accident takes the lives of Lissa's parents and brother, she's able to bring Rose back to life by using *spirit*, a mysterious fifth element that gives her healing powers. This act results in a one-way psychic bond. Rose is able to read Lissa's mind, sense her location, and even slip into Lissa's head and experience the world through her eyes. While intrusive, being "shadow-kissed" helps Rose be an even better guardian to her friend.

Q&A WITH RICHELLE MEAD

DID LISSA'S PARENTS INITIALLY HAVE A PROBLEM WITH THEIR PUREBLOOD MOROI DAUGHTER HAVING A DHAMPIR AS A BEST FRIEND? WHAT HELPED THEM ACCEPT ROSE AS A PART OF THEIR FAMILY?

A lot of people wonder how Lissa's parents could have been so accepting of Rose and Lissa's friendship, particularly considering what we know about the divisions in Moroi and dhampir society. The biggest taboo in this area is actually when it comes to love and romance. That's when Moroi-dhampir pairings become dangerous. Friendships aren't looked down upon as much, and it's actually pretty common for guardians who have protected a family long enough to be treated as just another family member. This is certainly what happened with Rose and the Dragomirs. Lissa's parents also were understandably concerned about Lissa's safety, and they knew that having someone like Rose—who was devoted as both a friend and guardian—would be the best way to ensure Lissa was always protected.

RICHELLE, ON THE BOND BETWEEN ROSE AND LISSA:

When I set out to write the series, I had a lot of characters' stories and subplots in my head, and I had to decide early on how I was going to address those. Rotating characters with a third-person narrative certainly lets you get a lot of stories out there—but can also leave you with a thousand-page book if you're not careful. I ultimately decided Rose was the character I was most interested in and that her story really formed the heart of the series. I chose her as my narrator but was still drawn to Lissa, both because she's fascinating in her own way and also because of her close connection to Rose. I soon realized, though, that their very connection would let me get away with slipping in another character's narrative. Rose's ability to see the world through Lissa's eyes allows us these moments of third-person POV that we wouldn't ordinarily get in a first-person series. I ended up with a sneaky kind of hybrid style of storytelling that was ultimately told with Rose's voice but expanded the world beyond her own experiences. This system became a really useful tool in *Blood Promise*, when Rose and Lissa were separated for the first time. Even though Rose was by far and away nearly everyone's favorite character at that point in the series, I think we all would've been sad to have a book where we didn't know what was going on with Lissa, Christian, Adrian, and the others. The bond let me continue keeping track of everyone, which became even more essential in later books as Rose and Lissa began to increasingly follow their own paths.

"You've been kissed by shadows. You've crossed into Death, into the other side, and returned. Do you think something like that doesn't leave a mark on the soul? . . . You should have stayed dead. Vasilisa brushed death to bring you back and bound you

to her forever." —*Victor Dashkov on the bond the girls share,*
Vampire Academy, page 317

When Lissa's spirit ability—although at the time they still didn't have a name for it—puts Lissa's life and mental health in serious danger, she and Rose run away from St. Vladimir's Academy and hide in the human world for two years, until guardians find them and forcibly bring them back to the school.

The more Lissa uses spirit, the more it wears on her mentally, threatening her sanity. Without realizing what she's doing, Rose begins to absorb her friend's darkness, saving Lissa but endangering herself for a time.

While Rose is able to know everything about Lissa through the bond, it doesn't work both ways. When Lissa finds out Rose has been keeping her relationship with Dimitri a secret, she's hurt that her best friend hadn't confided in her. She's even more hurt when Rose chooses to leave her behind to go on a quest to find and kill Dimitri when he's turned into a Strigoi. Rose never wanted to have to choose between the two people she loves most in the world, and it's a terrible, heart-wrenching decision for her. But when it comes to Dimitri, she's never had a choice.

The mental bond still allows Rose to check in on Lissa while she's away, and this connection is all that helps save Lissa's life long-distance when she's targeted by Avery, another spirit user, who wants to kill Lissa and bring her back to life in order to create another psychic bond.

Lissa accompanies Rose on her next quest to find out how to restore a Strigoi to life, an act that will rely completely on Lissa's spirit magic. While Rose draws the line at putting her friend in direct danger at the hands of a Strigoi, Lissa is determined to save the man her best friend loves. However, when the restored Dimitri then looks at Lissa as a goddess, Rose can't help but feel jealous.

While they have their share of difficulties—as all long-term friendships do—their devotion to each other never wavers. Rose pledged to give everything she has to keep Lissa safe, and she proves beyond a shadow of a doubt that's true when she throws herself in front of Lissa to save her from being shot—and is shot instead. This time it isn't Lissa's spirit magic that heals her. It's Rose's own willpower. The act of successfully bringing herself back from such a close brush with death breaks their psychic bond once and for all.

Despite a severed shadow-kissed bond, the friendship between the two girls is stronger than ever, and Rose officially becomes Lissa's guardian as she embarks on her new life as a university student and queen.

LISSA & CHRISTIAN

THE PRINCESS AND THE OUTCAST

Christian Ozera isn't exactly the kind of guy who normally ends up with a princess. Stigmatized by the choice his parents made to become evil Strigoi and looked down on by other students who assume he's a Strigoi-in-waiting, he prefers to be alone and has built up a snarky sense of humor to act as his armor against the rest of the world.

When Lissa finds Christian's hiding spot in the chapel attic, he realizes it might be possible to open up his heart to the beautiful blond princess. Christian battles self-doubt when it comes to

Q&A WITH RICHELLE MEAD

WHILE CHRISTIAN AND LISSA'S RELATIONSHIP HAS ITS PROBLEMS, THEY'RE NORMAL PROBLEMS THAT ANY TEEN MIGHT EXPERIENCE, LIKE JEALOUSY OR MISUNDERSTANDING. WAS IT INTENTIONAL TO HAVE A MORE DOWN-TO-EARTH ROMANCE IN THE BOOKS TO CONTRAST THE EPIC DRAMA OF ROSE AND DIMITRI?

Lissa and Christian, while far from being a "normal" couple, were meant to be a contrast to Rose and Dimitri (and even Rose and Adrian). I wanted to show that not every romance is fraught with epic, world-shattering problems! That isn't to say things were always easy for Lissa and Christian. They certainly had their share of difficulties throughout the series, and it was important for me to highlight the typical ups and downs that any couple, vampire or human, might have. Some people might argue that if I'd really wanted something to contrast with Rose's disastrous love life, I should have given Lissa and Christian a perfect, problem-free romance. There was no way I could do that, though. Aside from the fact that it wouldn't be realistic, I also think those little relationship kinks and difficulties are what end up making Lissa and Christian such a power couple. Facing problems together ends up strengthening both their love and themselves as individuals.

Lissa's true feelings for him, never feeling worthy enough to be with her. But his strong feelings for her, and a sense of wanting to protect her, lead him into a real relationship.

Lissa likes Christian because he doesn't love her for her popularity—he loves her for *her*. With him she can really be herself and feels at peace. Although Rose initially tries to keep the two apart, thinking that Christian's a dangerous influence on her best friend, it's clear that they're destined to be together.

> *Christian dragged his eyes from me to her, and as they regarded each other, I felt such a powerful wave of attraction, it was a wonder it didn't knock me over. Her heart was in her eyes. It was obvious to me he felt the same way about her, but she couldn't see it, particularly since he was still glaring at her.*
>
> —*Vampire Academy, page 168*

Christian and Lissa's relationship is not without its trials and tribulations, though.

Christian is jealous of other guys Lissa spends time with, especially Adrian, whom he sees as everything he's not, especially when he hears the rumor that the queen herself wants the two to get married.

When Avery befriends the group and turns Lissa on to drinking and partying—pretty much changing her personality into that of a shallow party girl—Christian feels he has no choice but to break up with her. This isn't the girl he fell in love with. It takes a while, despite a ton of stubbornness on both of their parts, before they finally get back together.

While Christian still deals with being treated like an outcast, he finally fully accepts that he has won the love of the Dragomir princess . . . and future Moroi queen.

Q&A WITH RICHELLE MEAD

CHRISTIAN'S PARENTS TURN STRIGOI, AND HIS AUNT IS A MURDERER. HOW DOES HE MANAGE TO COPE WITH ALL OF THIS, ESPECIALLY AFTER BEING SHUNNED FOR YEARS AT SCHOOL? DOES HE EVER BELIEVE THAT HE TOO COULD BE CAPABLE OF EVIL ACTS IF IT RUNS IN HIS FAMILY SO MUCH?

Christian has one of the most interesting pasts of any of the characters—which is saying something, with this cast! From the moment we meet him, he has the legacy of his parents' decision to turn Strigoi hanging over him. Later, he must contend with his aunt's treason. These things go a long way to explain why Christian has such a prickly, rebellious nature. He doesn't doubt himself or worry that he'll follow in the steps of his family. The problem is that although he knows the kind of person he truly is, that's not enough for some people. Since childhood, he's been defined by others' expectations of him. Everyone assumes he's going to behave a certain way, and it's incredibly frustrating to him since he often feels there's no way he can convince others he's different from the rest of his family. After a while, this is kind of what drives his tendency to act out. He figures if people think he's bad, then maybe he should act bad! Fortunately, Lissa's influence has had a huge impact on him. Although he's still troubled by others' opinions, she's convinced him that going forward and being who he truly is will eventually convince others of his real nature.

CHAPTER 9

Allies & Monsters

MOROI

Moroi are mortal, living vampires—born, not made. Physically, they are tall and have very pale skin, the kind of skin that blushes and burns easily. Since they are vampires, they must drink blood daily to keep up their strength but require normal food as well.

While Moroi can withstand sunlight, it weakens them, and they must limit their exposure. Because of this, their schedules are usually opposite to the human world—for example, midnight would be noon to a Moroi.

Moroi have superhuman sight, smell, and hearing and can wield elemental magic. Moroi view this magic as a gift and part of their souls that connects them to the world. As such, they believe that it should be used peacefully. There was a time when Moroi used their magic more openly, for defense, to avert natural disasters, and to help with food and water production. But now, rules surrounding their magic are strictly enforced to help keep their existence a secret.

ELEMENTAL MAGIC

While all Moroi have a low-level ability over all four (main) elements, in their teens they begin to specialize in one element in

Q&A WITH RICHELLE MEAD

WHAT INSPIRED YOU TO USE RUSSIAN AND ROMANIAN MYTHOLOGY TO CREATE THE WORLD OF VAMPIRE ACADEMY THAT INCLUDES BOTH LIVING AND UNDEAD VERSIONS OF VAMPIRES?

I took a class at the University of Michigan on Slavic folklore and mythology. One of the units we studied was on vampires, and we had the opportunity to read some really great stories and examine a lot of the symbolism behind these old tales. Years later, when I decided to write a vampire novel, I decided I wanted to base my series out of that same region. So, I went searching through Eastern European mythology again and eventually found a reference to Moroi and Strigoi that I thought could really make a great foundation for a vampire society. Dhampirs are a little more widespread in pop culture, and I'd heard of them before, though they too come from this same region. What's funny is that I decided early on that my kickass heroine would be a dhampir, simply because I liked the mix of human and vampire traits. Later, I learned that in a lot of Eastern European myths, dhampirs have a reputation for being great vampire hunters. There were those who believed that if an evil vampire was causing trouble, you needed to recruit a dhampir to come get rid of him or her. So, without even realizing it, I'd cast Rose into a traditional warrior role!

particular. It has long been forbidden to use this magic in anything but a peaceful manner, although some Moroi do begin to question this stance when it comes to fighting back against Strigoi.

EARTH   Earth users are able to manipulate the ground—causing mini-earthquakes—rot wood, and throw rocks or balls of mud using their minds. Earth users can also charm silver objects or jewelry with compulsion spells.

AIR   Air users can manipulate the air by doing everything from creating mild breezes to suffocating an enemy by removing all the air from a room.

WATER   A water user can manipulate water, moving it through the air to drown someone where they stand. A less-violent use could be to melt snow so slush falls on passersby.

FIRE   The most effective Moroi power to be used in combat against Strigoi, fire can be used to warm air, create fireballs, and light objects and/or people ablaze.

SPIRIT   Spirit users need to pull their magic from their own essence rather than the world around them, which makes the power taxing both physically and mentally. Using spirit can often lead to insanity, and spirit users typically develop different ways to cope with the aftereffects of their magic (for example, projecting dark moods onto an individual with whom one has bonded, self-medicating, turning Strigoi). Among other abilities, spirit users can heal plants and animals, dream-walk, see auras, and compel others with great intensity. In fact, their compulsion abilities are so strong that they can make others experience powerful hallucinations through super-compulsion. A spirit user can also create healing charms, including a silver stake that, when wielded by its creator, can restore Strigoi to their former life. Most of all, spirit users can bring someone who has recently died back to life, thereby making that person "shadow-kissed" and bound to the spirit user.

Q&A WITH RICHELLE MEAD

IF YOU WERE MOROI, WHICH ELEMENT WOULD YOU CHOOSE TO SPECIALIZE IN?

People often ask, "If the Moroi don't use magic for fighting, what do they use it for?"

The answer is that in recent history, most Moroi have simply used their powers for ordinary, day-to-day tasks. That might seem like a waste to some people, but if I had the chance to use air magic, I would do it in an instant! I absolutely hate blow-drying my hair and would love to be able to use a little magic to zap it into place each morning.

ST. VLADIMIR'S ACADEMY

A boarding school attended by both royal and non-royal Moroi as well as dhampirs who are in training to become their future guardians, St. Vladimir's is in backwoods Montana. The school has wards—magical protective borders—in place to keep Strigoi well away from the gated iron fence that borders the school grounds.

Since access to blood is an important part of a vampire's daily life, a "feeding room" is located adjacent to the cafeteria, containing willing human volunteers who are well cared for.

Moroi and dhampir students attend classes apart in the morning and together in the afternoon.

Q&A WITH RICHELLE MEAD

WHAT WAS THE PROCESS FOR BUILDING THE WORLD OF ST. VLADIMIR'S ACADEMY?

St. Vladimir's serves a lot of different purposes in the series, so I had to consider all of them for its creation. It's not just a school; it's also a sanctuary of sorts. Moroi parents who choose to send their children here are trading family time for safety. Students attend almost year-round and hardly ever see their parents. With those things in mind, I had to put St. Vladimir's in a location that would preserve that high level of safety—both from Strigoi and curious humans. Backwoods Montana—with its vast forests and mountains—became an ideal setting. At the same time, I also had to keep in mind that students at a school like this don't quite have the same experiences that "normal" students at a private boarding school would have. There's no easy way to get off-campus. Field trips are few and far between because safety won't allow it. Once Moroi and dhampirs are there, they pretty much stay there. As such, it was essential to make sure the school was the kind of place where they could live happily. Everything there is the newest and best, despite the façade of historic buildings. Computer labs, athletic facilities, and medicine—all of it is state-of-the-art. Academics are much more extensive than ordinary schools, in the hopes that there's something there for everyone to be interested in. Equally important are the touches of ordinary home life, like religious services, movie lounges, and lots of open green spaces. The message one walks away with is yes, you *do* have to spend a lot of time at St. Vladimir's... but you'll like it.

MOROI CLASSES consist of artistic learning, language, and control over their elemental powers. Sample classes include

American Colonial Literature, Ancient Poetry, Basics of Elemental Control, Russian, Creative Writing, and Culinary Science.

DHAMPIR CLASSES consist of fighting techniques and strength training for the guardians-in-training, known as "novices," such as Advanced Guardian Combat Techniques, Bodyguard Theory and Personal Protection, and Weight Training and Conditioning.

In their senior year, novices get six weeks of field-experience training. Throughout that period, they are not obligated to take classes. Instead, they are assigned to a Moroi student whom they are required to protect twenty-four hours a day, six days a week. During that time, they are regularly "attacked" by adult guardians to test what they've learned while at St. Vlad's.

SHARED CLASSES are subjects that will benefit the learning of Moroi and dhampirs alike and include Precalculus, Advanced Calculus, Animal Behavior and Physiology, Moroi Culture, and Slavic Art.

Q&A WITH RICHELLE MEAD

IF YOU WERE A STUDENT AT ST. VLAD'S, WHAT WOULD BE YOUR FAVORITE CLASS?

I'd probably take as many history and literature classes as I could! I love that kind of stuff, and one of the great things about the Moroi is that they have a much greater emphasis on their past and heritage than the rest of us tend to have. This makes a lot of sense when you look at what the Moroi have gone through. They've been hunted by the Strigoi and forced to spread out all over the world, sometimes hiding in isolation and sometimes mixing into human cities. When your people live with that kind of danger, preserving your culture becomes imperative. It's that shared heritage that continues to unite the Moroi as a people and allow them to persevere.

MOROI ROYAL COURT

Situated in Pennsylvania, near the Pocono Mountains, the Moroi Royal Court is a collection of beautiful, ornate buildings modeled off the fortresses and palaces of St. Petersburg, Russia. Here, representatives from each royal family serve as Council members who vote on decrees and laws and are officiated by the king or queen.

The Court features administrative buildings, ballrooms, guest rooms, restaurants, small stores, offices, a coffee shop, and a luxury spa. The children of those who live at Court do not attend formal schools. Instead, they are tutored and live year-round in town houses with their families.

At Court, there are also on-site prison facilities and a courtroom where the queen presides over important Moroi trials.

MOROI ROYAL COUNCIL

Although Moroi live inside human-run countries and are subject to those governments, they're also ruled by a king or queen elected from one of the twelve royal Moroi families. The eldest member of a royal family has the title of "prince" or "princess" and gets a seat on the Moroi Royal Council. The prince or princess is responsible for electing the Moroi king or queen, a position held until death or retirement.

Moroi royals are always given a dhampir guardian—often more than one—but non-royals are assigned guardians in a lottery system controlled by the Guardian Council.

THE 12 ROYAL MOROI FAMILIES

In order from smallest to largest:

DRAGOMIR

BADICA

CONTA

OZERA

TARUS

DASHKOV

VODA

LAZAR

DROZDOV

ZEKLOS

SZELSKY

IVASHKOV

Q&A WITH RICHELLE MEAD

IS THE MOROI ROYAL COURT MODELED ON OR INSPIRED BY ANY REAL-LIFE LOCATION? WHAT WOULD YOU COMPARE IT TO IN OUR WORLD?

I always picture the Moroi Royal Court resembling some of the old, sprawling universities found in the U.S. and Europe. I see lots of stone walled buildings and ivy, spread out on wide green lawns. We have to always keep in mind that the Moroi are living in a human world, and if they want to stay secret, they can't really have anything that screams "royal palace." Modeling their Court on a prestigious university gives them both a cover for humans and a presence that's still very regal.

DHAMPIRS

Dhampirs were originally the offspring of Moroi and human couplings, but since vampires retreated from the human world, they are now a mix of Moroi and dhampir—a mix that will still produce a half-human/half-Moroi dhampir. Dhampirs are unable to reproduce with each other and need Moroi in order to have children.

Dhampirs get strength and endurance from their human side and enhanced senses and fast reflexes from their Moroi side. Dhampirs can't work magic like a full Moroi, but they're also free from certain Moroi constraints—like needing blood and being easily damaged by sunlight.

Moroi men seek out dhampir women for sex, but it's extremely rare—practically unheard of—for there to be a more serious relationship between the two. Most Moroi prefer to marry their own kind to keep their bloodlines pure. A dhampir woman who lets Moroi men drink blood while having sex with them is called a blood whore.

GUARDIANS

With the mix of human and Moroi traits, dhampirs make the ultimate bodyguards. Many train to become guardians to protect Moroi from the threat of Strigoi.

Dhampir women often become single mothers, because Moroi men relish the freedom to have flings with them—without a real possibility of a lasting relationship. These women often choose to leave guardian training to raise their children, making female guardians rare.

Guardians are extremely serious about their jobs, in part because they need the Moroi race to survive so they're able to have children. In fact, the guardian mantra when it comes to protecting Moroi is "they come first." These are words many a guardian has lived and died for.

Dhampirs who do not complete their training do not receive their promise mark. Those who still kill Strigoi as a vigilante or hire themselves out as freelance bodyguards are deemed "unpromised." These are dhampirs who are rebels by nature or those who are actively against the enforced social structure of the Moroi world, which to many means that dhampirs are treated like second-class citizens.

Q&A WITH RICHELLE MEAD

IF GIVEN THE CHOICE, WOULD YOU PREFER TO BE A MOROI, A DHAMPIR . . . OR A STRIGOI?

I'm pretty content to be a human, but if forced to choose between the three races in the VA world, I'd probably choose to be a dhampir. I like the sun too much and am too grossed out by the idea of drinking blood to really get excited about that! The one downside is that I'm not sure how well I'd do in combat training. In fact, I'm fairly confident I'd break my hand the first time I tried to punch someone.

MARKS & TATTOOS

Guardians have several official marks they use to acknowledge their achievements, and all are applied to the back of the dhampir's neck.

PROMISE MARK — Also known as the graduation mark, dhampirs receive this tattoo to show that they have successfully finished their training and are now an official guardian. It's described as a twisting line, sort of like a snake.

MOLNIJA MARK — For every Strigoi a guardian kills, the guardian receives a *molnija* mark, a tattoo that looks like two streaks of jagged lightning (*molnija* is Russian for "lightning"), crossing in an *X*.

ZVEZDA MARK — Also known as the battle mark, it's a star-shaped tattoo (*zvezda* is Russian for "star"), which is given to a guardian who's fought in a battle and killed many Strigoi.

Q&A WITH RICHELLE MEAD

WHAT WAS THE INSPIRATION FOR THE GUARDIANS' TATTOOS?

The guardian tattoos came about for a couple different reasons. One was that I wanted a way to establish rank and honor among the guardians. I wanted people to know, at a glance, who the most powerful dhampirs are. It was also important to me to establish a unique culture for the dhampirs. So much of what they do is in service to the Moroi that it's easy to forget the dhampirs are their own people. The tattoo system and its ceremonies give the guardians an opportunity to have something that is totally their own. What I most certainly did not expect was that readers would start getting those same guardian tattoos permanently applied in real life! I've seen some pretty amazing tattoo work at my signings that I never envisioned when I started the series. I just hope my readers are still glad they got those tattoos twenty years from now!

ALCHEMISTS

In the Middle Ages, some people were convinced that if they found the right formula or magic, they could turn lead into gold. While they didn't succeed, they continued to pursue other mystical and supernatural subjects that eventually led them to—vampires.

Now Alchemists work with the Moroi to help cover up their existence from the rest of the world—and even have techniques and potions to get rid of Strigoi bodies. They are given a special tattoo made from gold and Moroi blood, which gives them traits similar to those of the Moroi themselves: a long life and excellent

283

health. Because the tattoo is also charmed with water and earth compulsion magic, it prevents the Alchemist from speaking about Moroi in any way that could endanger or expose them.

Alchemists tend to be religious and feel it's their duty to God to protect the rest of humanity from evil creatures of the night. They think anything remotely vampiric—be it Moroi, dhampir, or Strigoi—is evil and unnatural. Despite working for vampires, Alchemists try to stay apart from the vampire world as much as possible. Dhampirs aren't told about their existence until graduation.

A career as an Alchemist is something that's passed down through one's family—if one's mother or father was an Alchemist, then there's no other career choice available. And once you're a part of the Alchemist organization, you're in it for life . . . whether you want to be or not.

STRIGOI

If Moroi are the living, peaceful, mortal vampires, Strigoi are the undead, evil, immortal kind and are completely unable to withstand sunlight.

Strigoi are driven by their desire for blood—and while, yeah, they like human blood, it's *Moroi* blood that's their favorite kind. It will make them stronger and harder to destroy.

Apart from the red rings around their pupils and their chalky white skin, it's difficult to tell Strigoi are undead since they appear to talk and walk the same as they did before their transformation. If they were Moroi before being "awakened," which is the Strigoi term for being turned—rather appropriate since they no longer require sleep—they lose their connection to elemental magic. They also lose their auras, as only the living have auras, and are unable to enter holy ground.

Q&A WITH RICHELLE MEAD

AS THE NARRATOR OF *BLOODLINES*, SYDNEY IS THE COMPLETE OPPOSITE OF ROSE IN SO MANY WAYS. IS IT FUN, OR MORE OF A CHALLENGE, TO WRITE THIS CHARACTER?

Sydney is a really great character to have as a narrator, especially because she's so different from Rose. I loved writing Rose, but it's nice for an author to be able to switch voices and try something new. I also think having someone like Sydney to tell the story for a while will give us new insight into the VA world. Rose has grown up among Moroi and dhampirs, and from the very beginning, we're influenced by her perceptions—mainly, that vampiric life is perfectly ordinary. For Sydney, it's most certainly not ordinary. So, we get the perspective of someone who's an outsider, looking at this world through human eyes. Sydney's also much more of a careful observer than Rose is at times, so that too will provide some new insight. From a craft point of view, Sydney isn't easier or more difficult to write—she's simply different. After writing six books with one character, I've definitely fallen into a comfortable familiarity with Rose. I can jump right in and know exactly how she'll respond. With Sydney, I'm still getting to know her, but I have no doubt that within a couple of books, I'll know her just as well as I do Rose.

Strigoi have better strength, reflexes, and senses than dhampirs and are almost impossible to kill. While a Strigoi's power and strength increases with age, they rarely live together and frequently turn on each other when in groups.

HOW STRIGOI ARE CREATED

BY FORCE

Humans, dhampirs, or Moroi can forcibly be turned Strigoi after a single bite if they drink (voluntarily or by force) the Strigoi's blood in return.

BY CHOICE

Moroi tempted by immortality could become Strigoi by purposely killing another person while feeding. This is considered dark and twisted, the greatest of all sins against Moroi life and nature itself.

HOW STRIGOI CAN BE KILLED

SILVER STAKES

Silver stakes are a guardian's deadliest weapon. To forge a silver stake, Moroi must charm it with magic from each of the four main elements. Stabbing a Strigoi through the heart with a silver stake means instant death. HOWEVER, should the stake be charmed with a spirit user's healing magic and be wielded by the spirit user him- or herself, the Strigoi will be restored to their former Moroi state.

DECAPITATION

To cut off a Strigoi's head (or anyone else's, for that matter) will result in death.

FIRE

Lighting Strigoi on fire (via fire-magic or flame thrower, to name just a couple of options) is an effective way to destroy them.

Q&A WITH RICHELLE MEAD

WHAT INSPIRED THE IDEA THAT A SPIRIT-CHARMED SILVER STAKE COULD RESTORE A STRIGOI?

Silver has a long history in many cultures' folklore as a magical substance. Probably the most well-known application, that's still present in today's stories and myths, is the use of silver bullets to kill werewolves. A lot of those same stories simply say any stake through the heart will kill a vampire, but I wanted it to be a little more difficult in my series. Putting in the silver requirement maintained ties to mythology and also made Strigoi that much harder to kill. Charming those silver stakes with magic added one more obstacle and also tied into the idea of duality that's present in a lot of ancient vampire stories. Those stories place a big emphasis on the balance of life and death, and in the VA world, magic is associated with life since only Moroi can use it. It therefore makes sense that infusing those stakes with that same "life" would be needed to destroy the undead.

CHAPTER 10

The Quiz

THINK YOU'VE GOT THE STUFF TO BE AN OFFICIAL
GUARDIAN? WILL YOU MAKE THE GRADE AND GET YOUR
PROMISE MARK . . . OR WIND UP IN HEADMISTRESS
KIROVA'S OFFICE?

NOVICE LEVEL (10 QUESTIONS)

1. What is a Moroi?

A) A TYPE OF FISH FOUND IN THE ATLANTIC OCEAN

B) A LIVING VAMPIRE

C) A MOUNTAIN RANGE IN MONTANA

D) THE GHOST OF SOMEONE WHO RECENTLY DIED

2. If a dhampir and a Moroi have a baby, what will it be?

A) DHAMPIR

B) MOROI

C) HUMAN

D) STRIGOI

3. Who is St. Vladimir?

A) A MOROI SAINT FOR WHOM THE ACADEMY IS NAMED
B) A VERY FAMOUS STRIGOI
C) A HUMAN SAID TO BE BENEVOLENT TOWARD ALL VAMPIRES
D) A CURRENT STUDENT WHO THINKS REALLY HIGHLY OF HIMSELF

4. What is a sure sign of a Strigoi?

A) A RED RING AROUND THE PUPILS OF THE EYES
B) THE ABILITY TO TURN INTO A BAT
C) THE DESIRE TO SLEEP IN A COFFIN
D) A GREAT AFFECTION FOR VIOLIN MUSIC

5. What is Adrian Ivashkov's bad habit?

A) SMOKING
B) DRINKING HEAVILY
C) SNEAKING INTO ROSE'S DREAMS
D) ALL OF THE ABOVE

6. Who is given the nickname "little dhampir"?

A) ROSE
B) JANINE
C) ALBERTA
D) MASON

7. If you're a guardian who kills a Strigoi, what do you receive?

A) A PROMISE MARK

C) A PROMOTION

B) A *MOLNIJA* MARK

D) A SHINY MEDAL

8. What is Dimitri's affectionate nickname for Rose?

A) ROSIE

C) ROZA

B) ROSITA

D) PETUNIA

9. Why does everyone dislike and distrust Christian Ozera?

A) HE'S A JERK.

B) HIS PARENTS CHOSE TO BECOME STRIGOI.

C) THEY'RE JEALOUS OF HIS RELATIONSHIP WITH PRINCESS VASILISA.

D) ALL FIRE USERS ARE SHUNNED AT SCHOOL.

10. Why does Victor Dashkov kidnap Lissa in Vampire Academy?

A) SHE CAN HEAL HIS DISEASE WITH SPIRIT.

B) SHE'S A REALLY GOOD COOK.

C) SHE'S HIS LONG-LOST DAUGHTER.

D) HE WANTS RANSOM MONEY FROM THE SCHOOL.

The Quiz

QUALIFIER LEVEL (10 QUESTIONS)

11. At the beginning of Vampire Academy, *how many* molnija *marks does Dimitri have?*

A) TWO   C) SIX

B) FOUR   D) EIGHT

12. What nationality is Rose's mother, Janine Hathaway?

A) IRISH   C) TURKISH

B) SCOTTISH   D) AMERICAN

13. How old was Dimitri when he beat up his abusive Moroi father?

A) NINE   C) EIGHTEEN

B) THIRTEEN   D) TWENTY-FOUR

14. What is Headmistress Kirova's first name?

A) MARY   C) JANICE

B) HELEN   D) ELLEN

15. What element does Mia Rinaldi specialize in?

A) AIR

B) WATER

C) FIRE

D) EARTH

16. In Frostbite, what is the name of the perfume Adrian sends to Rose that she chooses to keep?

A) PINK SUGAR

B) ETERNITY

C) AMOR AMOR

D) PURE POISON

17. Which is the largest and most influential royal Moroi family?

A) OZERA

B) DRAGOMIR

C) IVASHKOV

D) DASHKOV

18. What is the Nightingale?

A) A CLUB IN ST. PETERSBURG

B) A BIRD LISSA RAISED FROM THE DEAD

C) ROSE AND DIMITRI'S LOVE SONG

D) A CODE WORD USED AMONG GUARDIANS

19. What is an Alchemist's tattoo made from?

A) NORMAL-COLORED INK

B) HERBS AND WINE

C) SILVER AND PAINT

D) GOLD INK AND MAGIC

20. What is the name of the prison Victor Dashkov is sent to?

A) SARANSK

B) ALATYR

C) TARASOV

D) ZHUKOV

BADASS GOD LEVEL (10 QUESTIONS)

21. In Frostbite, *how many victims were found at the Badica residence?*

A) ONE GUARDIAN, FOUR MOROI

B) TWO GUARDIANS, EIGHT MOROI

C) THREE GUARDIANS, SEVEN MOROI

D) FOUR GUARDIANS, NINE MOROI

22. According to Queen Tatiana in Shadow Kiss, *how many times in the last fifty years has a Moroi purposefully become a Strigoi, as Christian's parents did?*

A) NINE TIMES IN FIFTY YEARS

B) SIX TIMES IN FORTY YEARS

C) TEN TIMES IN SIXTY YEARS

D) IT HAPPENS AT LEAST ONCE A YEAR

23. In Shadow Kiss, *how many Moroi and dhampirs were carried away the night the group of Strigoi attacked St. Vladimir's?*

A) SEVEN

B) NINE

C) ELEVEN

D) THIRTEEN

24. In Blood Promise, *what kind of car does Sydney buy in Russia?*

A) 1985 HONDA

B) 1976 MINI COOPER

C) 1972 CITROËN

D) 1990 TOYOTA

25. What is the name of the river Dimitri falls into after Rose stakes him near the end of Blood Promise?

A) OB
B) YENISEY
C) LENA
D) VOLGA

26. If you ask for your drink "spiked" at a Moroi bar, what do you get?

A) AN EXTRA SHOT OF ALCOHOL
B) A SHOT OF BLOOD
C) AN OLIVE SKEWERED ON A SILVER STIR STICK
D) ICE CUBES CHARMED WITH WATER MAGIC

27. Which book does Abe give Rose to read while she's awaiting her murder trial?

A) *ROMEO AND JULIET*
B) *TO KILL A MOCKINGBIRD*
C) *JANE EYRE*
D) *THE COUNT OF MONTE CRISTO*

28. What is the name of the young, famous Moroi queen whose statue Abe had blown up to aid Rose's escape from Court?

A) ELIZABETH

B) ALEXANDRA

C) GALINA

D) MAYA

29. What is the standard epitaph on a guardian's gravestone, which is written in Russian, Romanian, and English?

A) ETERNAL SERVICE

B) REST IN PEACE

C) WITH US IN MEMORY

D) CHERISHED PROTECTOR

30. What are Lissa's two middle names?

A) RACHEL SARA

B) SABRINA ROCHELLE

C) REINA SABRINA

D) SABINA RHEA

The Quiz

Answers:

NOVICE LEVEL

1-B, 2-A, 3-A, 4-A, 5-D, 6-A, 7-B, 8-C, 9-B, 10-A

QUALIFER LEVEL

11-C, 12-B, 13-B, 14-D, 15-B, 16-C, 17-C, 18-A, 19-D, 20-C

BADASS GOD LEVEL

21-C, 22-A, 23-D, 24-C, 25-A, 26-B, 27-D, 28-B, 29-A, 30-D

SCORES

1–10 CORRECT ANSWERS

While you have some knowledge of the world of Vampire Academy, it's quite obvious that you just got here. We'd suggest unpacking your bags in the freshman dorm and getting ready to study hard for your next challenge. Watch out for Strigoi on your way home. You *do* know what they are, right?

11–19 CORRECT ANSWERS

You're scraping by, but you're probably attending way more parties than classes—come on, you can admit it, we won't tell! Detention is probably in your future, so you should cram in a bit more studying if you really want to make the grade. Sorry, but it's doubtful that Dimitri would give you extra after-school sessions with *this* score. Besides, you should spend that time studying!

20–25 CORRECT ANSWERS

Well done! You attend your classes and get good grades. You could probably hold your own in a fight against a Strigoi, but we're not saying you're about to get a *molnija* mark out of it or anything. Still, you're well on your way to kicking serious butt!

26–30 CORRECT ANSWERS

You rock! You know the world of Vampire Academy like the back of your silver stake! Dimitri himself would agree you're going to make one badass guardian. Get ready to receive your promise mark; you've graduated top of your class!

Pop-Quiz Answers

VAMPIRE ACADEMY

1) SCREAMS; 2) A RAVEN; 3) FIRE;
4) EDDIE CASTILE; 5) WESTERN NOVELS; 6) SANDOVSKY'S
SYNDROME; 7) DRESSED; 8) HER FAVORITE LIP GLOSS;
9) JESSE AND RALF; 10) NATALIE DASHKOV

FROSTBITE

1) QUALIFIER; 2) THE HEART; 3) DECAPITATING;
4) MARTIAL ARTS; 5) LORD; 6) MIA RINALDI; 7) FALSE;
8) SPOKANE, WASHINGTON; 9) MASON, EDDIE, AND MIA;
10) AN AQUARIUM

SHADOW KISS

1) VICTOR DASHKOV; 2) EDDIE CASTILE; 3) THE MOROI ROYAL
COURT; 4) BY BRINGING A PLANT BACK TO LIFE; 5) ADRIAN;
6) TREASURE; 7) SUICIDE; 8) THE MÂNĂ; 9) BURIA; 10) LOVED

BLOOD PROMISE

1) FLOWERS AND LEAVES; 2) SIMON; 3) SONJA; 4) ZMEY;
5) EASTER; 6) BAD ENEMY; 7) AARON; 8) HESITATE; 9) GALINA;
10) VICTOR DASHKOV

SPIRIT BOUND

1) MOROI ROYAL COURT; 2) MIKHAIL TANNER; 3) HUMAN FEEDERS;
4) ALWAYS; 5) SPIRIT; 6) THE WITCHING HOUR; 7) TO SEE ROSE;
8) THE DEATH WATCH; 9) SIXTEEN; 10) ABE MAZUR

LAST SACRIFICE

1) BECAUSE LISSA ASKED HIM TO; 2) MCDONALD'S; 3) DANIELLA
IVASHKOV; 4) THE TAINTED; 5) JOSHUA; 6) TASHA, CHRISTIAN,
AND ADRIAN; 7) THREE; 8) COUSINS; 9) HURTS; 10) MIA RINALDI

CHAPTER 11

Glossary

ALCHEMISTS   A group of humans who work with Moroi and dhampirs to hide the existence of vampires from the world. Alchemists bear a charmed tattoo on their faces made from gold ink, Moroi blood, and magic, which gives them special abilities to help in their work and prevents them from speaking to others about the vampire world.

AURAS   All living people—humans, Moroi, and dhampirs—have different-colored auras that surround them and show their mood. Spirit users are able to see these. Strigoi do not have auras because they are not technically alive.

AWAKEN   The term used by Strigoi to describe changing from what they'd been before: human, Moroi, or dhampir.

BLOOD WHORE   An insulting term for a dhampir, male or female, who allows a Moroi to drink their blood while having sex. It's also an unfair slur often applied to single dhampir mothers who choose to raise their children instead of becoming guardians.

BONDMATES — Those who are bound together after one is brought back to life by the other's use of spirit—like Rose and Lissa. It is possible for a spirit user to have more than one bondmate, but in all cases, the bond only works one way.

BURIA — Russian for *storm*, this is a code word guardians use among themselves to warn of a Strigoi attack.

CHOTKI — A bracelet-sized rosary.

COMPULSION — A Moroi or Strigoi's ability to mentally influence others. Those who specialize in spirit are the most skilled at compulsion.

DEATH WATCH — This is a secret, ancient Romanian ceremony to honor the dead which has been passed on through the oldest bloodlines of the Moroi elite.

DHAMPIR — Someone who is half-human and half-Moroi.

EARTH CHARMS — Objects charmed with earth magic and often tied to compulsion spells—such as the lust-charmed necklace that Victor Dashkov gives Rose.

ELEMENTAL MAGIC — The power all Moroi possess to magically harness earth, fire, earth, air, or—rarely—spirit.

FEEDER — A human who willingly donates blood to a Moroi. Feeders usually become addicted to the drug-like endorphins in a vampire's saliva, which give intense pleasure when bitten.

GUARDIAN | A dhampir who trained as a bodyguard for the Moroi.

GUARDIANS COUNCIL | The group that makes decisions on behalf of guardians and assigns them to Moroi.

THE KEEPERS | Moroi who prefer to keep to the old, more backward ways and traditions. They live together in communes, far away from the rest of society, and marry whomever they like—be it Moroi, dhampir, or human.

THE LOST | The term the Keepers use for Strigoi.

THE MÂNĂ | A secret society formed by Moroi royal students to feel special and elite, whose name means "the hand" in Romanian. The *Mânǎ* can be found at most schools.

MOLNIJA MARK | The Russian word for *lightning*, it's a tattoo emblazoned on the back of a guardian's neck as a reward for each Strigoi he or she has killed. Each looks like a tiny *X* made of lightning bolts. The more marks, the more experienced a guardian is.

MOROI | Living, peaceful, mortal vampires who are born with elemental magic.

NAZAR | A small blue eye made of glass that will bring protection to the one who wears it, according to old Middle Eastern superstition.

NOVICE   A dhampir who is in training to become a guardian.

PROMISE MARK   A tattoo that resembles a twisting snake, marking a dhampir as a guardian and given upon successfully completing trials at graduation.

PSI HOUND   Wolf-like creatures that are mentally connected to each other, aiding their ability to hunt.

ROSE LOGIC   Dimitri's term for Rose's counterpoints to serious arguments, usually going against the (arguably) more sensible opinion (usually his).

SANDOVSKY'S SYNDROME   A terminal illness that afflicts Moroi. It attacks the lungs first before dragging the rest of the body toward death.

SHADOW-KISSED   One who has died and been brought back to life through the use of spirit. The shadow-kissed will be psychically bonded to the spirit user who saves them.

SILVER STAKE   A lethal weapon charmed with magic from each of the four elements. Such a stake can instantly kill both Strigoi and Moroi if it pierces their hearts. Slightly shorter than a forearm, a stake has a hand grip at the bottom and a thick, rounded body that narrows to a point like an ice pick.

SPIRIT   The elemental magic that allows a Moroi to use

very strong compulsion and heal both plants and animals, enough to bring something or someone back from the dead. Some spirit users are able to dream-walk, use telekinesis, and charm silver objects with compulsion or healing spells. Unfortunately, the overuse of this ability can lead to depression and insanity.

STRIGOI   An evil, undead vampire that is created when a Moroi, dhampir, or human is bitten by a Strigoi and then drinks the Strigoi's blood in return or if a Moroi kills another person while feeding.

ST. VLADIMIR'S ACADEMY   A boarding school in Montana for Moroi students and the dhampir students training to become their guardians.

THE TAINTED   What the Keepers consider those Moroi who've abandoned the old, traditional ways to join up with the modern world.

TARASOV   A maximum-security Moroi prison, currently in Alaska, containing prisoners in two sections—criminal and psychiatric.

UNPROMISED   A dhampir who has never completed his or her training and therefore doesn't have a promise mark but still kills Strigoi without answering to anyone. Unpromised are usually hired bodyguards or vigilante Strigoi hunters.

VRĂJITOARE Teller of fortunes; a witch.

WARDS Created when four Moroi, each one strong in a different element, walks around an area and lays the magic in a circle on the ground, creating a protective border. The life in a Moroi's magic keeps out Strigoi, who are devoid of life. Wards fade quickly and require a lot of maintenance. Driving a silver stake through a ward line in the ground will pierce the ward and cancel out the protective effect.

ZMEY Russian for *serpent* or *snake*, it's the nickname for Rose's dangerously influential father, Abe Mazur.

ZVEZDA MARK The Russian word for *star*, it's the battle mark, a tattoo shaped like a star, that is given to a guardian who has fought in a battle large enough to lose count of Strigoi kills.

Vampire Academy
MERCHANDISE
INSPIRED BY THE INTERNATIONAL
BEST-SELLING SERIES FROM
RICHELLE MEAD

APPAREL

ACCESSORIES

JEWELRY

BOOKS & POSTERS

TO SEE MORE STYLES AND TO ORDER, VISIT:
WWW.VAMPIREACADEMYBOOKS.COM/MERCH